VICIOUS
LittLe
DarLings

VICIOUS
Little
DaRLINGs

KATHERINE EASER

BLOOMSBURY

NEW YORK BERLIN LONDON SYDNEY

First published in the United States of America in June 2011
by Bloomsbury Books for Young Readers
www.bloomsburyteens.com

For information about permission to reproduce selections from this book, write to
Permissions, Bloomsbury BFYR, 175 Fifth Avenue, New York, New York 10010

Library of Congress Cataloging-in-Publication Data
Easer, Katherine.
Vicious little darlings / by Katherine Easer. — 1st U.S. ed.
p.   cm.
Summary: Sarah Weaver, a jaded seventeen-year-old from a broken home, leaves
California to attend an all-women's college in Massachusetts, where she befriends a
mysterious pair of legacy students and learns a shocking secret that could lead to murder.
ISBN 978-1-59990-628-7
[1. Friendship—Fiction.   2. Secrets—Fiction.   3. Colleges and universities—Fiction.
4. Family problems—Fiction.   5. Massachusetts—Fiction.]   I. Title.
PZ7.E126723Vic 2011   [Fic]—dc22   2010038024

Book design by Danielle Delaney
Typeset by Westchester Book Composition
Printed in the U.S.A. by Quad/Graphics, Fairfield, Pennsylvania
2 4 6 8 10 9 7 5 3 1

All papers used by Bloomsbury Publishing, Inc., are natural, recyclable products
made from wood grown in well-managed forests. The manufacturing processes
conform to the environmental regulations of the country of origin.

For D. L.

VICIOUS
LittLe
DarLings

1

Where to?" the cabdriver asks. He's middle-aged with cracks in his face and weary eyes and he's squinting at me through the rearview mirror.

"The nunnery," I say.

The cabbie doesn't blink or laugh or say anything.

"It was a joke," I explain.

He just keeps squinting at me.

I give up and say, "Wetherly College."

Nodding, he starts the engine and pulls away from the curb, looping around the airport toward the nearest exit.

"You a freshman?" he asks, once we're on the highway.

"Yeah." I check his nameplate. JIMMY FORD, it reads. He looks about ten years younger in his license photo: fewer grooves in his face, perkier eyes. When he looks at me in the mirror again, I consider sliding over to the left side of the car, out of his field of vision, but decide it's too hostile a move.

Instead, I roll down my window, letting in a blast of fresh dung. It's 5:47 PM and still hot out. Aside from a couple of big rigs, the highway is empty.

Yup, I'm really here, in humdrum New England. Where there are cows. Brown ones, black ones, and spotted ones, all happily grazing next to the highway. I'm three thousand miles away from my crazy Lutheran grandmother's crappy Spanish-style complex in the slums of Beverly Hills—south of Wilshire—with its peach stucco and fossilizing tenants. And now I'll be spending the next four years at a women's college instead of UCLA, all because Nana caught me with Brad Taylor, the most popular guy at my Lutheran high school. Nana basically gave me two choices: Wetherly (her alma mater) or a college of my choice, except she wasn't going to pay for Option B and she wanted me out of the house by September. All I can say is, Brad totally wasn't worth it. He was *so* not my type. I only hooked up with him because I was trying to see if popularity could be sexually transmitted. Turns out it can't.

So I blew it. I screwed up the one blood relationship I had. Not that Nana even cares. She used to tell me I was just like my mother, and she hated my mother. But can I blame her? I hate my mother too. I haven't seen or heard from the woman in twelve years, but if she called or visited me, I'm pretty sure I'd still hate her.

Jimmy turns on the radio and starts whistling along to "Close to You" by The Carpenters. Suddenly I feel like crying. Despite everything, I miss Nana. I miss the way she snorts whenever she laughs and the way she fixates on the TV during *As the World Turns.* Even when I think of all the mean things she did—like buying me a push-up bra for my tenth birthday even though I didn't have any breasts yet, and telling me to wear makeup because God doesn't like an ugly face—I still miss her. I guess it's because she's all I have.

"Hey," Jimmy says, "what's a pretty girl like you doing going to an all-girls school?"

I can't help but snort. *Pretty?* I have skin like death—pale with visible blue veins—and dyed jet-black hair. I'm wearing torn Levi's, a black tank, and combat boots. If pretty were the point, I would be wearing pink blush and a dress made of doilies.

"I guess you can kiss your social life good-bye, huh?" he says.

"No kidding." It's ironic: sex is what got me here, and now, for the next four years, I won't be having any. But maybe that's okay. Sex always seems to get me in trouble. Maybe I should make it my goal to be celibate until summer.

"Or maybe you're one of those lesbians?" While looking into the mirror, Jimmy raises his eyebrows suggestively.

Now there's a thought. If celibacy gets to be too hard, I could always become a lesbian.

"Sir," I say, "if it's okay with you, I'd like to meditate now."

"Sure. Fine. Knock yourself out." He turns up the radio.

I close my eyes and try to relax, but I can't stop picturing Nana's permanent look of disapproval. Here's something I've learned from seventeen years of living: there's nothing you can do to make someone love you.

When I open my eyes, Jimmy is exiting the highway. He makes a sharp turn and drives down a private, tree-lined road. It's dark and eerie and feels as though time has stopped. We pull up in front of a sinister-looking wrought-iron gate with a plaque that reads WETHERLY COLLEGE 1871.

Wetherly. The name makes me think of Waspy women wearing white gloves and sipping Earl Grey with their pinkies thrust into the air. I can't help but sit up straighter.

Jimmy turns off the radio. "Which house?" he asks, suddenly all business.

I unfold my campus map. "Haven House," I say. "It's in the quad."

We drive past the gate and under a brick archway. Then we circle a courtyard with too-perfect lawns and trees with gnarled trunks, finally stopping in front of a massive, ivy-encrusted building. I step out of the cab. Jimmy stays in the car while I haul my own luggage out of the trunk, so I return the kindness with a one-dollar tip.

"Good luck," he says ominously before speeding off.

I look up at Haven House. It's impressive, all brick and ivy, ivy and brick. It sort of looks like Harvard—or at least like what I know of Harvard from the movies—both welcoming and intimidating at the same time.

I drag my suitcases to the door and ring the bell. A minute later, the door opens and a girl with curly brown hair sticks out her head.

"You must be Sarah," she says. Before I can respond, she motions for me to enter and begins talking in a rapid, no-nonsense way while I lug my suitcases into the foyer. "You're the last one to arrive. Everyone else is at the dinner. I almost thought I'd have to miss it. I'm Caitlin, by the way. I'm the head resident of Haven House. Your room's up on the fourth floor, and your roommate is . . ." She glances at her clipboard. "Madison Snow. But you already knew that. You probably e-mailed each other over the summer, right?"

"Not exactly," I say, closing the door behind me. "I e-mailed her, but she never wrote back."

Caitlin checks something off on her clipboard and says, "You're going to have to work that out with Madison." Reaching into the back pocket of her plaid Bermuda shorts, she pulls out a small envelope and hands it to me. "Here are your keys. The gold one's for the front door and the silver one is for your room. I'm going over to Belmont Hall to see if there's any food left. I suggest you drop off your bags and do the same." She hands me a brand-new campus map, pointing to a building in the southwest corner. "That's Belmont Hall. See you there."

A quick wave and she's out the door, leaving me behind in the musty entryway.

I look around. The wood paneling, dim lighting, and faint scent of leather remind me of a funeral home. Above the door hangs a banner that reads WELCOME FIRST-YEARS.

One at a time, I drag my suitcases up the stairs, stopping in front of the door that bears my name and hometown on a star-shaped piece of pink construction paper: SARAH WEAVER, BEVERLY HILLS, CA. It's strange seeing "Beverly Hills" next to my name. It makes me sound like some kind of princess, which I'm not. Nana was a teacher until just a few years ago, and when Grandpa was alive, he owned a plumbing-supply store in Culver City.

Next to my star is another that reads MADISON SNOW, NEW YORK, NY.

I place my hand on the cool doorknob. *Relax*, I tell myself. *It's just four years.*

I open the door, a little surprised to find it unlocked and a *lot* surprised to find a guy and a girl in the middle of the room doing something I really shouldn't be seeing. The girl is on her knees with her back to me, oblivious to the fact that there's a stranger in the room. The guy, on the other hand, is looking right at me. My first impulse is to bolt, but I'm too stunned to move—the guy is so incredibly good-looking. He's tall, with dark hair and green eyes, and I can barely take my eyes off him. He brings a finger to his lips and winks at me. *Hot*. Too bad he's an asshole. I turn and walk out, making sure to slam the door behind me.

I find the communal bathroom, a large, basic room with six sinks, four toilets, three shower stalls, and a bathtub. I wash my hands vigorously even though they're not dirty, and after washing and drying them three times, I feel refreshed—that is, until I look in the mirror and see what a mess I am. I've got dark circles under my eyes, chapped lips, and a frighteningly bad case of airplane hair. Shit. I hope that guy couldn't tell I was attracted to him. But guys are kind of smart that way. Even when they're clueless about everything else, they can always tell when a girl is into them. I know because I've slept with a lot of guys: some cute, some not-so-cute, and even a couple of teachers—Mr. Johnson, who taught US history, and Mr. Christopher, who taught physics and then had the nerve to give me a B for my final grade.

Suddenly the bathroom door flies open and the girl walks in. She's tall, with long, blond hair, gray eyes, and a rounded forehead like Botticelli's *Venus*. Her beauty startles me. She didn't seem beautiful at all when she was down on her knees. Who knew she had such luminous skin and high cheekbones? Even in her simple outfit of dark-wash jeans and a white T-shirt, she exudes sophistication.

"Are you Sarah?" she asks.

I hesitate. "Yeah."

She marches right up to me and extends her hand. She's so close I can smell her green-apple shampoo. "I'm Maddy," she says. "I'm going to be rooming with you."

"Nice to meet you." I shake her hand even though I really don't want to, considering where her hand has just been. Inwardly, I cringe and hope she'll leave soon so I can wash my hands again.

But she doesn't leave.

She just stands there picking at her short, midnight-blue fingernails, saying nothing. The awkwardness of the situation feels all too familiar and I get a flashback of Nana walking in on Brad and me midcoitus. Mortifying.

"Look," I say, "you don't have to worry. I didn't really see anything."

Maddy exhales. "Thank goodness. I didn't hear you come in, and I thought you were at the dinner."

"Yeah, I kind of missed orientation."

"I'm so sorry." She covers her face with her unwashed hand. "It's just that my boyfriend, Sebastian, is leaving for Cornell tonight and we're not going to be able to see each other for a couple of weeks, so . . . you know."

"Yeah," I say, though I'm not quite sure what I'm agreeing with.

She runs a hand through her hair. "The thing is, we haven't had sex yet, and I know it's frustrating him. And now he's going to be so far away! I mean, you saw him. He's gorgeous, right? Girls fawn over him. But I'm just not ready to . . . you know. We do other stuff, though," she says reassuringly, "and I know he's not going to cheat on me or anything, but still . . ."

I'd hate to be the one to break it to her, but I'm pretty sure her boyfriend cheats on her. I could see it in his eyes.

"Anyway," she says, "Sebastian's getting ready to leave, and I'd really like to introduce you to him properly."

"Oh, okay." I *so* want to wash my hand, but I don't because Maddy seems nice and I don't want to make her feel any worse.

She checks her reflection in the mirror. "By the way, I'm sorry I didn't e-mail you back. I had a very busy summer."

"No problem," I say. But I wonder, Who's too busy to answer an e-mail?

We walk back to our spare, garretlike room and find Sebastian on the floor doing sit-ups. The guy is ridiculous.

"Sweetie," Maddy says, "come and meet Sarah, my new roommate."

Sebastian jumps up and extends his hand. "Sebastian. Pleasure to meet you."

While shaking his hand, I stare at his long, black lashes and pray that my eyes won't give me away. But it's hopeless. Despite myself, I *am* attracted to him and I know he can tell. I turn and smile uncomfortably at Maddy.

"So anyway, I have to get back to Ithaca," Sebastian says, rubbing his hands together. "Can I drop you ladies off in town somewhere? I think you might've missed dinner."

"That's a great idea, sweetie," says Maddy. "There's supposed to be a yummy Italian place in town. I think it's called Antonio's." She turns to me. "It's not that far from here. Sebastian will drop us off and we can walk back. Sound good?"

"Yeah," I say, "just let me go wash my hands."

2

Sebastian drives a tricked-out Porsche SUV, metallic black with a red and gray leather interior. He's just finished explaining to me the car's various features: twenty-four-carat-gold cup holders, wood imported from the Ivory Coast, cable TV, and custom massaging suede seats. It's an obnoxious car, disgustingly ostentatious, the kind of car you'd expect Snoop Dogg to drive. I'm tempted to say this out loud, but Sebastian would probably take it as a compliment, and the last thing I want is to pay him a compliment, so I quietly lean back into my vibrating seat. I hate to admit it, but the shiatsu action does feel pretty good.

Sebastian turns to Maddy, who's riding shotgun. "*¿Dónde es la restauranto?*" he says in a wannabe-Spanish accent.

Maddy laughs. "Sweetie, it's, *Dónde está el restaurante.*"

"Oh, yeah." He playfully slaps his forehead.

"It's next to the movie theater, remember? We drove by it earlier today." Maddy turns around and rolls her eyes at me. "Sebastian wants to major in Spanish."

Stupidly, I ask, "Are you Spanish?"

"No, *señorita,*" he says, chuckling. "I'm three-quarters English, two-thirds French, and one-eighth Dutch. Or something like that."

I can't do the calculations—at least not without a pen and paper—but I *do* know that all those fractions add up to more than one person. It's a good thing Sebastian is not majoring in math. But how the hell did he get into Cornell?

He looks in the rearview mirror. We make eye contact. "You know why I'm majoring in Spanish?"

"Why?" I smile into the mirror.

"Well, I got this boat—a real beauty—and next summer I'm going to sail it to Spain. Maddy's coming with me. Right, babe?"

"I'm not sure yet, sweetie," Maddy says. "You have to learn how to sail first."

"Anyway," Sebastian continues, "I figured it'd be useful to learn Spanish for when I go there, even though everybody speaks English nowadays. And then I thought, since I'm gonna be studying Spanish for a whole year, I might as well major in it too."

I nod politely, though I think Sebastian is an idiot, and I almost lose it when I catch him winking at his own reflection in the rearview mirror.

Maddy leans toward him and begins to stroke his arm. I feel a twinge of jealousy, which is a real surprise to me since I've never liked boneheads. But despite how annoying Sebastian is, I can't deny that I have this uncontrollable urge to run my fingers through his hair. I can even imagine how it would feel—thick, soft, slightly damp. And what would it be like to kiss him? Warm. Warm and rough.

But I shouldn't be thinking about stuff like this. Sebastian is Maddy's boyfriend, not mine.

He plugs his iPod into the car stereo. Josh Groban. Singing in

Italian. Kill me now. Sebastian starts singing along, and he's got this blissful look on his face. "I love Spanish music," he says.

This is Italian, I want to say. But I can't because now I'm perversely intrigued by Sebastian. Yes, he's cheesy, but he's cheesy in such a fresh, weird way. I think I'm in love.

Or not.

Sebastian drops us off two blocks from the restaurant; it's easier for him to get on the highway. He's quite the gentleman.

"Nice meeting you," I say, and jump out of the car before he can respond.

It takes Maddy another five minutes to extricate herself from the pimpmobile. As I'm standing outside, the car windows start to fog up. When Maddy finally opens her door, she's got bed hair and an embarrassed look on her face. Before she can step out of the car, Sebastian leans over and licks her face—is he trying to be a dog or a Neanderthal?—and Maddy's embarrassment quickly turns to annoyance. Even I'm annoyed just having to *watch* this.

Maddy climbs out of the car, eyes lowered, face pink.

"Love you, babe," says Sebastian. "You're my girl." He blows her a kiss.

"Love you too," Maddy says, shutting the door.

We hear a muffled "*¡Adiós, chicas!*" before the car screeches away from the curb.

Maddy smooths down her hair with one hand and wipes her cheek with the back of the other. "Sorry about that."

"*No problemo*," I say in a mock Spanish accent, instantly regretting it.

After an awkward silence, Maddy lets out a tiny laugh. "You're funny," she says, and we begin our walk toward civilization.

She tells me that the town of Wetherly is basically this one long, dull street. Beyond it, the roads lead to forestland and open space. Depressing. We pass a used bookstore, a tea shop, an ice cream parlor, and several restaurants, all of which appear to be closed. When we finally arrive at Antonio's, I'm not exactly shocked to find it closed as well.

"Shoot," Maddy says, "it's Sunday."

"So?" Through the restaurant window I see a ceiling-high wine rack and pillar-candle chandeliers.

"Town closes on Sundays."

My stomach growls. "All of it?"

"Most of it. Anyway, don't worry, I'm sure we'll find a place," Maddy says. "Let's keep walking. I think I see something up ahead. See that blue light?"

I nod, and we walk toward the light.

It hits me that I haven't seen a single guy since Sebastian. I know Wetherly is a women's college, but does that mean the town is all-female as well? Because I don't think I could survive in a place where there aren't any men. I've never even had any female friends. I usually try to avoid girls because I'm afraid of them. When guys are mad at each other, they duke it out and then forget about it, but when a girl is mad at you, she'll ruin your life. That's exactly what happened to me when Brad Taylor's frigid and super-popular girlfriend, Sophie, found out I'd slept with him. She and her girl posse stole my backpack, egged Nana's Oldsmobile, and smeared dog shit on our front door. They terrorized me until I stopped going to school. Luckily, Nana was oblivious to my ditching, and my teachers just thought I had premature senioritis.

We stop in front of a pub where a man (finally!) in jeans and a black leather jacket is guarding the door. He's bald and muscular, and he lets us in without checking our IDs.

Inside, the place is packed. Maddy slides into a round red-leather booth, and I scooch in next to her. It's dark, the room lit by just a handful of tiny red lanterns. The air is clammy and smells a lot like feet.

I spot a few guys. A couple of them are cute. Then again, everyone looks cute from afar. There's one guy in particular who catches my eye. He's baby faced and a little on the short side, and he's standing in the corner clutching a beer. He's got an adorable button nose like River Phoenix's—which is great for me because I love River Phoenix. He may be dead but he's still hot, I always say. I first fell for River a few years ago when I saw him in *The Mosquito Coast*, which just happened to be on TV that day. It was fate. I loved everything about him: his dirty-blond hair, his blue eyes, his pouty lips, even his name. I mean, how great is a name like River? It's grand and sexy. River and I, we'd make the perfect couple. If he weren't dead, that is.

No matter. I still carry a picture of him in my wallet: a tiny, black-and-white glossy I cut out of *Entertainment Weekly*. It's an intense portrait: tight and very noir. His hair is slicked back, and there are these huge shadows around his eyes so you can't really tell if he's looking at you. God, I wish he were still alive.

Back to the cute guy in the corner. He has honey-colored hair and he's wearing a long-sleeved T-shirt with a regular T-shirt over it. Since I'm feeling kind of brave, I think I'll go talk to him.

As far as I'm concerned, there are two ways to get a guy to like you: act dumb or be slutty. If you do a combination of the two, the guy will practically fall in love with you. Sad but true. I usually opt for slutty because I hate acting dumb, and I would never do both because I don't want anyone to fall in love with me. I've never been in love before, but my parents were supposedly in love once, and the last thing I want is to end up like them: divorced and miserable. Plus, I really don't want some guy calling me twenty times a day. Or licking my face.

I glance back at the River look-alike. He's still standing in the corner. And he's still cute. Unfortunately, he seems to be checking out some girl at the bar. But here's the bigger problem: he has breasts. Not man boobs, *breasts*. River Jr. is a *girl*! I can't believe I didn't realize this earlier. It's dark in here, but still.

"I'll be right back," I say to Maddy, and hurry to the restroom, where I rinse my eyes out with cold water. *Much better.*

When I return to the table, I find Maddy sandwiched between two rough-looking guys. One has a greasy ponytail, and the other has a shaved head and a pockmarked face.

"Hi," I say, standing in front of the booth.

"Hey, Sarah," Maddy says. "So, the bad news is they don't serve food here, but the good news is that Bobby and Joe bought us some drinks."

Bobby and Joe smile at me.

"Great. Thanks," I say, although it appears that Joe, the one with the shaved head, has already chugged down the drink he bought me.

"Sit," Bobby orders. I don't know where he expects me to sit since he and his friend have taken up the entire booth, so I snatch a chair from a neighboring table and plop down at the end. Bobby is sitting very close to Maddy, staring at her lips while his tongue darts in and out of his mouth, lizardlike. Maddy, looking uncomfortable, turns away from him, but he counters by grabbing her hand, which she jerks away. Bobby snickers at Joe.

A few seconds later, Bobby begins to stroke Maddy's hair. I should probably be feeling pretty scared right now, but instead I'm just pissed. Can't Bobby tell that Maddy isn't interested?

She's trembling, for God's sake. And what right does he have to touch her?

I take a deep breath and try to calm down, but it's useless. When I'm mad, it's like I'm possessed; I never know what I'm going to say or do. The *nerve* of this guy for even thinking he has a chance with Maddy. Where does his deluded sense of confidence come from?

"Hey." I wave at Bobby to get his attention. "Maddy has a boyfriend, so maybe you should go hit on someone else."

He withdraws his hand from Maddy's hair and looks at me. "Do *you* have a boyfriend?"

"No."

"Well, I'd give you a shot, but I'm not into scrawny chicks." He laughs hard, pounding the table with his fist.

Joe lets out a guffaw.

"That's okay," I say. "I prefer guys with brains anyway."

Bobby stops laughing. His chest begins to heave and his biceps appear to be flexing of their own accord. Now I'm a little scared. I wait for him to say something.

A whole minute passes before he says, "Care to repeat that?"

Still possessed, I say, "I think you heard me the first time."

His nostrils flare. "I know what your problem is, sweetheart. You've never been with a *real* man."

A bead of sweat trickles down my back. "Actually, I have."

"Yeah? Why don't you tell me about it?"

"It's none of your business." I glance at Maddy, who has turned an unnatural shade of pale.

Bobby looks at Maddy and then back at me. "Tell you what, tough girl, I'll make you a deal. You tell me about the last time you spent the night with a real man, and I'll leave you and your friend alone. Okay?"

Or we could just walk out of here. Unfortunately, Maddy is wedged between these two yahoos.

Sensing my fear, Bobby smirks. "Well?" He turns and makes a kissy face at Maddy.

Out of nowhere, a small, bony hand reaches forward and grabs Bobby by the ponytail. His head jerks back. "What the fuck?" he yelps.

Standing next to me is a short, anorexic, homely-looking girl with a dark brown bob and a death grip on Bobby. She leans in close to Bobby's face and whispers something in his ear, and then, surprisingly, Bobby gets up and leaves with Joe trailing closely behind.

"How did you know we were here?" Maddy asks the girl with the bob.

"You weren't picking up your cell, so I called Sebastian," the girl says.

Maddy slides out of the booth. "But I told Sebastian we were going to Antonio's."

"It was closed. I drove around until I found this place. Come on. Let's get out of here."

I follow the two of them outside, where Maddy introduces me to her friend Agnes Pierce. Although I'm grateful to Agnes for sort of having saved my life, I instantly know that I'm not going to like this girl. There's just something about her. She's got small, hateful blue eyes and an unnervingly steady gaze. Her lips are thin and unsmiling, her cheekbones sharp, and she's wearing the strangest outfit for a girl our age: a boxy, baby-blue cashmere sweater set, cream-colored pants, and pearls. From the crook of her elbow hangs a quilted ivory Chanel bag. She looks like she could be her own mother.

"We should go," Agnes says.

Her black Mercedes sedan is parked right in front of the bar. I reluctantly climb into the backseat, which feels like a coffin: chilly and airless.

"I know a place," Agnes says, starting the car. She turns on the stereo, blasting classical as though it were gangsta rap.

I once read that listening to classical music was supposed to make you smarter. This was when I was still in high school, about a month before I had to take the SATs, so naturally I was curious about the theory. Every day for a week, I listened to those old guys: Bach, Beethoven, Mozart, Tchaikovsky—but by the end of the week I didn't feel at all smarter. And then I started thinking, why do I want to be smarter? Smart people are never happy, and since I'm already depressed, classical music could have serious repercussions for me. What if I were to end up in a bloody tub one day all because of Brahms? So, I no longer listen to classical music. Unless it's forced upon me, like right now.

Agnes lowers the volume and rolls her shoulders.

Maddy says, "Let's just go back to the house."

"But you haven't had dinner and you have to eat, Maddy," says Agnes, in a soft, nurturing voice, different from the one she was using earlier. This new voice sounds fake and it makes me dislike Agnes even more. You just can't trust people with multiple voices. Multiple voices are like multiple personalities: scary.

3

There it is," Agnes says, as we approach a huge, silver, bullet-shaped structure, flickering in the distance like a UFO.

We're in the middle of nowhere and Agnes is whipping down the dark highway with the ease of a madwoman.

"What is it?" Maddy asks.

"A diner," says Agnes. "I doubt the food will be any good, but seeing as how nothing else is open at this hour . . ."

It's a truck stop. Agnes squeezes the car in between two semis and we step out. My stomach is queasy from her insane driving, but Agnes looks invigorated: cheeks pink, pupils slightly dilated.

"Do you always drive that fast?" I ask her.

"Only when I'm in a hurry," she says, slamming the door. So she's a bad driver *and* a smart-ass. Wonderful.

"Do you think we could go a little slower on the way back?" I say, clutching my stomach for effect. "I wouldn't want to get sick all over your nice leather seats."

"Don't worry. No one's allowed to get sick in *my* car." She lets out a deranged cackle. Freak.

It's eleven o'clock and the diner is bustling with ranchers, truckers, and rugged-looking people in denim and corduroy, with faces warped by boredom and a few too many Massachusetts winters. With her Chanel bag and matching ballet flats, Agnes looks completely out of place here, but she doesn't seem to care or notice. Country music twangs from the overhead speakers and all the waitresses wear the same sassy expression—like they don't give a shit. The place is so bright it kind of reminds me of California, where the oppressive sun could melt your face off.

After a few minutes of just standing around waiting, Agnes begins to tap her foot against the tile floor. She stops a middle-aged waitress passing by with two coffeepots and says, "Is someone going to seat us . . . today?"

The waitress snaps, "Excuse me, Your Highness, but can't you see my hands are full? I'll be with you in a minute." And with that, she disappears into the kitchen, never to return.

"A minute here is like a New York *day*," Agnes mutters.

We seem to be getting a lot of stares from oily, middle-aged men, many of whom have perked up ever since Maddy walked through the door. Maddy doesn't seem to care, demurely looking away anytime someone tries to make eye contact with her. I'm sure she's used to getting attention from men, though these aren't the kind of guys I'd imagine *any* girl being interested in, much less a beautiful girl like her. Agnes, on the other hand, seems to be annoyed that Maddy is being ogled. I can tell because she's got a scowl on her face and she's nervously picking lint off Maddy's back, like it's her way of claiming Maddy or something.

"Stop," Maddy finally says, pushing Agnes away.

I scan the diner. There's no one interesting except for a guy who's sitting alone in a corner booth, making paper-doll chains. He's bone pale, dark haired, in his early twenties, and dressed entirely in black. He looks a lot like Edward Scissorhands. I try not to stare at him.

By the time we're seated, I'm ravenous. Maddy and Agnes sit down on one side of the booth and I sit on the opposite side. Maddy and I order cheeseburgers, fries, and strawberry shakes from a tired waitress with frizzy, coppery-gray hair. Agnes orders a cup of hot water. Who is she kidding? Like she doesn't eat? When the waitress walks away, Agnes's eyes bore into me. She's studying me, looking for flaws. Someone should tell her it's rude to stare.

I look at Maddy, who's been quiet ever since we left the bar. I ask, "So how did you two become friends?"

Maddy smiles. "Our moms were best friends. They met at Wetherly, and Agnes and I practically grew up together. We're more like sisters than friends."

"*Best* friends," Agnes adds haughtily.

So they're legacy students. I nod and try to look interested, but of course the real question I want to ask—and the thing that's been on my mind for the past half hour—is what Agnes whispered to Bobby to make him go away. But I get the feeling that Agnes won't tell me anyway, so I don't ask.

Maddy goes on to tell me her life story. She's an only child from New York whose parents died in a car accident three years ago. Apparently, her parents were divorced and having an affair with each other after her mother had already married Maddy's stepdad, a well-known Manhattan shrink. Her stepdad didn't learn of the affair until the day Maddy's parents died, and apparently he's still angry about it. He feels especially betrayed by Maddy because she kept her parents' affair a secret, and to this day he still calls her, whimpering into the phone. Now she lives with her aunt and uncle—both of whom are high school teachers—in Queens. The quiver in Maddy's lip tells me her life is not a happy one, and shortly after mentioning her aunt and uncle, she tenses up and stops talking altogether. Poor girl. Her life has more drama than *As the World Turns.*

The waitress returns with our food. "Here's your hot water," she says icily to Agnes. "You sure you don't want a tea bag to go with that?"

"I'm sure," Agnes says with a smirk.

The waitress stalks off.

Agnes takes a sip of her water and makes a face. "Luke-warm." She pushes the mug toward the edge of the table.

"You're not hungry?" I ask.

"No," she says curtly while stealing a fry from Maddy's plate. "I'm a vegetarian."

O-kay.

Maddy then starts telling me Agnes's life story as though Agnes weren't here. I learn that Agnes comes from a prominent New York family who can trace their roots back to the Mayflower. She had a precious upbringing: maids, butlers, trips around the world, homes in New York, Massachusetts, and Connecticut. Apparently, her father owns half of Massachusetts and most of Connecticut, blah, blah, blah. Although I do find some of the story interesting, it's impossible to concentrate, what with Agnes mad-dogging me.

When Maddy finishes talking, Agnes leers at me and says, "So what do *your* parents do?"

I pause, trying to think of how I should answer this. The truth is, my parents, when I knew them, were alcoholics who struggled to hold down jobs. My mother left when I was five, never to be heard from again, and my father currently lives in Vegas with his stripper girlfriend. Sometimes he sends postcards, but never money. Even Nana thinks he's a loser, and he's her only child. I'm so tempted to tell Agnes my parents are big Hollywood producers or famous plastic surgeons, but I can't decide which way to go, and then I start worrying that I won't be able to pull it off anyway, so I just say the next thing that comes to mind: "My parents are dead." I glance at Agnes to gauge her reaction. She looks completely unaffected, stoic as a monk.

"I'm sorry," Maddy says, looking down at the table and then at Agnes. "I definitely know how you feel."

"It's no big deal," I say, hoping she'll drop the subject before I start feeling guilty. The last thing I want is for Maddy to feel sorry for me when she's the real orphan. Plus, she's got a dumb ass for a boyfriend. She deserves my sympathy.

"Are you a scholarship student?" Agnes asks, squinting at me as if I'm some kind of alien.

My ears grow hot. "No."

I look down, not wanting her to see the lack of privilege and breeding in my eyes. But, like a bloodhound, she keeps sniffing, keeps searching my face for clues. I want to ask her why she's such a bitch—does it come naturally to her or did it take years to cultivate?

"Who's paying for your education?"

My God, she just won't quit.

"Agnes," Maddy scolds, "you're being nosy."

"It's okay," I say. "I don't mind." But I *do* mind. I contemplate telling them the truth: about Nana, about our life in California and how Nana used up a large chunk of her savings to pay for my education, not because she cares about me, but because she wanted to get rid of me. But I can't make myself say the words. I won't be bullied by this spoiled brat no matter who her dad is, so I say, "My parents left me some money."

"Oh." Agnes looks bored as hell. "So, what made you decide to come to Wetherly?"

Brad's naked body pops into my mind. But instead of telling her about the stupid incident that led me here, I just shrug.

Agnes smirks. Whether she's impressed by my apathy or simply annoyed, I can't tell. She glances at Maddy. Something passes between them, but I'm not sure what it is. It seems like all night they've been mostly communicating nonverbally. It's like one can give the other a look and the other will know exactly what she's thinking, the way twins do. Or lovers. I envy their closeness. What would it be like to have a best friend who knows everything about me and still likes me? I chew on a fry while contemplating this.

"You're from California," Agnes says.

"How'd you know?" It was naive of me to think the interrogation was over.

"Your accent gave you away."

"She doesn't have an accent," says Maddy.

"Yes, she does. It's part Valley Girl, part surfer." Agnes snickers. We make eye contact. "Are you from Los Angeles?"

I nod, not sure where she's going with this.

"I knew it," she says, beaming.

I roll my eyes, but Agnes is too busy giving Maddy another nonverbal cue to notice. Then she touches Maddy's hair and leans in to whisper something in her ear. To me, it sounds like, "See? I'm psychic too."

Is she mocking me?

Maddy responds by giving Agnes a shove, and then the two of them burst into giggles like children.

"So what did you say to Bobby to make him leave?" I finally ask.

Agnes stops laughing. "Who?"

"Bobby. The guy at the bar."

"Oh, *him*. I'd rather not say."

"Tell her," Maddy says, sending Agnes another telepathic signal.

Agnes glances back at Maddy and then at me, and leans forward. She motions for me to do the same. She covers her mouth like she's going to whisper the answer and then . . . nothing.

I wait, craning my neck further.

Finally, Agnes whispers, "Boo." She laughs hysterically.

I shrug and act like I don't care, but all I can think is: *bitch*.

"That was mean, Agnes," says Maddy. "Stop joking around. Tell Sarah what you said, what you always say when you're in trouble."

Agnes shrugs. "Fine." She looks me in the eye. "I told him I had a gun in my purse and that I wasn't afraid to use it."

"And he believed you?" I ask.

"Why wouldn't he?" Agnes says. "It's true. Of course, I did have my purse slightly open so he could see it poking out. But I think he would've believed me regardless."

I glance at Maddy, who's busy stirring her shake. She doesn't look up, so I turn back to Agnes. "You have a gun? Why?"

Agnes chuckles. "Don't you watch the news? It's a crazy world out there, and security is *very* important to me."

Still stirring her shake, Maddy deadpans, "Better not get on Agnes's bad side."

"Very funny," Agnes says. "It's not like I carry it around with me all the time. But I'm sure glad I had it tonight."

Agnes looks at me and then does something really scary: she smiles. It's a sinister smile, crooked and laced with malice. Her lips are pressed together so tightly that they're starting to turn white, and her eyes are smug, arrogant, not at all inviting. It's probably the best she can do; I doubt she's had much practice. The thing that surprises me is that she seems to be warming up to me. Did I pass her test? I didn't think it would be this easy, and—as much as I hate to admit it—I'm kind of flattered. That's how it is with mean people: they have all the power because they simply do not care. The minute they're nice to you, you feel all honored—like you did something right, like you won them over with your charm or wit or intelligence—when all you did was fall into their trap.

I don't trust Agnes one bit.

I look over at the Scissorhands guy, who is stretching a doll chain across the table. With a magnifying glass, he examines each doll. When he glances back at me, I turn and look out the window.

The ride home is speedy, as expected. Agnes is in a great mood, humming along to another opera. Even with our headlights on, the highway is incredibly dark. We might as well be wearing blindfolds.

Suddenly Maddy yells, "Stop!"

There's a loud bang, followed by a horrible crunching sound. We've hit a boulder or something.

"What was that?" Agnes says calmly.

She pulls over and slips her gun into her pocket before getting out of the car. Maddy and I follow her out to the middle of the highway, where a fawn is lying on the ground, trembling, blood oozing from one of its legs. Maddy shrieks and kneels down beside the animal as it yelps and bleats in an excruciatingly high pitch. The sight of blood alone is enough to make me sick, but coupled with the animal's screeching, it is just too much.

I turn toward the forest. A pair of eyes stares back at me. An owl, I think. I wish someone would put this young deer out of its misery. Then maybe it could be reincarnated as a bear or a mountain lion. What was it doing crossing the highway anyway? Especially at night. Didn't its mother teach it not to do that? Well, at least the fawn won't have to suffer when it's dead. Death is the ultimate escape from all that sucks in the world.

The squeals continue. I try to block them out. I've learned that it's best to ignore the sad things in life, because if you let yourself feel every single sad thing out there, you'll lose your mind. It's true. Besides, successful people are guided by logic and reason, not feelings. And maybe they aren't the nicest people in the world, but at least they're not going around having nervous breakdowns. I don't really care about being successful, but I do care about my sanity.

There. I feel nothing.

I turn toward Agnes, who's examining her car for damage. There's blood everywhere.

"Agnes, do something!" Maddy wails.

"What do you want me to do?" Agnes says, fingering a tiny dent on the door.

"Anything. You're premed. You of all people should know what to do." Maddy removes her thin white jacket and covers the fawn with it. The jacket slowly turns scarlet.

The fawn's eyes, I notice, are liquid, desperate—a little like Maddy's.

"She's in so much pain," Maddy whimpers. "We have to take her to a hospital."

"Can't do that. They'll send us home," Agnes says. "I doubt it has health insurance."

"That's not funny," says Maddy.

"I'm just saying hospitals don't admit venison as patients," Agnes says, suppressing a smile. "Besides, I don't think this deer is going to make it. It's bleeding pretty heavily."

"What about an animal hospital?" I suggest.

"We're in the boondocks," snaps Agnes. "There are no animal hospitals here."

"Well, we can't just leave her here to be eaten by wild animals, can we?" Maddy trembles. "You did this, Agnes. You have to fix it. We can't just abandon her. We can't!" She's practically delirious. She must really love animals.

Agnes goes over to Maddy and pats her on the head, as though Maddy were a small child. It's an odd, slightly condescending gesture.

"Do something," Maddy whines again, looking up at her.

"Agnes," I say, "do you have a first-aid kit in your car?"

"Of course." She pops open the trunk and takes out a large blue box. She then crouches down next to the fawn and expertly bandages its injured leg with a long strip of gauze.

But the fawn continues to bleat.

"I've stopped the bleeding," Agnes announces. "Now what?"

Suddenly another deer—a much larger one—appears out of the darkness, probably in answer to the fawn's wails. Maddy notices it first and whispers to me, "It's the mother." Agnes is still hunched over the fawn, her back to the mother deer. The mother deer leaps toward Agnes.

"Watch out!" Maddy screams.

"What?" Agnes turns around. The mother deer, standing two feet away, shrieks angrily at Agnes. Agnes calmly gets up and reaches inside her pocket. As the mother deer inches toward her,

Agnes slowly backs away and pulls out her gun. She's going to shoot it?

"No, Agnes, don't hurt her," Maddy pleads.

"I'm not going to," Agnes says, annoyed. "God." She points the pistol in the air and fires it. The sound is so tremendous that my whole body shakes.

The mother deer sprints back into the forest, into the night, and leaves her offspring half-dead on the empty highway. Mothers. Why am I not surprised?

"Let's take her to the house. We can nurse her back to health there," Maddy says, wiping away tears with the back of her hand. Her T-shirt is soaked with the deer's blood and she's looking a little like Stephen King's Carrie right now.

"They allow pets in the dorm?" I ask.

"No, but you don't mind, do you, Sarah?" Maddy pleads. "She won't bother us and we'll just keep her until she gets better. Then we'll bring her back to the forest. *Please?*"

I don't know what to say. I never had a pet growing up, but who knows? Maybe my childhood would have been more tolerable with a cat or something. Nana claimed to be allergic to anything furry, especially if it moved, but she was just lying to me so I wouldn't bug her about getting a dog. But if she really knew me, she wouldn't have bothered. I never would've asked for a dog—they're too hyper. But fawns are pretty mellow, right?

"Okay," I say reluctantly. Relief spreads across Maddy's face. Agnes looks to the ground and shakes her head.

What if the fawn has ticks? What if it can't be litter-box trained?

"I'm going to name her Hope," Maddy says cheerfully. She sweeps the fawn into her arms and carries it to the car.

"Wait," Agnes says to her, opening the trunk again. She takes out a piece of tarp and drapes it over the backseat. Then she and Maddy maneuver the fawn into the car.

Silently, we drive away.

4

It's Sunday night and I'm in my room with Maddy and Agnes. The first two weeks have flown by and I have more or less settled into my life here.

Our room is on the small side, sparsely furnished with identical sets of everything—beds, bureaus, desks, chairs. It's a cozy space, with dark wood floors, a sloping roof, a bay window, and a window seat. Maddy's poster of Monet's "Water Lilies" hangs above our desks, and her red Persian rug fills the space between our beds. What the room really needs is my River Phoenix poster, which is still rolled up in the closet, but I'm not ready to share that side of myself with Maddy and Agnes yet. They might think I'm some kind of deranged fan.

Maddy is sitting cross-legged on the floor, feeding Hope chunks of Brie while flipping through the latest issue of *Vogue*. Agnes, who never sits on the floor unless there's something separating her from it—like a cushion or a textbook—is sitting at Maddy's desk, using her laptop. I'm sitting on the window seat, reading *Us Weekly* and trying hard to ignore Agnes, who's been whining about her roommate, Crystal Buckley, a Texas cheerleader type with long, dirty-blond hair and acrylic nails. The first time I saw Crystal in the hallway, I thought, Wouldn't it be funny if Agnes were forced to share a room with someone like her? Then, when I found out Crystal actually *was* Agnes's roommate, I couldn't help but think I was psychic. I'm pretty intuitive when it comes to stupid things.

"She borrowed my Kelly bag without asking," Agnes says. "Then she had the nerve to return it to me filthy."

"Filthy?" I ask.

"There were little specks on the strap."

"Specks?" I repeat.

"Yes! They were disgusting. I don't know what they were." Agnes sighs. "I have to move out. I can't bear another minute with that beast."

Maddy looks up from applying face cream to one of Hope's hooves and says, "Don't you think you're overreacting?"

Agnes just looks at her. "What in God's name are you doing?"

"What?" Maddy asks. "Her paws looked dry."

"That's Crème de la Mer!" Agnes exclaims. She shakes her head disapprovingly, but she doesn't fool me: her eyes are full of adoration.

"Hope is worth it," says Maddy. "Aren't you, Hope?" She moons at the deer.

Hope gives Maddy a blank look. I guess fawns only have one expression because I haven't seen Hope look anything but blank since the night we ran her over. Luckily, she's doing a lot better now, but having a pet deer is not much fun. The room is starting to smell like a zoo: dank and strangely fishy, no matter how much Jo Malone Maddy sprays into the air. And since Hope failed our litter-box training session, she basically goes to the bathroom wherever she wants. The odor is so bad I'm surprised our housemates haven't complained yet.

Another annoying thing about Hope is that she likes to walk around the room at night, making it impossible to sleep. As cute as she is, she has horrendous breath, which for some reason she enjoys blowing on me in the middle of the night. I've been fantasizing about a speedy recovery for her so we can take her back to the forest. But I wonder how Maddy will handle it. She and Hope are practically codependent now. Even Agnes is starting to warm up to her, despite her aversion to animals, shyly petting her now and then when she thinks no one's looking. Once I caught her feeding Hope champagne truffles. "What?" she said when I gave her a funny look. "Champagne gives me migraines. I guess my mother forgot about that when she was putting together my care package." Agnes frowned, fed Hope another truffle, and added, "But at least someone likes them."

"There," Maddy says to Hope. "Your paws are properly hydrated now."

Agnes grins at her. "You mean *hooves*."

"Oh, right." Maddy laughs.

Agnes turns back to her laptop and says, "It's good to see you happy, M."

It's obvious to me now that Agnes is in love with Maddy—she practically coos whenever she speaks to her—but I wonder if Maddy sees it. She'd have to be clueless not to, but if she does, she's definitely not acknowledging it.

"She's so vile," says Agnes.

"Who?" I ask.

"Crystal. Haven't you been listening to me?" snaps Agnes. It amazes me how fast she can go from zero to bitch.

"If she's so horrible," I say, "why don't you just shoot her with your gun?" I snort and look over at Maddy, who isn't laughing.

Agnes keeps staring at her computer screen. My joke hangs in the air.

A minute later, Agnes whines, "Maddy, how am I going to get into med school with that bimbo for a roommate? I can't even study in my own room. Did I tell you she sleeps twelve hours a night and can't tolerate any light?"

"You've told us a million times," I say.

Agnes purses her lips. "I was talking to Maddy. You're just lucky you got Maddy for a roommate and not some freak."

Agnes is right. Maddy is a great roommate. She's considerate and easy to live with—minus the whole fawn fixation, of course. Her obsession with hair is a little annoying—she trims her split ends with a pair of Winnie the Pooh scissors while talking on the phone to Sebastian—but nobody's perfect. I could have done a lot worse. I could have gotten Agnes.

Maddy rests her face in her hands, a gesture that makes me think of Audrey Hepburn, and says to Agnes, "It'll get better. You just need time to adjust is all."

"How can I adjust to someone who tweezes her pubic hair in front of me? Why doesn't she have the decency to get waxed in a salon, or at least do it in the bathroom where I don't have to see it? The really abominable part? She doesn't put the tweezed hairs in the wastebasket. She just throws them on the floor, where they get stuck between the floorboards." Agnes turns red with agitation. "I can't sleep at night knowing those wretched pubic hairs are scattered across our room. It's like she's marking her territory. I have to move out."

This is the first time I've seen Agnes lose her cool. Obviously she has a bad case of OCD, and in a weird way, that's comforting to know. But I also feel for her. I wouldn't want somebody's pubic hair all over my room either.

"But you can't move out," I say.

"Why not?" says Agnes.

"First-years aren't allowed to live off-campus."

"Let's just say the rule doesn't apply to you when the school's expecting a large donation from your parents. I don't think they'd object to my living in Zimbabwe if that's what I wanted."

I try to picture Agnes in Zimbabwe, dressed in her twinset and pearls, riding an elephant. The image makes me shudder.

Agnes glares at me. "What?"

"Nothing." I look at Maddy, who's moved on to cuddling with the fawn.

"Oh my," says Agnes, pointing at her computer screen. "Come and look at this house."

I get up from the window seat. On-screen is an image of a large white Victorian house that reminds me of the Haunted Mansion at Disneyland.

"This is the one," Agnes says. "M, come look."

Maddy untangles herself from the fawn and comes over. "Oh, wow. I like the porch. How many bedrooms does it have?"

"Four. So that's one for each of us, plus an extra room for Hope."

"You're going to rent this house?" I ask Agnes.

She nods.

"Why?"

"Because I want my own place, and this way we can all live together."

"Yay!" Maddy says, clapping her hands.

"But . . ." I trail off. Live together? Is she serious? Would the college even allow me to live off-campus? They're certainly not expecting a large donation from Nana. And even if they allowed it, I wouldn't be able to afford the rent.

Agnes says, "Let's go drive by."

"Now?" Maddy asks.

Agnes nods.

"Okay," says Maddy.

Agnes raises her eyebrows at me. "Coming?"

"No," I say. "I have a lot of reading to do."

"Oh, come on, it'll be fun," Maddy coaxes.

"I have to read three psych chapters by tomorrow."

"Well, in that case," Agnes says, "enjoy the stench."

"Hey," Maddy says, slapping Agnes's arm.

"We won't be long anyway," says Agnes, snatching her car keys off Maddy's desk. "Don't forget to lock the door."

"Why?" I ask.

"Security," Agnes says.

I ignore the warning. We live in an all-female dorm at an all-female college. What could happen?

Maddy kisses the top of Hope's head. Then she comes over to me and kisses the top of mine. "Sure you don't want to be with us?"

I can't help but wonder about her choice of words: *be with us.* Are we not allowed to be apart?

"I'm going to stay here," I say.

Agnes opens the door and "Down Boy" by the Yeah Yeah Yeahs blasts into the room from across the hall.

"I like this song," I say.

Agnes immediately closes the door. "Sorry, but I can't hear. Come on, M."

"You know," Maddy says, stroking my hair, "I think you'd look really cute with a pixie."

"What?"

"Like Winona Ryder in *Girl, Interrupted*."

I shake my head. "I've never had short hair before."

"It would look *so* good on you. Here, I'll show you a picture." She grabs a hair magazine from a pile on the floor.

Agnes taps her foot. "Can we do this later?"

"Just a sec," says Maddy.

"I'll be outside," Agnes says, opening the door again and disappearing into the hallway.

Maddy holds up a picture of a waif with short, spiky hair. "Isn't that adorable?"

"On her, yes. On me, it would look stupid."

"Are you kidding? With your bone structure? It'd look even better on you."

Her compliment makes me uncomfortable, so I say, "Shouldn't you get going?"

"Yeah, I guess. We can talk about this later."

Can't wait.

Finally Maddy leaves, closing the door behind her. Alone at last. Well, sort of. Hope is looking at me with her wet, dopey eyes.

I think of Nana and picture her sitting on her rat-colored La-Z-Boy, feet propped up, chain-smoking, eyes glued to the TV. Should I call her? We haven't spoken since the day I left California. I don't really feel like talking to her, but I'm almost broke and the check she promised to send still hasn't arrived. Before I left, I asked Nana if she thought she'd get lonely without me. She just shook her head and said, "I could always get a dog." *You told me you were allergic,* I wanted to say but didn't. Nana's a bitch. I don't get it: aren't grandparents supposed to love their grandchildren? Isn't it one of the laws of nature or something?

I decide not to call her.

Not knowing what to do with myself, I open the door to the large walk-in closet Maddy and I share. I study her clothes: Marc Jacobs, Chloé, Louis Vuitton, Proenza Schouler, and a bunch of designers I've never heard of. Most of the pieces are unworn, with their tags still dangling at their sides. I reach for one of the price tags: $3,175 for an Azzedine Alaia dress. It's worth more than my entire wardrobe. I let my fingers run over the mistlike fabric.

Then a pink gown with spaghetti straps catches my eye. It's incredibly soft and looks like something Paris Hilton might wear on a rare good day. It's not something I would ever wear, even if I had the body for it, because it's just not me—I hate pink—and yet I have the urge to put the dress on.

So I do. I know it's weird, but I can't seem to stop myself.

Maddy is way taller and curvier than I am, so the dress hangs on my body like a drop cloth. But does that stop me from prancing around the room like a debutante? Sadly, no. I feel amazing in the dress, completely transformed. So this is what it feels like to be Madison Snow. Life suddenly appears a lot sweeter.

I step in front of Maddy's full-length mirror and do a shimmy. Then I pull the dress taut against my body and pile my hair on top of my head. Maybe Maddy was right. Maybe I should think about cutting my hair. I could use a change, and short hair would be so much easier to manage. Plus, with no guys around, who is there to impress?

I can't stop staring at myself. Is this what heiresses do? Pose in front of mirrors all day long?

Suddenly I feel a twinge of panic. I feel strange and disoriented and I can't breathe. It's like I'm being consumed by Maddy. This dress, which was once on her perfect body, is now on mine. I've crossed a line.

I try to distract myself with the framed photograph of Sebastian sitting on top of Maddy's dresser. It's a black-and-white snapshot of him lying in bed, looking unbelievably sexy, like he's just woken up. I put down the frame, then open the top drawer of Maddy's dresser. It's a minipharmacy, with everything from Adderall to Zoloft. Is she depressed? Well, who isn't? I pick up the bottle of Zoloft, but before I can open it, there's a knock at the door.

Shit.

I try not to panic, remembering the door is unlocked. I put the bottle back into the bureau and slam the drawer shut.

"Maddy? Can I come in?" It's a guy's voice. *Sebastian?* But Cornell's so far away.

I try to undress as quickly as possible. But then the zipper gets stuck. I tug and tug on it until it *really* gets stuck. *Damn.* I sprint toward the closet just as the doorknob begins to turn.

5

$f$rom inside the closet, I hear the door open. I hope that whoever he is will go away once he realizes no one is here.

"Hello? *Hellooooo*. Anybody home?"

He definitely sounds dumb enough to be Sebastian.

"Maddy, are you here? Maddy? Baby?" He starts to whistle, and then I hear him mutter, "Oh, yeah. Uh-huh."

I stick my head out of the closet.

Yup, it's Sebastian, and he's checking himself out in Maddy's full-length mirror. As much as I hate to admit it, he does look pretty cute today. His hair is deliberately messy and he's wearing jeans and a lime-green T-shirt. He sniffs his armpits and then looks up.

When he notices me, he takes a step back. "Whoa, you scared me. Didn't see you standing there."

"Don't you knock?"

"I *did* knock. You didn't hear me?" He scratches the back of his neck.

"I'm trying to get dressed."

"I'll close the door."

"No!"

But it's too late. The door is closed, and now Sebastian is busy locking it. He turns to face me, then leans seductively against the wall.

We're alone and it's suddenly very quiet.

"There, that's better," he says with a wink. "Now you can get dressed."

"Do you mind?"

"No, I don't mind. I don't mind at all." He gives me a toothy grin.

Is he flirting with me, or am I hallucinating? I feel a bit light-headed. I glare at him. "What are you doing here?"

"I came by to surprise Maddy. Is she hiding in that closet with you?"

My face goes hot. "Maddy went out with Agnes, but they'll be back soon. Why don't you wait for them downstairs? In the Poetry Room."

"Why don't I just wait here?"

"Because I'm changing," I say.

"That's okay. Take your time."

Before I can protest, he's kicking off his shoes and making himself comfortable on my bed. How am I going to get rid of him? I could yell "rape" or "misogynist," which would surely result in a stampede of angry feminists but I don't think Sebastian deserves that harsh a punishment. *It'll be okay*, I tell myself. I just need to get out of Maddy's dress.

I close the closet door and say, "I'll be out in a sec."

In the dark, I fumble for the zipper at the back of the dress, tugging at it vigorously. It doesn't budge. I try pulling the dress up over my head, but the narrow waist gets stuck around my chest and restrains both of my arms in a ridiculous upright position. The rest of the dress is wrapped around my head so I can't see a damn thing. Aside from cutting the dress open, I don't know how I'm going to get out of it. And now I'm starting to sweat. Fabulous.

The closet door suddenly opens and light from the room filters in through the pale pink fabric.

"Get out!" I shout.

Ignoring me, Sebastian slips inside and shuts the door behind him. My throat closes. The sound of his breath, slow and heavy, pounds in my ears. I want to die. I can only imagine how stupid I look, mummified in Maddy's dress with my ass hanging out.

"Whoa," he says. "It's dark in here."

"Would you please leave?"

"It looks like you need some help." He chuckles.

"I don't need your help."

"You know, you're not being very nice. After I drove all this way too. Here, let me help you. Why *are* you wearing Maddy's dress anyway?"

"I'm not," I say.

"Uh, yes, you are. I was with Maddy when she bought this dress."

Fuck. "This isn't what it looks like," I stammer.

I'm beyond mortified, so I don't struggle when Sebastian helps me unzip the dress, and I don't object when he lets the dress slide to the floor, leaving me in my bra and panties. And I don't cringe when his clammy hands linger on my hips.

What happens next, of course, is no surprise. Sex is practically inevitable when you're standing half-naked in front of a horny, sexually deprived guy. Even if you have cellulite. It's true—guys don't care, at least not while you're having sex. God, if I'd known sex was on today's menu, I would have shaved my legs. My psychic powers must be waning.

Ten minutes later, we're done. Sebastian is not much of a lover, but I'm relieved because if he'd lasted a minute longer, I would have been plagued by guilt too soon, ruining the whole experience. Surprisingly, not once did I think of Maddy or how wrong it was to screw her boyfriend. Until now.

The closet floor feels like a block of ice against my back. I can't believe I had sex with Maddy's boyfriend! Why did I do this? I really like Maddy, and it's not like I'm after Sebastian— God, no. Maybe I was scared that Sebastian would tell Maddy about the dress. But I wasn't *that* scared. And Maddy is not the kind of person who would stop being my friend just because I raided her closet. Maybe the act of wearing Maddy's dress was just too intimate and it made me temporarily insane. I don't know. I am a mystery to myself.

Maybe it's Wetherly's fault. Maybe deprivation of the opposite sex results in bad, desperate behavior. That's probably it. Now if only I could figure out a way to get rid of this guilt . . .

Sebastian is lying on the floor, slapping his belly. I get up and open the closet door.

"Was it good for you?" he asks, sounding like a sleazebag. Who says that kind of stuff?

"Look, Sebastian, I feel horrible about this," I say, while trying to locate my jeans. I find them on the bed and scramble into them. Then I pull a T-shirt over my head. "This was a mistake. It can't happen again. Maddy's my friend and I would never do anything to hurt her."

"But you have to admit, it *was* pretty fun," he says with a smirk.

"You need to get dressed. They'll be back any minute."

He gets up. "Okay, okay. Don't get me wrong, Sarah . . . I'm not a bad guy. I don't go around doing stuff like this. But I am a guy. Stuff happens. It doesn't mean I don't love Maddy. She's still my girl."

The words sting. I'm unable to speak. Then I regain my composure and say, "Good. Then you won't tell Maddy I was trying on her dress?"

"I don't know. I'll need to think about that," he says, pulling on his black, semisheer Gucci boxers. *Ick.* "Of course, if you gave me a massage, like, on my butt—that area's very tight—I might be more agreeable . . ."

I look at him, not sure if he's kidding.

"Oh, relax. I won't say anything." He steps out of the closet and finishes getting dressed.

His eyes, I notice, aren't that pretty a green. And his body is a lot softer than it looks clothed—all muscle turned to fat. He's got a gut and a ton of chest hair. But as disgusted as I am with him, and myself, and his body, and even those stupid boxers, he still is pretty cute. Cute in a cheesy boy-band way. When he's not talking. Oh, who am I kidding? He's gross.

"There she is," Sebastian says.

I panic and lunge toward the window. "Where?"

"I meant the deer. I didn't notice her before. She's so quiet. But she reeks. At first I thought it was me. I told Maddy you guys should've just shot her."

"That's nice. You know where the Poetry Room is, right?"

"Yeah, yeah. I'll find it."

When Sebastian finally leaves, I lock the door. If I'd just

listened to Agnes and locked it in the first place, none of this would've happened. *God*. Now I have to desex this room pronto.

I throw open the windows and frantically spray Maddy's Jo Malone over everything: the beds, the rug, and especially inside the closet. My efforts are probably unnecessary, since the stench from the fawn could mask any odor.

I look at Hope: cute, innocent, curled up on Maddy's bed. Is it me or is her face a little angry, a little accusatory? Does she know I just betrayed Maddy? Either she's smarter than she looks or I'm really starting to lose it. There's an empty can of pâté on the rug and next to it, a puddle of diarrhea. I can't think of a more perfect metaphor for how I feel right now.

"Great. See what you did?" I say to Hope, pointing at the mess. She turns away. "What? You won't even look at me now? Well, fuck you!" Then, feeling slightly moronic for swearing at a fawn, I say, "Sorry."

Hope meets my gaze. Now she looks kind of sad. The poor thing has been throwing up a lot lately, thanks to all the junk Maddy feeds her. I examine the puddle, trying to figure out the best way to attack it. A shiver runs through my body. What's wrong with me? I should be glad to be cleaning up this mess. It's the least I can do for Maddy after fucking her boyfriend. I grab the nearest magazine, an *Us Weekly* with Justin Timberlake on the cover, and scoop up the mess. I never did care much for Justin Timberlake.

6

maddy's key slices into the lock and my two friends tumble inside. I look for traces of suspicion on Maddy's face. For a second, she seems preoccupied but then she flashes me a big smile.

"Guess what?" she says to me.

"What?" I try to stay calm.

"We just saw Sebastian. He drove all the way from Cornell just to give me a kiss. Isn't that sweet?"

"Yeah," I say, forcing a smile.

Maddy sighs dramatically. "I love him so much. I'm really lucky to have him." She goes over to the window seat and opens it, taking out a bottle of liquor. "Vintage scotch. Fifty-five years old. That's like all of our ages combined!"

"You shouldn't drink, M," scolds Agnes.

Maddy places the bottle on her bed and closes the window seat. "This is a special occasion. You rented a house! The three of us are going to be living together. It's going to be like one big slumber party every night," she says, clapping her hands.

The house—I completely forgot. "You already rented it? How?" I ask. "It's Sunday night."

"I called the owner. He met us there, gave us a tour, and now he's reviewing our application. He'll let us know tomorrow."

"Oh, it's definitely ours," says Maddy, filling three shot glasses. She hands me one and I down the scotch, determined to erase Sebastian from my system.

Agnes warns Maddy, "You know what alcohol does to you."

"Don't be such a downer, Agnes. I feel like celebrating!" Maddy hands Agnes a glass and refills mine.

I start to feel warm, relaxed: *Sebastian who?* I sit down next to Maddy on the floor. Agnes places several magazines on the rug and sits on them. She doesn't touch her scotch. For a while, we sit in silence.

"I know what we can do!" exclaims Maddy. "Let's play Skeletons in the Closet!"

I know the game, although I've never played it. It's the one where you tell all your dirty secrets. I've heard that it can get pretty intense, and I have absolutely no desire to play, especially after what just happened in *our* closet. Lucky for me, Agnes doesn't seem interested in playing either.

But Maddy insists. "I'll start," she says. "Sebastian has a really big penis. I'm talking eight inches, ladies."

Agnes scowls. "That's great, Maddy. Congratulations. Can you tell us something less revolting next time?"

Wait. Maddy's lying. Sebastian's penis is nowhere near eight inches. It's average, maybe even on the small side. Why would Maddy lie about something so stupid?

"Sarah, it's your turn," Maddy says.

I hesitate before taking another shot. I'm already giddy and light-headed and if I get too relaxed, I might end up confessing what I just did with Sebastian. I try to think of a truth that won't reveal too much, but my brain feels like mush.

Before I can stop myself, I blurt out, "I've slept with fifteen guys." It's only half-true. I've actually slept with more, but I stopped counting after twenty. It's good I lost count, otherwise I'd be too ashamed. At least I've always practiced safe sex, except with Sebastian—which happened so fast, so unexpectedly, that I didn't have time to think about protection. Suddenly a very scary thought enters my mind: what if Sebastian gave me an STD? I've seen pictures of gonorrhea and it is *not* pretty. Looking at those pictures could turn a person off sex for life—this one *and* the next.

But Sebastian can't have gonorrhea. He's Maddy's boyfriend and she would never date a guy with VD.

"You slut!" Maddy exclaims, laughing. "All this time, I thought you were a virgin like me. I guess I'm the only chaste one here."

Agnes shoots Maddy a dirty look while clenching her untouched glass of scotch. I'm stunned. Agnes isn't a virgin? Since when? I can't imagine her having sex with anyone.

"It's your turn, Agnes," says Maddy.

"This game is stupid," Agnes grumbles.

Maddy nudges Agnes with the back of her hand. "Come on, we both went. You have to go too."

"Fine." Agnes takes a sip of her scotch. "I don't know . . . What do you want to hear? That I'm a hermaphrodite?" She snorts.

I laugh too, but Maddy just pouts. "Be serious."

"What should I say? That I'm adopted? You already know everything about me, M. There are no secrets between us." She gazes intently at Maddy before turning to me. "So, yes, I'm adopted. It's no big deal. In fact, I really lucked out because my parents are great. I'm not scarred or the least bit curious about my biological parents. I'm perfectly fine." The way she says it makes me think otherwise, and the tiny red hives crawling up her neck confirm it. But the fact that Agnes is adopted doesn't surprise me. I suspected there was more to her; I knew there had to be a flaw to her seemingly perfect life.

"Okay, my turn," Maddy says. "Now this one shouldn't be much of a surprise." She licks her lips. "I want to marry Sebastian and have his babies."

"Not this again," sputters Agnes. "Stop lying to yourself, Maddy."

"I'm not. I really love Sebastian."

"You're in denial," Agnes says. "You're only with him because you think he's the kind of guy you're *supposed* to be with. You don't even really like him—"

"Oh, really? Are you me? How would you know how I feel?"

Agnes puts a finger to her lips. "I don't think the whole quad needs to hear this." She gets up to close the window. "I know you, Maddy. I know you're afraid—and that's okay—but don't fool yourself. You need to start thinking about what you really want, what's good for you. *He is* not good for you."

Blood rushes to Maddy's cheeks. "You don't understand what we have together. You're jealous because you don't have someone who loves you as much as he loves me."

Agnes winces.

"What do *you* know about love anyway? You've never experienced it. You're the last person who should be giving me advice." Maddy shakily pours herself another glass of scotch. "You already know I'm going to die young, so why can't you just let me be happy?"

Die young? What is Maddy talking about? I feel dizzy all of a sudden, disoriented. I shouldn't have drunk the scotch so fast. Maybe old scotch is more potent than young scotch, because all I seem to want to do right now is lie down.

Maddy drains her glass. "Do you think it's fun worrying about death all the time? At least Sebastian makes me laugh."

Agnes rolls her eyes. "Sebastian's a loser. And you're not going to die young, so stop saying that—"

"Wait!" I exclaim. "What are you guys talking about?"

"Nothing," snaps Agnes. "It's none of your business."

"You're so rude, Agnes." Maddy turns to me. "I'm sorry. I should've told you earlier, but I didn't want you to think I was a freak." She looks down and swallows. "Ever since my parents died, I've had the feeling that my life would be cut short and I would be joining my mom and dad in the afterlife sooner rather than later. I just feel it in my bones. It's like I gained a sixth sense after they died. I get feelings about things, and I'm usually right. Like, I had a good feeling about you when we met, and that turned out to be true. And tonight, when we were at the house, I felt a sense of peace. But the night we ran over Hope, I knew something bad was going to happen." She shudders. "This must sound really weird to you."

"No," I say quietly. I don't know what else to say. I'm skeptical and curious at the same time.

"Don't listen to her, Sarah," Agnes says, finally gulping her scotch. "Maddy's just paranoid. I mean, it's natural to feel uncertain about life after something as traumatic as your parents' death, but the truth is, no one knows what the future holds."

"I know I'm going to die young. It even says so on my palm." Maddy thrusts her hand toward Agnes's face. "See my short lifeline?"

Agnes glances at her hand, then looks away. "I've told you a million times, palm reading is not a science."

"That's easy for you to say. You have a long lifeline." Maddy turns to me. "Sarah, let me see your hand."

"Which one?" I ask.

Maddy grasps my left hand and traces her finger over my palm. "You have a long one too. You're lucky." She drops my hand and, with a wistful look in her eye, says, "I'm just glad I have Sebastian. Sometimes I think he's the only thing keeping me going."

"You don't love him!" Agnes snaps back. "You don't even know what love is. Love isn't pretty, Maddy. It's complicated and messy and sometimes not so desirable, but that doesn't mean it's inferior or any less real. You can't deny love just because it doesn't fit perfectly into your life."

Maddy gets up. "I don't want to talk about this anymore."

"Fine," says Agnes, sighing.

Maddy turns toward her. "I'm sick of you breathing down my neck. You drain me, you know that? Sometimes I wonder why I'm still friends with you."

"That's nice," Agnes says, looking away.

Maddy crosses her arms over her chest.

A heaviness fills the room. I don't know what I could say to make the situation better. This sure isn't what I had in mind when I applied to Wetherly. The brochure said nothing about angst-filled dorms or psychic roommates. I feel a bit overwhelmed.

"I'm sorry, M," Agnes says in a low voice.

Maddy heads toward the closet, then stops and turns around. "It's . . . too . . . late," she stammers. Tears spill down her red cheeks, leaving behind stark white lines. She sways from side to side, struggling to regain her balance. Then she grabs her jacket and bolts out of the room.

Agnes and I try not to look at each other. After a while, she gets up and leaves without saying a word.

* * *

The next morning I wake up with the biggest hangover of my life. It feels like there's a truck parked on my head. I keep my eyes closed for another minute, trying to ignore the irritating stabs of sunlight coming through the window.

Last night suddenly returns—and with it, an asphyxiating sense of dread. The last thing I remember is Agnes chasing after Maddy. I must have passed out after that. And then I had a disturbing dream. We were in a forest: Maddy, Agnes, and I. We were walking in the dark, single file, with Maddy leading us. There were dead swans everywhere. "Where are we, Maddy? What are we doing here?" I kept asking over and over, but she wouldn't answer me. We came to a tunnel. We had to swim through it to get to the other side. At the end of the tunnel, on a patch of dry land, was Hope, lying in a coffin. And then I woke up.

I open my eyes and turn toward Maddy's untouched bed.

7

It's a little after six and the dining hall is nearly empty. Johnny Cash's "I Walk the Line" is playing on the jukebox. I'm eating dinner alone since Maddy and Agnes have been gone for the past five days. I have no appetite whatsoever, and my head is flush with questions. Where the hell did they go? Should I call the police? Tell our head resident? Why did they take Hope with them? I called both of their cells, but couldn't leave a message because their mailboxes were full. Who, I wonder, has been filling up their mailboxes? I'm worried, pissed off, and confused all at once and there doesn't seem to be a damn thing I can do about it.

I poke at my food: tempeh and limp broccoli in brown gravy. It's the vegan meal option. The food at Wetherly is devoid of flavor, yet loaded with fat. I've been gaining roughly two pounds a day—which I'm sure is some kind of record—so I started opting for the vegan entrees, and now I get dirty looks from the *real* vegans of Haven House. Who knew vegans could be so mean?

But it's not the food or even the mean vegans that have me so upset. Both would be tolerable if Maddy and Agnes were here. Now that they're gone, everything at Wetherly is bland. I actually cried in the shower this morning, although I'm sure that was partly due to the nasty surprise I found in the drain: a large clump of hair with contributions from everyone who had showered before me, a kind of Haven House hair ball. It was so gross that I had to take a follow-up shower in a different stall immediately afterward. I probably should file a complaint at the next house meeting. That is, if I even go.

To pass the time, I've been going to class. I'm taking drawing, film theory, microeconomics, and psych 101, but drawing is the only class I care about. It's like a language I was born understanding. When I was little, the other kids would watch me sketch and ask, "How do you do that?" They'd shout out their requests: *Draw a pony licking an ice-cream cone! Draw a dog eating my homework! Draw Tommy farting!* I liked being really good at something. And no matter what was going on around me, drawing always seemed to calm me down.

Unable to eat another bite, I put down my fork. I take my tray into the kitchen. After scraping my plate, I hand it to the auburn-haired girl who's rinsing off dishes. She's a fellow housemate who's on the work-study program and she looks flushed and tired. She avoids my eyes. After rinsing off my plate, she takes another from the top of a huge stack and grimaces at the hardened mixture of cheese, gravy, and marinara sauce stuck to its surface. My body tenses: this girl could be me in a few weeks if Nana's check doesn't get here soon.

I go up to my room. I lie in bed and try to relax, but being in my room only triggers anxious thoughts of Maddy and Agnes. What if Maddy found out I had sex with Sebastian? What if she and Agnes hate me now?

No. I've got to distract myself from these paranoid thoughts. *But how?* I've already done all my homework, read every magazine

I want to read, pushed back my cuticles, and trimmed my nails. I guess I could redye my hair, but I feel like I'm standing at the edge of a cliff, and I doubt that the tiny act of dyeing my hair will keep me from falling. No, I've got to do something active. It's Friday night. I should be out having fun, not cooped up in my room by myself. Who knew college would be like this? It's weird being alone all the time.

The problem is that I'm not close to anyone here other than Maddy and Agnes, and even though it's only the third week, it's already too late to make new friends. Everyone bonded during Orientation Week and these are the friends they're going to have for life. Through graduation, marriage, children, divorce, and death. It's all so arbitrary. You're going to be BFFs with someone just because you started a conversation with her in the bathroom late one night, when you were brushing your teeth and she was washing her face in the sink next to you and you were both feeling a little homesick. The bond will form instantly and it will be permanent.

I reach for my sketchbook, but decide on a whim to take a walk instead. I slip on my black Chucks and hurry out the door.

It's seven o'clock, still light out. I've been wandering around campus for the past forty minutes, but I'm no less tense.

There's a guy walking toward me who looks familiar. He's wearing all black, has pale, pale skin and glossy black hair. Of course! He's the guy from the diner my first night here, the Edward Scissorhands look-alike with the paper dolls.

He stops in front of me and smiles. "Hey, haven't I seen you somewhere before?"

"No." I keep walking.

"Wait," he calls after me. "I remember now. The diner by the highway. You were with two other girls."

I turn around. He *is* kind of cute—not in an obvious, classic way, but in a quirky, interesting way. He has high cheekbones and a prominent Adam's apple.

"You were there?" I say. "I don't remember you." Why did I lie?

He grins. "You sure?"

"Yeah."

"What's your name?"

"Sarah."

"Hmm," he says, "I could've sworn we made eye contact."

I don't know what to say to this, so I tuck a lock of hair behind my ear. "Do you go to school here?" I ask.

"Here?" He laughs. "No. I'm not a female. In case you were wondering."

I'm an idiot.

"Actually, I'm a senior at Hampshire," he explains. "But I like the libraries here."

"Even on Friday nights?"

"Yup, I'm a nerd. I'm busted." He covers his face in mock shame. "Anyway," he says, lowering his hand, "would you consider having dinner with this nerd?"

"Now?"

"If you're free."

Yes, yes, yes, I think. But I don't want to appear too eager, so I say, "You're a stranger."

"I'm no stranger. We've met twice. And we've already established that I'm a nerd. Nerds are harmless. The worst they could do is analyze you to death."

"Well, in that case . . ."

"Great." He touches my elbow. "Come on. I parked on Maple Drive."

After dinner at Hunan Garden, the only Chinese restaurant in town, we go to his place. Scissorhands lives in a big, yellow Victorian with green trim on a street lined with willow trees. His apartment is on the first floor. When he bends over to put his key in the lock, I take the opportunity to check out his ass. Kind of flat, but not bad.

As we walk into his place, I scan the narrow living room. The apartment smells of popcorn and turpentine, and there's a Lucite coffee table supported by a female mannequin on all fours. The mannequin is naked and has a big, gaping, blow-up doll mouth.

"Nice coffee table," I say.

"Ridiculous, isn't it? It was a birthday present. I'm getting rid of it, though. Do you know anyone who needs a coffee table?"

"Are you kidding? I go to Wetherly. I'm probably breaking some kind of feminist code just being in the same room with this thing."

He laughs. He's cute when he laughs. "I should have known. I'll be right back," he says, and walks down the hall toward what I assume is the bedroom.

He comes back carrying a white sheet, which he proceeds to drape over the coffee table so that the freaky mannequin is no longer visible.

"Better?" he says.

I nod. Our eyes meet. The lighting in here must be amazing because he looks really good.

His other furniture is modern and masculine: black leather

with cherry accents, a metal drafting table in the corner. I'm impressed that his place looks like a real, grown-up apartment—not the dirty, pizza box–infested bachelor pad I was expecting. Stacks of art books line the floor and a wooden easel sits in the corner. There's no TV.

"Do you have a roommate?" I ask.

"No. I live alone. I like it." He pauses. "Have a seat. Can I get you something to drink?"

"Water would be great," I say.

"Ice?"

I nod.

As he fixes my drink in the adjacent kitchen, I sit down on the couch and try to imagine him alone in his surroundings. Does he lie on the couch while he's reading his art books? Does he eat in the kitchen or in bed? His life seems kind of quiet, but I guess all lives appear quiet when they're not filled with people.

He comes back with my water, and I realize that we haven't spoken for at least two minutes. I should probably say something.

"So, what's your major?" I ask, cringing at my lack of originality.

"Studio art."

"Me too. At least that's what I *want* to major in. I haven't officially decided yet, but art seems to be the only thing I'm good at. Not that I'm really good at it." I take a sip of water. "Can I see some of your work?"

He doesn't respond, and I start to think that maybe I'm being too forward. I would never show anyone *my* work unless I knew them pretty well.

He opens a filing cabinet and takes out a sketchbook.

"I don't normally show my stuff on a first date, but since you're an artist too . . ."

He hands me the sketchbook.

"You sure?" I ask. "Because—"

"Yeah. Go for it."

His drawings are disturbing, to say the least. Francis Bacon-esque renderings of the female form: twisted, grotesque, amputated. Skinny women with missing arms and legs, some missing a breast or two. What do these drawings mean? He's obviously some kind of misogynist. He probably has mother issues too. Doesn't everything lead back to the mother? I feel inadequate all of a sudden, as a woman and as an artist. I'm not as skinny as these girls, and my drawings aren't nearly as gutsy. Who are these women? Past girlfriends? Models from his class? The women of his dreams?

I close the sketchpad. There's no way I'm sleeping with this guy. "Wow," I say. "Very interesting."

"You hated them."

"No, I liked them. I just, well, you have to admit your work *is* kind of disturbing."

"It's supposed to be." His eyes bore into me.

It occurs to me that this probably wasn't such a brilliant idea, coming to a stranger's apartment alone at night. If art is a reflection of a person's mental health, then I'm definitely in trouble. What if he's angry with me for not liking his work? What if he tries to amputate *me*? I force myself to stay calm.

"Do you have a boyfriend?" he asks.

I shake my head.

He clears his throat. "I just got out of a two-year relationship."

"Oh?"

"Actually, I didn't *just* get out of it. It ended about six months ago."

"Oh." I'm curious to know what happened with his ex, but I don't ask and we don't say anything for several minutes. I reach for my water as he sits down next to me. There's about a foot of leather between us. As soon as I place my water glass back down on the coffee table, he pounces on me. He covers my neck with kisses and runs his hands down the length of my body. We kiss and it's surprisingly good, even though he tastes a bit like kung pao chicken. When I feel his erection against my leg, I start to panic. I hardly know this person; he could have a million diseases. Maybe I shouldn't be doing this.

But then thoughts of Sebastian swoop in to torture me. I fucking hate that he's the last guy I slept with, and at least Scissorhands is nice and seems to like me. So I kiss him harder and he responds by squeezing my breasts. Then he whispers in my ear, "You're so beautiful," and even though I know that compliments from a guy don't mean as much when they're uttered right before sex, hearing this one makes me smile. I run my hands up his back, through his feather-soft hair and around to his face. With my fingertips, I feel his sandpapery Adam's apple and say, "Do you have a condom?"

He nods and kisses me once more before getting up. "Come on," he says, offering me his hand.

I take it and follow him into the bedroom.

I sleep until six in the evening the next day and feel like shit when I wake up. Last night, after the sex, Scissorhands did something weird: he tried to cuddle with me. I let him do it for a few minutes and then I freaked out. I've never cuddled with anyone before, and he was so tender about it that it made me feel totally vulnerable, and I started worrying that if he kept doing that, I would fall in love with him or something. So I made him drive me home immediately. He probably thinks I'm certifiable, but who cares? I hardly know the guy. I don't even know his name, for God's sake.

And yet I can still feel him inside me. It's like the sexual version of phantom-limb syndrome. Bizarre.

After my shower, I go down to the dining hall. It's dinner-time, but I head straight for the cereal boxes, which are laid out on the buffet table like fine silver. I take my bowl of Cap'n Crunch and sit by the window. No matter how hard I try to block them out, I can't stop playing back scenes from last night. Sex is weird. Just when you think you can no longer be affected by it, you get affected. My whole body feels inflamed. I feel like sex on legs; sex personified; living, fire-breathing sex. Even my hands smell of sex—despite my shower—and I can't tell if it's his smell or mine.

"Is anyone sitting here?"

I look up from my bowl. Standing in front of me is Keiko Yamada, a first-year from New Jersey. Her long, black hair is pulled back into a sleek ponytail and she's wearing her signature red cat's-eye glasses. She sets her plate down across from me. A second later, Amber Parker, a first-year from Boston, wearing head-to-toe J. Crew in matching earth tones, takes the seat next to me.

"Hey there," she says in her thick Boston accent.

"Are you going to the Yale party tonight?" Keiko asks me.

"I didn't even know about it."

"Come with us," Amber says. "It should be interesting."

"It's a naked party," adds Keiko.

"A what?" I ask.

Keiko takes a bite of her mashed potatoes and, mouth full,

says, "A naked party. Everyone has to go naked. Guys *and* girls. I've never been to one, but I heard they're fun. You just have to leave before it turns into a massive orgy."

Amber lets out a short laugh. "The good thing is you don't have to worry about what to wear. Any old trench coat will do."

Trench coat? I don't even own a *regular* coat. She can't be serious. Who would show up at a party in nothing but a trench coat? "What if you don't want to go naked?" I ask.

Keiko grins. "Well, then you have to pay the fine. It's, like, five dollars."

"That's not so bad," I say.

"Yeah," says Amber, "but the whole point is to go naked."

The thought of going naked scares me. But aside from that, do I even want to be partying with a bunch of naked people while I'm fully dressed? Wouldn't that be awkward? Still, I'm desperate for a distraction, so I say, "What time are you leaving?"

"Around eight," says Keiko. "My roommate's driving us. We'll swing by your room before we leave, okay?"

"Okay," I say, and hurry back upstairs.

When I open my door, I'm shocked to find Maddy and Agnes packing up the contents of the room. Maddy emerges from behind a tall stack of cardboard boxes, runs up to me, and hugs me forcefully, nearly knocking me over. Agnes stays in the corner at first, and then comes over and gives me a kiss on the cheek. It's an odd gesture, completely out of character for someone who has never even touched me before.

"Where did you guys disappear to?" I ask, feeling strangely shy. The week apart has made things tense. Do I even know these girls anymore?

"We went to New York to buy furniture for the house," Maddy says.

"For the whole week?" *Liar*. "Why didn't you call? I was worried."

"I'm sorry," says Maddy. "We were just so busy. And we wanted to make the house nice for you. As a surprise."

I glance at Agnes. "So you got the house?"

"Of course," she says. "I told you I would. Now help us finish packing. We're moving in tonight."

I shake my head. "I can't. I'm going to a party."

"Seriously?" Agnes furrows her brow. "Why would you want to go to a party *here*?"

"I'm not going to a party *here*. It's at Yale and it's supposed to be good," I say.

Agnes looks skeptical. "Who are you going with?"

"People."

"Who?"

"Nobody you know."

I glance at Maddy. She looks troubled—no, it's more than that—she's . . . angry. Why? Just because I'm going to a party without her? When she notices my gaze, she tries to regain her composure and says, "Why don't we move your stuff for you? You can come to the house after the party. We'll pick you up."

"The thing is . . . I'm not sure I want to move," I say, annoyed that they packed my things without asking me first. "I kind of like it here."

Agnes looks at me like I've said something amusing, then tosses Maddy's Pucci-printed headband into an unsealed box.

"Don't be mad at us, Sarah," Maddy says, throwing Agnes a nervous glance.

"I'm not mad," I say. But I *am*. They abandoned me for an entire week. Did they think they could make it all better just by coming back? And then to lie to me on top of everything. Buying furniture? Do I look that dumb? I have a life here now. I'm making new friends. I'm going to a naked party. I don't need them.

"You'll love the house, Sarah," says Maddy. "It's really spacious and it's got a fireplace in every room. It's almost completely furnished and Hope is already settled in, and she loves it. You'll have your own room, which is twice as big as this one . . ." Maddy trails off, probably sensing I'm not impressed. She's right; I'm too angry to be impressed. "Don't you want to be with us?" she asks.

Again those words: *be with us*. She's good at guilt-tripping, but I'm not falling for it this time.

"I don't know," I say. "I can't discuss it now. Keiko and Amber will be here soon."

Agnes rips off a piece of sealing tape. The sound is loud and aggressive. She finishes taping up a box and says, "Forget it, M. Let her do what she wants."

Maddy looks deflated.

And then I start to feel bad. Her wounded look always gets me. The poor girl has had such a tragic life. And she actually believes she's going to die young. I can't help but worry I just shaved off a few more hours.

Still, I don't back down.

"Okay," Maddy finally says. Her tone is curt. She turns away from me toward Agnes, and an awkward silence fills the room. Then Maddy turns back around and flashes me a wide grin. I'm not sure what to make of it.

Before things have a chance to get any weirder, I grab my jacket and leave the room.

The naked party turns out to be a bore, with all the ugly guys naked and all the cute guys fully dressed. I keep my clothes on and pay the five dollars, while Keiko and Amber strip down to nothing and get in for free. They're surprisingly fit. They must work out constantly.

Toward the end of the night, I meet a guy named Finn—a naked Yalie with curly red hair and chewed-up nails—who's kind of dull and looks like a cross between Richard Simmons and Little Orphan Annie. But does that stop me from making out with him?

Sadly, no.

8

When I get home from the party, I find a cream-colored envelope on my bed. I tear it open. Inside is a note written in Agnes's perfect cursive:

Sarah,
    I need to talk to you. It's important.
    Call me ASAP.

                Agnes

I pick up the receiver on my desk and dial Agnes's cell.

Five minutes later, she's at my door. She looks flustered and her white button-down shirt is slightly wrinkled. Right next to her nose is a huge zit, haphazardly covered with a big glob of cakey concealer. Funny, I didn't notice that earlier. I didn't think Agnes ever got zits. She must be stressed. I try not to stare at it (though it's difficult)—not because it would embarrass her, but because staring at zits is a risky thing to do. If I so much as look at a zit, or even think about zits, I'll wake up with my very own cystic nightmare the next morning. Zits are telepathically contagious.

"You're looking at my blemish," Agnes says accusingly.

"No, I wasn't."

"I saw you looking at it."

"I wasn't looking at anything," I say, keeping my eyes locked on hers.

"Well, don't look at it."

"I won't."

"Fine."

"So, are you going to tell me what's going on?"

"Not here. Let's go for a drive."

"It's late," I say, yawning emphatically. "I don't want to go out again. Can't we just talk here?"

"Too risky."

I feel a twinge of anxiety. "Why? What's going on? Is it Maddy?"

"Maddy's fine. She's sleeping. Let's go to that diner next to the highway."

"No," I say a little too quickly. I can't risk running into Scissorhands.

"Why not?"

I shrug.

"Come on."

"Fine," I say. But damn, he'd better not be there.

Everything at the diner looks exactly the same, including the people. The same frizzy-haired waitresses. The same greasy truckers.

The waitress leads us to our table. I scan the diner one more time to make sure Scissorhands isn't hiding in a corner booth.

When I see that he isn't, I feel an unexpected surge of disappointment. I sit down opposite Agnes.

"So, are you going to tell me what this is all about?" I ask after we've ordered. Paranoid as ever, Agnes refused to talk about Maddy in the car. To Agnes, it makes more sense to talk about private matters in bright, crowded diners.

She looks at me. "I wanted to tell you what really happened last week. You probably figured out we weren't just furniture shopping the whole time."

"That was pretty obvious," I say.

"We did shop on the last day—yesterday. God, it feels so long ago. But the rest of the time we were in Vermont."

I think of trees and outlet malls and people dressed in L.L. Bean. "What were you doing there?"

"Well," she says, licking her lips, "remember how hysterical Maddy was that night she stormed off?"

"You mean, after you bad-mouthed Sebastian?"

"I didn't bad-mouth him. But I'm no fan, that's for sure." She looks out the window, then back at me. "I thought Maddy was having a breakdown that night. She can be pretty unstable at times. It worries me. Did you become obsessed with death after your parents passed away?"

My right eyelid starts to twitch, and I blush with shame. "My parents aren't actually dead." I look away. "But they might as well be."

"I see." She seems both unfazed and uninterested. Which means there will be no further questions. Thank God.

The waitress appears out of nowhere and slams Agnes's pancakes and my burger onto the table. The noise is jarring. Agnes glares at the waitress, who has orange hair and Tammy Faye eyelashes, but the woman is oblivious.

"Country bumpkins," Agnes mutters with a sigh.

I take a huge bite of my burger and watch Agnes pick at the edges of her pancakes.

She puts down her fork. "Remember when Maddy ran out of the room and I went to look for her?"

"Yeah," I say, my mouth full, "but I don't remember anything after that."

"Well, I searched the whole dorm but couldn't find her anywhere, so I decided to take the car and drive around campus. That's when I realized my car key was missing and I just *knew* Maddy had taken it. When I got to the car, there she was, sitting in the driver's seat, ready to drive off to God-knows-where. I was lucky to have found her in time. Who knows what she would've done?

"So we came back to the room. By that time you had passed out. I thought of leaving you a note, but we were in a hurry, and, besides, I wasn't sure where we were going. Maddy was delirious and I was getting panicked myself, so I snatched the fawn and we got in the car and drove and drove until we ended up in Vermont. We stayed at an inn overlooking a small lake. The surroundings were good for Maddy. Almost immediately she went back to her normal self. Having the fawn there also seemed to help. Otherwise I would've let the poor thing go. I'm not fond of that animal at all—the mess and the awful smells—but at least it's quiet. I'd go nuts if I had to listen to it yap all the time."

"Me too," I say, nodding. I take a bite of my pickle and look at Agnes. "So then what happened?"

"Things were fine until about the fourth day, when Maddy became hysterical again. She started coming up with all sorts of nutty ideas. She composed a list of all the things she wanted to do before she died."

"Like what?" I lick my fingers.

"There was something about skydiving and meeting the Dalai Lama." Agnes pauses. "And losing her virginity," she says, looking flustered.

"To Sebastian?"

"To *anyone*. She wanted to find a random Vermonter and take him back to our room."

I cringe and semi-lose my appetite. Sure, I could see myself doing something like that—but Maddy the virgin?

"It didn't happen," says Agnes. "I wasn't going to let it happen. That's why we left Vermont. You're lucky you weren't there. Maddy was such a wreck. She kept rambling about suicide and the afterlife. I couldn't calm her down and I became quite edgy myself. At one point, she started screaming and pulling out her hair. I didn't know what to do, so I started talking about the house—all the fun things we were going to do and how great it was going to be with the three of us living together. That seemed to work. She got very excited and stopped talking about death—it was a miracle—and then suddenly she wanted to go buy furniture and house stuff so we went to New York."

I put my burger down. "Why didn't you call me?"

"I know. I should have, but there was nothing you could've done." Agnes picks up her fork and starts poking holes in her pancakes.

I wipe my fingers on my napkin and take a sip of water. "Did you call Maddy's aunt and uncle?"

"Are you kidding? They don't care about her. They only care about her parents' money. If they had seen her in that manic state, they would've had her committed."

"Does Maddy go to a shrink?"

"No," she says, swallowing visibly.

"Then how did she get all those prescription pills?"

"From her stepdad. He's a psychiatrist."

"He treats her?"

"No, he just sends her whatever medication she wants."

"I thought he was still mad about her parents' affair—"

"He's getting over it. Maddy calls him whenever she misses her mom. She doesn't really take those pills, other than the occasional Ambien. Trust me, Maddy is not a pill popper. But having them in her drawer gives her comfort, knowing she doesn't have to suffer if she doesn't want to. Personally, I don't like drugs of any kind; I won't even take an Advil when I have a headache. But if having pills around is reassuring to her, then I guess that's fine."

I scratch my head.

"Anyway, once we got to New York, she was okay. We got a room at the St. Regis, left the deer there, spent the whole day shopping, eating, and wandering around Soho, and Maddy's spirits seemed to improve."

"So, that's it?"

"No, I'm just getting to the disturbing part." She licks her lips. "So, last night we had dinner in Chinatown. As we were leaving the restaurant, Maddy bumped into an old Gypsy woman, knocking her bag off her shoulder. Everything spilled onto the street. Maddy, of course, helped the woman, but instead of saying 'thank you,' the Gypsy said, 'Your parents miss you too.' Well, Maddy just froze. We both stood there in shock, not knowing what to say. I don't usually trust those Gypsies, but this woman was different. Of course, Maddy insisted on having a reading."

I get a chill.

"But the woman refused, saying it was late. I had to do something, so I took out all my cash—a little less than two thousand—and offered it to the woman. She became very nervous. At first she refused the money. I thought maybe she suspected it was counterfeit, so I took one of the bills and held it up to a street lamp. Of course, it was dark and you couldn't really see anything, but I wanted to show good faith.

"And it worked. She took the money, and we walked a couple of blocks to her dingy apartment. Maddy and the old woman went into a back room to do the reading, and since I wasn't allowed to sit in, I waited in the living room. It was such a strange room, Sarah. There were candles and Catholic knickknacks everywhere. Imagine hundreds of Jesuses and Marys staring at you."

"Weird," I agree. "So what did the Gypsy tell her?"

"I don't know!" Agnes throws up her hands. "She came out of the reading with a big smile on her face, but when we got back to the hotel, she wouldn't tell me anything—except to say that the Gypsy had confirmed what she'd known all along."

"What's that supposed to mean?"

"I have no idea." Agnes rubs her temple. "That's why I'm worried. I hope the Gypsy didn't confirm Maddy's delusions about dying young. That would be evil, and yet it's exactly the kind of thing Maddy would want to hear."

"Maybe the Gypsy told her the opposite, and Maddy was relieved."

"I hope so." Agnes pauses. "But Maddy wouldn't have been so happy if that were the case."

I rest my head in my hands. "Why is she so eager to die anyway? I can't even imagine dying at our age. I've never even had the chicken pox."

"Her parents' death really unhinged her. But there's also a part of her that just wants to be right. She desperately wants to believe in destiny and in her own intuition. I'm not even sure how good her intuition really is. What if she's getting bad signs? And what if her beliefs end up becoming a self-fulfilling prophecy?"

"Like what?" I ask, reaching for my water.

"I'm just worried she'll do something rash, like give up on life just because of what a Gypsy said. You've got to help me convince Maddy that she has a long life ahead of her. She trusts you, Sarah." Agnes stops to chew on a nail, then looks at me. "Will you move in with us? Maddy said she wouldn't leave Haven House unless you moved in."

Is this why Maddy seemed irritated with me earlier? Because she really wants me to live with them?

"The rent is paid for," Agnes says. "My father's accountant is taking care of it, so you wouldn't have to pay anything, if that's what you're worried about. I know your family isn't very generous with you financially."

Not knowing what to say, I look out the window.

"Here. Take this," Agnes says, sliding a key across the table. "Say you'll move in."

I can't help but feel that I'm getting in way over my head. I don't know how I'm supposed to convince Maddy to live if she really wants to die. And it doesn't seem right that she should have all those pills when she's potentially suicidal. The whole situation is kind of frightening. And yet a part of me thinks that Maddy is just acting, creating all this drama to get attention.

"Please?" Agnes begs.

Agnes never begs. How can I say no? So, ignoring my fears, I take a deep breath and say, "Okay."

"You won't regret it," she says with a smile.

God, I hope not.

9

It's a Wednesday, two in the afternoon, and I'm alone in the new house. My first nude self-portrait for drawing class is due tomorrow and I haven't started yet. I'm a little annoyed that Professor Connelly is making us do this. What could I possibly learn from studying my own naked body? I already know that I have flabby thighs. Professor Connelly is a sadist.

I go downstairs to get a Coke from the fridge and then drink it at the counter.

The new house is amazing. Every morning I have to pinch myself; I can't believe this is where I get to live. The house is rustic, elegant, and sparsely decorated in Agnes's minimalist style: bare walls, sleek couches in beige and taupe, tables with long, skinny, brushed-aluminum legs. The only room with any color is the downstairs bedroom, which came with bloodred walls. Agnes wanted to repaint them ecru, but Maddy insisted that she liked the red, so Agnes deferred to her like she always does. Since Hope sleeps on a dog bed in the den, we turned the fourth bedroom into a library. Every night we gather there in front of the fireplace on Maddy's Persian rug. We talk and drink hot chocolate and read from our favorite poets; it's all very old world and romantic. I'm happy that I finally have a place I can call home, and it's hard to explain, but I feel right with Maddy and Agnes. We fit together like the sides of a triangle, each almost dysfunctional without the other two.

The additional three bedrooms are upstairs. Agnes's room is next to Maddy's and faces the front of the house. My room is the most private—separated from Maddy's by a bathroom that we all share—and faces the backyard, where Hope spends her days.

The best part of our living arrangement is that Agnes cooks dinner for us every night. Even though she's vegetarian, she cooks nonvegetarian meals for Maddy and me. Complicated dishes like lobster risotto, braised short ribs, and grilled lamb. I'm in awe of how self-sacrificing Agnes can be when it comes to Maddy—it's hard to imagine a vegetarian touching raw meat without wanting to vomit. And who knew Agnes was so domestic? Cooking seems to relax her, and since she only needs four hours of sleep a night, and is always caught up on schoolwork, what else is she going to do with her time?

But I know that everything Agnes does is for Maddy. I'm just tolerated because Maddy happens to like me. And though she won't admit it, I know Agnes is desperately in love with Maddy, but it's a repressed love, totally one-sided. Maddy never shows her any affection aside from a hug now and then. It's tragic, really. Thank God I'm not part of that equation.

Another weird thing is that Agnes always pays for everything. Maddy doesn't chip in, and I can't afford to. I'm afraid to even guess how much our weekly food bill is. But Agnes never says anything about it, never asks us to pay our share. I'm starting to worry that I'm going to owe her my life by the end of the semester, but what can I do? Nana's check still hasn't arrived. I got so desperate I called California the other day, but the phone just kept ringing and ringing. Where could Nana be? I know for a fact that she would never leave her wet bar for more than a few hours at a time. After all, even Jesus drank, Nana used to say.

Back to my assignment. I go upstairs and stare at the blank page. It's two fifteen. Agnes has lab until four and Maddy has art history until three, so I've got about forty-five minutes to get my portrait done. I lie on my white sleigh bed—which Agnes picked out and paid for—and try to get into a depressed state of mind, because depression is absolutely necessary for art-making. I stare at the ceiling and the crown moldings, and think of Nana's popcorn ceiling and the perpetually dim, dank condo we called home. Now I'm depressed.

I strip out of my jeans and my I AM EVIL T-shirt and stand in front of the full-length mirror mounted on the inside of my closet door. I've been gaining a lot of weight. For the first time in my life, I have actual hips and breasts. But I'm more pear-shaped than hourglass, and although I look like a woman, I still feel like the scrawny kid I was up until a month ago. This new body does not fit my personality.

Suddenly there's a knock at the door.

"Sarah? It's me, Maddy. Can I come in?"

"Just a sec." What is she doing home so early? I slip into my robe and say, "Come in."

Maddy saunters in, rosy cheeked, wearing white jeans and an indigo peasant top. Her walk kind of reminds me of Sebastian. *Weird.*

"Hey," she says, "I just finished tying a kabbalah string around Hope's ankle to protect her from the evil eye."

I snicker. "The evil eye? Who would envy a fawn?"

"I don't know. The shar-pei next door?" She smiles. "Why are you wearing your robe?"

"Oh." I tighten my sash. "I was just getting ready to draw."

"Yeah?" she says. "I left class early. It's too beautiful out. I didn't feel like being in a stuffy classroom, listening to another boring lecture." She sighs, goes over to the window, and opens it. "Some fresh air would do you good. Look, the leaves are starting to turn."

I peer out at the giant red-and-gold-leafed maple tree in our backyard.

"Hey," Maddy says, "do you want to go to town for some ice cream?"

"I wish I could, but my assignment's due tomorrow."

"You're so studious. That's one of the things I like most about you. You're a true Capricorn—diligent, serious, and loyal."

"How did you know I was a Capricorn?"

"By your actions, of course. Why? When's your birthday?"

"December twenty-fifth."

"See? I was right. Poor thing. It must be hard having your birthday on Christmas."

I shrug. "It's fine."

"I thought *I* had it bad. My birthday's on December twenty-first. But I'm a Sagittarius. We're honest, open-minded, and trusting. Agnes is the one we have to watch out for—she's a Gemini!" Maddy giggles. "Come on, take a break. We poor little orphan girls need to have fun once in a while. Right?"

I bite the inside of my cheek. "Actually, my parents aren't dead," I say, surprised that Agnes never mentioned that to her.

She turns toward the window. "Oh, I know all about that. Agnes told me. But your parents aren't in your life, so basically you're all alone, just like me."

Confused, I nod.

"So, are we going to get ice cream?" she asks.

"I can't. Anyway, I need to go on a diet. My ass is getting huge."

"Don't be silly." Maddy looks away. "You're superskinny."

She's totally lying. But I guess she's just trying to spare my feelings.

"It's okay if you don't want to go," she says. "Can I watch you draw?"

"Well . . . I have to do a nude self-portrait."

Flipping her hair, she says, "Why don't you draw me? I've always wanted to have my portrait done, and it's not like your professor knows what you look like naked, right? A body's a body, after all."

Before I can begin to consider how awkward it would be to draw Maddy naked, she's already taking off her clothes. It's not so much her nakedness that bothers me—it's the intimacy of drawing someone I know, naked *or* dressed.

Surprisingly, Maddy's body is not perfect. Her breasts are slightly asymmetrical, her legs are a little on the skinny side, and she doesn't have much of a waist. But somehow her imperfections only seem to heighten her beauty. It's so unfair. If I weren't her friend, I'd hate her.

I consider telling Maddy I don't want to do this. But I can already imagine how crushed she would be. She's so damn sensitive. Agnes and I always have to tiptoe around her, and yes, it's exhausting, but what choice do we have? She's had a tragic life.

I dig around my art box for a fresh stick of charcoal.

"How should I pose?" Maddy asks, now fully nude and facing me.

I try not to look at her as she adjusts her breasts.

"Should I do a sexy pose?" she says, squeezing her breasts together and cocking her head to one side. I feel my cheeks getting warm.

"Why don't you sit on the floor facing me? Wait, I'll go get a towel." I really just want to get out of this room.

"No need. The floor's clean," she says, sitting down yoga-style. "We could practically eat off it, thanks to Agnes."

"But you might get splinters."

"Don't be silly," she says, laughing. "Just draw."

I sit on the floor facing her and press my charcoal into the paper. It's strange at first. We're so close and her nipples are right there and her stomach puffs out a little every time she exhales. I can even smell her strawberry-scented lip balm.

But soon I lose myself in the drawing. Maddy doesn't exist anymore. I see lines, shapes, and shadows. And then nothing at all.

"Maybe you should get naked too. Wouldn't that be fun?"

I ignore her. I'm free, floating, at peace.

"I think Sebastian's cheating on me."

I drop my charcoal. "What?"

"He hardly calls me anymore. I always have to call him, and when we do talk it's always brief because he's so busy. He'll say he has to go to the library or to a meeting or to a study group. I know he's lying. I mean, it's not like I don't know him. Sebastian in a library would be like Agnes in a Walmart. He's definitely avoiding me, and I think it's because there's someone else."

I start to panic. I never should have slept with Sebastian. It was a stupid, stupid thing to do. The sex wasn't even good, and now it's going to ruin my friendship with Maddy. I've got to reassure her of Sebastian's fidelity.

"But what if he really *is* studying?" I say, fully aware of how ridiculous that sounds. This is a guy who thinks Spanish and Italian are the same language. So I add, "People change. Maybe being at an Ivy is making him more studious."

I pick up my charcoal and force myself to continue drawing.

Maddy shakes her head. "I've known Sebastian for two years. He won't read a book unless it has pictures in it. I don't know what to do, Sarah. I love him so much. I can't lose him."

"Don't worry," I say, redoing her clavicle. "He's probably just busy."

"Yeah, with some slut." She pounds the floor with her fist and groans. "It's just that he's so irresistible to girls. I wish he was uglier," she says in a bratty voice. "I wish he had a big scar on his face."

"Don't say that."

"Well, don't you think he's cute? If he wasn't my boyfriend, wouldn't you go out with him?"

I stop drawing. "No." My face goes hot. "We all have our type, I guess."

"And he's not your type? He's gorgeous; he's everyone's type." She gives me a probing look, then lowers her eyes. "But he's picky. He might sleep with you, but that doesn't mean he'll like you."

Ouch. Where did that come from? Does she know I had sex with him? Or am I being oversensitive because I'm guilty?

Maddy gives me a sheepish smile and then unties her pony-tail, letting her hair cascade down her shoulders and over her breasts. "So, I was thinking of surprising him this weekend. I have to find out who this other girl is. Come with me, Sarah. Please? I need you there for moral support." She twists her hair into a haphazard knot.

My heart contracts. "I don't think you should go. It's never a good idea to drop in on someone unannounced. And you shouldn't accuse him of cheating just because he's been a little distant lately."

"But I know it. I *feel* it. I'm psychic, remember?"

Shit, shit, shit.

"I just need to find out what's going on. If he's seeing someone else, I have to know so I can figure out how to win him back." She starts picking at her cuticles. "Will you come with me?"

Do I have a choice? I sigh. "Okay."

Maddy beams. "Thank you, Sarah. You're such a good friend." She gets up and hugs me, and her naked body so close to me surprisingly doesn't bother me because I'm too busy figuring a way out of this mess.

I toss and turn. Finally I flip on the lights. It's one in the morning. What am I going to do? I have to warn Sebastian somehow. Of course he's been cheating on Maddy. He'd sleep with anyone. If I don't warn him, they'll have some big confessional conversation, and he'll end up telling Maddy the truth about us.

I tiptoe downstairs. I look for Maddy's cell phone, which she normally leaves on the dining table. My plan is to copy down Sebastian's number and call him tomorrow from campus.

Light shines from under the basement door. *Damn.* I thought Agnes would be asleep by now. The basement is her personal study area, where no one else is allowed. I'll have to be quiet. Maddy's phone gleams from the dining table. I pick it up and scroll through her contact list. I find Sebastian's number and write it on my palm.

"What do you think you're doing?" a voice behind me says.

I freeze.

10

I slowly turn to face Agnes. How am I going to explain myself? What good reason could I give her for snooping through Maddy's cell phone?

She's standing in front of the basement door and even though it's dark, I can tell she's scowling. When she flips on the light I notice her pajamas: an adult-size onesie. She looks like an old baby, and it's such a disturbing image that for a second I consider telling her the truth.

"Well? What are you doing?" she repeats.

I hold up Maddy's phone. "Trying to make a call."

"To whom?"

Think, think, think. "My grandmother."

"With Maddy's cell?"

"Yeah. You know I don't have a cell phone. I've never had one. My grandmother doesn't believe in them."

Agnes raises an eyebrow. "Is she Amish?"

"No, Lutheran." I snicker.

Agnes doesn't crack a smile. "What's wrong with the landline?"

"Nothing." I shrug. "It's just more expensive. Maddy has a

ton of free minutes." I mentally pat myself on the back for the quick thinking and ask, "Why do you look upset?"

"Well, it's one in the morning and you're sneaking around in the dark. It's only natural that I'd be a little . . . alarmed." She squints at me. "Why are you calling your grandmother so late anyway?"

"It's only ten in California. I haven't been able to reach her during the day so I thought I'd have better luck at night."

"I see." Agnes almost looks disappointed. Walking past me toward the kitchen, she says, "I was just going to make some hot chocolate. Care to join me?"

"Sure," I say, relieved to be out of the hot seat. "On second thought, I'll just have some hot water with lemon. I've been gaining a lot of weight."

"I've noticed."

"Thanks."

"Just being honest."

Sure. "Actually, I wanted to talk to you about our meals," I say. "I think I need to start eating lighter."

"Fine. I'll make you salads from now on. I make an excellent Waldorf salad."

"Don't go to any trouble," I say. "Even I can make a salad."

"In my kitchen? I don't think so. I don't want anyone making a mess in my kitchen. Sorry, but that's my rule."

"Fine."

"But why *are* you gaining so much weight? Because it can't be *all* my fault. Lately, your appetite seems to have gotten . . . heartier." She gives me a weird look. "You're not pregnant, are you?"

"Pregnant? God, no." I laugh nervously. "How could I be pregnant? I haven't been having sex."

"You sure?" She looks serious.

"Yes! There aren't any men here. Who could I have slept with?" That, I realize, was a stupid thing to say. To my horror, my right eyelid starts to twitch and I can't get it to stop. If only I knew what Agnes was thinking. Does she know about Sebastian and me? Is she planning to tell Maddy? Could I actually be pregnant? The thought never even occurred to me. I *am* late, but I've always been irregular.

Agnes laughs. "Calm down. I was just joking. I almost got you though, didn't I?"

"Yeah, that was *really* funny," I say. "I'm going to bed."

"Oh, come on," she says. "Where's your sense of humor? I'm sorry. Stay. Call your grandmother."

"I'll call her tomorrow."

"Okay, but don't go to bed yet. Sit with me. I'll make you some chamomile tea."

I reluctantly pull out a chair and sit down. I try to appear calm but inside I'm a wreck. What if I *am* pregnant? I used a condom with Scissorhands, but not with Sebastian. It was just that one time, but still. On the other hand, it's not that easy to get pregnant. That's why there are so many fertility clinics everywhere. Even healthy young people have trouble conceiving. This is the Age of Anxiety, after all. A little stress and your body goes out of whack. And I've certainly been under a lot of stress lately.

But my breasts do feel a little tender, come to think of it. And the fact that they grew practically overnight is pretty unusual. God, I hate Agnes. Her words always get under my skin and wriggle around like ticks.

She opens the refrigerator and takes out a carton of milk, which she pours into a small saucepan. Then she places the saucepan on the stove and fills the tea kettle with Evian.

"There's something I want to talk to you about," she says with her back to me.

"No more jokes, please."

With the flick of a spoon, Agnes opens a tin of hot chocolate and turns to face me. "It's a business proposal."

"What do you mean?"

"I'll explain in a minute." She washes her hands.

What kind of business proposal could she possibly have for me? I search her face for clues but her small, sharp eyes betray nothing. I stare at her nose: thin, straight, patrician. I count three freckles under her left eye. Small, elfin ears that stick out in the most endearing way. She's not bad looking. You might even say she looks kind of exotic, like a pale, blue-eyed Eskimo. But most of the time she looks so severe. I guess it all depends on the angle. Like a hologram, she's pretty one minute and ugly the next. Like that French term: *jolie laide*. Pretty ugly. Not pretty gorgeous, but pretty in an odd, interesting way. She's the antithesis of Maddy's classic, universal beauty.

Agnes sets a cup of hot tea in front of me, then goes down to the basement.

She returns with the portrait I drew of Maddy.

"Where'd you get that?" I ask.

"From your room. I noticed it on your dresser when I was vacuuming the dust under your bed." She sighs. "It's exquisite. You really do have talent, Sarah. You captured a side of Maddy that I rarely get to see." Agnes pulls out a chair and sits down. "I want to buy this from you."

I rub my brow. "Are you kidding?"

"How much do you want for it?"

"It's homework, Agnes. It's not for sale."

"Everything's for sale. You should've learned that by now."

"Well, this isn't, so give it back. I have to turn it in tomorrow."

"I thought you were supposed to do a self-portrait."

"I was, but Maddy came in and asked me to draw her instead."

"So, technically, this isn't your assignment."

"No, but it's all I've got so I'm turning it in."

"I'll give you five hundred dollars for it."

What? She's out of her mind. Five hundred dollars for a stupid sketch? I shake my head.

"Why not? You can draw yourself another one before class. You still have time."

"But I don't *want* to draw another one," I say, irritated.

"How about a thousand?"

"You're crazy."

"Is that a yes?"

"No!"

"Look, I know a thousand dollars isn't a big deal, but it's extra cash and you might need it this weekend when we go up to Cornell." She exhales. "Take it."

I think of the forty-two dollars I have left in my account. I'm tempted, but I can't take Agnes's money. I'm already living in her house for free and there is such a thing as pride.

"Why do you want the drawing so much?" I ask her.

She doesn't answer. A second later, I hear a sizzling sound.

"Shoot," Agnes says, jumping out of her seat. The milk she was heating is now bubbling over the edge of the saucepan. Agnes puts the saucepan in the sink and begins a vigorous cleaning of the stove top.

I look at the portrait. It's actually pretty good. There's something about it that makes me want to keep looking at it. I'm surprised I was even able to finish it, what with the I-think-Sebastian-is-cheating-on-me bomb Maddy dropped on me. I was trying to capture Maddy's essence, as corny as that sounds. Looking at her, I saw big eyes—almost too big for her delicate, heart-shaped face—and a perfect button nose, and pouty, pink lips. Her beauty was overwhelming, but strangely, I couldn't connect with it. It was like looking at a beautiful mask; I felt nothing. But I started drawing anyway. I drew her head and her eyebrows and her eyes. And that's when I saw it—something sinister slithering behind the eyes. A darkness. A profound ugliness underneath all that beauty. That's what I drew.

As expected, Maddy did not appreciate the portrait. She pretended to, and forced a smile and even said she thought it was nice, but I know she hated it. I could almost hear her thinking, *This doesn't look like me at all.* And it's true; it doesn't look like her. It *is* her.

"You really like Maddy, don't you?" I say to Agnes, who is now mopping the kitchen floor.

"She's my oldest friend," she answers dismissively.

"You can have it," I say. I owe Agnes too much already. Giving her the drawing will, hopefully, make me feel like less of a freeloader.

"I'll get my checkbook."

"No," I say, "it's a gift." Then I hurry upstairs before she can thank me.

I sleep hard and fast, a dreamless sleep. When I wake up, I discover a check for a thousand dollars on my nightstand. I leave it there. I can't deal with it now. It's nine fifteen. I've got less than an hour before class, and I still have to do that other drawing.

* * *

Thirty minutes later, I'm running out the door, clutching my haphazardly drawn self-portrait. I didn't have time to shower and I feel beyond disgusting, but I don't want to fail the only class I like.

It's a sunny, cool day. As I run past the campus pond, amber-gold leaves crackle under my feet. I see all of this beauty, but I can't take it in. I have ten minutes before class, and I still need to call Sebastian.

I dash into the art building and find a phone booth. I open my palm. The numbers are faint and smudgy, but still visible. I'm shaking all over, but I know I have to do this. I take a deep breath and dial.

Then a crazy thought darts into my head.

What if I really am pregnant? That would make Sebastian the father of my baby! I hang up. I'm going to have to take an e.p.t. It's no big deal. I've taken them lots of times and they've always turned out negative.

But what if this one turns out positive? I'm not mom material. It's not in my genes. I don't take care of Hope; I don't even play with her. If by some stroke of bad luck I'm pregnant, I'll just have to get rid of it. There's no other way. God, how did I get into this mess? I don't have money for an abortion. I don't even know how much an abortion costs. And it would be a hassle, not to mention traumatizing. I'm seventeen; I can't be dealing with shit like this! Well, whatever happens, Sebastian will never know about it.

Again, I pick up the receiver and dial. I stay on the line this time, even though I feel like vomiting. On the sixth ring, Sebastian picks up.

"*Ciao,*" he mumbles in a groggy voice.

"It's Sarah."

I hear him yawn. Then, in a trying-to-be-sexy voice, he asks, "From last night?"

It kills me to think this creep could be the father of my baby. Bile rises in my throat. "This is Maddy's roommate," I say.

"Oh, sorry. Didn't recognize your voice." He laughs. "What's shaking?"

"I didn't call to chat," I say, trembling. "I just wanted to let you know that Maddy is planning a surprise visit to Cornell this weekend."

"Cool. Are you coming too?" I can actually hear him smiling into the phone. He obviously does not sense the gravity of the situation.

"Maddy is freaking out. She thinks you're cheating on her. I just called to warn you. So hide your bimbo and act surprised when you see her, okay?"

"What bimbo? I'm not cheating on Maddy. Besides, she's the one who wanted a time-out. Not me."

Huh? "What are you talking about?"

"She didn't tell you?" he asks. "I bet there are lots of things she doesn't tell you. Maddy's an enigma, a true enigma. I don't know what the hell's going on with her half the time. She said she wanted a break, so I gave her one."

"When did she say that?"

"I don't know. About two weeks ago."

"Why?"

"How the hell am I supposed to know?"

"You never told her about us, did you?"

"No! That's wack!"

"Then why would she want a break?"

"Maybe she wants to fuck some other guy. All she said was

88

she couldn't handle a long-distance relationship right now." He pauses. "She met someone, didn't she?"

"We go to a women's college, Sebastian. Who do you think she's going to meet?"

"Tell me who he is so I can kick his ass."

"There's no one. Look, I don't know what's going on with you guys, but she's coming to see you, so . . ." I glance at my watch. *Shit*. Late again. "Gotta go. Don't tell Maddy I called, okay? Bye."

"Wait . . . Sarah?"

"What?"

"Do you ever think about me?"

"Bye, Sebastian."

I hang up, totally confused. I don't know who's telling the truth. Maddy wouldn't lie to me, would she? She did lie once— about the size of Sebastian's penis—but that was a stupid lie, and one stupid lie doesn't make you a liar. Besides, aren't I the queen of stupid lies?

Still, I get the feeling that Sebastian is telling the truth. For starters, he's too lazy to lie. And he did seem genuinely jealous of this imaginary other guy.

What is Maddy up to?

After class, I go into town to buy an e.p.t. Then I dive into a bagel store and head straight for the unisex bathroom. I do the test. I wait. I pace the Ajaxed floor, biting my nails until they bleed. I want to scream, but don't. I think of all the ways I'll change my life if the universe grants me this one wish. I'll take better care of myself, exercise, floss more. I'll quit reading *Us Weekly*, quit having casual sex. I'll read to the blind, study harder, and be nicer to senior citizens, including Nana. I'll give Hope a bath when I get home. I'll never have sex with Sebastian again.

The test turns out negative.

When I get back to the house, Agnes isn't around and Maddy is still asleep in her room. I go to the backyard and look for Hope. I promised the universe I'd give her a bath, so that's what I'm going to do. I may be an atheist, but a promise is a promise.

Hope is sleeping on a bed of leaves under the maple tree. I check her food bowls, half-full of nuts and dried cranberries. Why does she eat so little and sleep so much? I know that's not a good sign, but at least she looks peaceful.

It's a beautiful day. The air smells of cut grass and nutmeg. The sun is out, the birds are chirping, a cool breeze grazes my face. I feel oddly content. I'm not pregnant, and everything is as it should be. I have friends who care about me, a home, my whole life ahead of me.

I hoist Hope up and carry her into the house. For someone who doesn't eat, she sure weighs a ton. Fifty pounds, I would guess. I wonder if that's normal for a fawn her age. I wonder if she misses her mother or the forest or any of her deer friends. She smells pretty rank. The kabbalah string Maddy tied around her right front leg is partly chewed, ready to fall off.

I take Hope upstairs to the bathroom, which has a claw-foot tub with an attached shower unit, a pedestal sink, and a stained-glass window facing the neighbor's house. Hope gets comfortable on the plush periwinkle rug and watches as I run the bath. I pour some bath gel into the water and wait for the citrus-basil scent to permeate the air. When it does, I take a deep breath. As the tub fills, weird shapes form on the surface of the water.

Skulls and laughing faces. WTF? I get rid of them by adding more bath gel. Now all I see are bubbles. You'd never guess there was scalding water underneath. It's the same with people: it's hard to know what's under all those layers.

I dip my hand into the water to check the temperature. It's so hot that, for a second, it feels cold. *Ow!* I add more cold water. Hope sniffs at the bubbles. When the tub is full, I check the temperature again and then lower Hope into the water. She fights me. She sloshes around and snorts bubbles and tries to jump out of the tub. I hold her down so I can scrub her back with Maddy's loofah, but her slippery body squirms away. Then she starts eating the bubbles.

"Stop," I tell her. "You'll give yourself diarrhea again."

I hold her head up, away from the bubbles. But when I take a step back, Hope leaps out of the tub and splashes water all over the floor.

"Great," I mutter. "Just great."

Her kabbalah string, I notice, is lying next to the toilet, and the bathroom floor is now a wading pool. Agnes is going to have a cow.

"I was just doing you a favor, but forget it," I say, my voice rising. "I don't need this. I should've just sprayed you with the garden hose. Shit." I grab my towel and wrap it around her, then carry her downstairs to the backyard.

"Happy now?"

She just looks at me with her blank eyes.

11

Cornell's off," Maddy announces, running down the stairs in her bathrobe. "Sebastian's coming *here* instead!"

"*What?*" Agnes and I say in unison from the dining table.

"He just texted me. He's coming for the weekend. I think he sensed I was coming to surprise him today. Soul mates can do that, you know." Maddy places her hand over her heart and looks at me. "Sebastian and I have such an amazing bond."

Not knowing how to respond to this, I just swallow.

"Well, that's great," Agnes says, a worried look settling into her face, "but where's he going to stay?"

"I don't know." Maddy tightens the belt to her robe. "We didn't get a chance to talk about that. Maybe we'll get a room at the Wetherly Inn."

"Or he can stay here," Agnes offers. "With us."

I blurt out, "Like one big happy family?"

"Sure," says Agnes. "Why not? It'll be fun. And much more comfortable than a hotel."

"What if Maddy and Sebastian want some privacy?" I say, hoping Agnes will get the hint. After all, Maddy just might want to lose her virginity tonight, and why would Agnes want to be anywhere near that?

"If they want privacy, they can go into Maddy's room," Agnes replies, missing the point entirely. "Right, M?"

Maddy beams. "I'm going to text Sebastian right now." She pulls her cell phone out of her pocket and starts typing.

"Good. Then it's settled." Agnes gets up to pour herself another cup of coffee.

"He hasn't left Cornell yet," Maddys says, staring into her phone, "so it'll be a while before he gets here. Perfect. That'll give me enough time to get a haircut. Anyone want to come with?"

"I'll go," Agnes volunteers. "I don't need a haircut, but I can keep you company."

Maddy looks up from her phone. "Sarah, you have to come too, because you actually *need* a haircut."

The two burst into laughter.

"Thanks a lot," I say.

"Sorry," says Maddy, "but it's true."

I tug at my ragged ends, parched from a recent dye job. I guess I could use a trim.

Two hours later, after a trip to Sally Jo's House of Beauty, the only salon in town, I am beyond furious. Somehow Maddy and I wound up with the same haircut. On a whim, I decided to chop off my hair and get that Winona Ryder pixie Maddy suggested, and the second Maddy saw me with my new hair, she told her stylist to give her the same cut. Never mind that her stylist had already snipped her long hair to shoulder length, blown it dry, and flat-ironed it. Maddy just *had* to have my haircut. Now we look like twins. Except she's blond and beautiful and looks chic with her new hair, and I look like a twelve-year-old boy with big thighs.

It's close to five o'clock when Sebastian arrives.

"What took you so long, Boo Boo?" Maddy says, opening the door.

"Traffic was bad, baby." Sebastian leans in for a kiss. When he sees Agnes and me standing in the foyer, he pulls away and grins, wiping Maddy's lip gloss off his mouth. "Hello, *chicas*."

"Hello," Agnes says in a bored tone.

I force a smile. "Hi."

He winks at me. I look away, hoping no one saw that.

Maddy grabs Sebastian's hand and pulls him into the house. He does a three-sixty in the foyer. "Nice place you got here, Agnes. Better than that crappy old dorm, that's for sure."

Agnes lets out a chuckle, but her eyes can't hide her contempt for Sebastian.

Suddenly Maddy claps her hands together. "Why don't we all go into the den?"

Sebastian pinches Maddy's ass as she leads the way. When their backs are turned, Agnes rolls her eyes at me and motions for me to follow them.

We enter the room just in time to see Maddy pushing Sebastian down on the sofa and straddling him. *Someone's desperate to lose her virginity.* Agnes and I sit on opposite armchairs and try not to stare at them.

"I missed you so much, Boo Boo," Maddy purrs. "Aren't you happy to see me? Aren't you going to compliment me on my hair?"

"It's short," he says.

"Do you like it?"

Sebastian puckers his lips and Maddy automatically leans forward to kiss him. The kiss quickly turns into a full-on tongue fest with groping hands and everything. Agnes and I turn away in disgust.

"We'll leave you two alone," Agnes says, getting up.

"Wait." Maddy looks at her while Sebastian continues nuzzling her neck. "We were thinking of ordering Thai food later. Want to join us?"

"No, Sarah and I have plans."

We do? I glance over at Agnes.

"We're going to catch a movie and then go out to dinner," she explains.

We are?

"Oh." Maddy pouts. "Well, have fun."

"You too," Agnes mutters before heading upstairs.

I give Maddy a quick wave and then I turn. But sensing she's still looking at me, I turn back around just in time to catch her scowling at me. Then, suddenly, she flashes me a big smile. What the . . . ?

Maybe the scowl wasn't meant for me. Maybe it was intended for Sebastian, who's still busily sucking her neck. Whatever. I give her a faint smile and exit the room.

Agnes is waiting for me at the top of the stairs. "Pack an overnight bag," she whispers.

"What? Why?"

"Just do it. I'll wait for you out front."

I throw some clothes into my backpack and slip five hundred dollars into my wallet. I ended up cashing Agnes's check after all. At first I felt bad for taking her money, but then I decided it was a fair trade. I needed the money, and she wanted the portrait. And now, for the first time, I've got money to burn. It feels good. I think I'll treat Agnes tonight.

I head out to the car, where Agnes is waiting for me in the driver's seat.

She exhales loudly when I get in. "Unbelievable."

"What?"

"The Wetherly Inn is completely booked for a conference. We have to find somewhere else to stay."

"Why? I thought you wanted us to be one big happy family."

Rolling her eyes at me, she says, "I just wanted to make her happy. But the minute I saw his face . . ." She grips the steering wheel. "How can she like him? A piece of cardboard has more depth. He's not even alive. He's a zombie like everyone else."

I shiver. Am I a zombie too? The thought scares me, so I tell myself to think about it later. "Let's get out of here," I say.

Agnes doesn't start the car. She just looks out the window without saying a word. What can I tell her? That she's too good for Maddy? That she should find someone else to love? I'm pretty sure that's the last thing she wants to hear right now.

"It's just a phase," I finally say.

She turns to me. "What is?"

"Sebastian. She'll grow out of him."

"You don't know anything, Sarah," she says, starting the engine.

The only place with a vacancy is the Full Moon Motel, ten miles outside of town. Unfortunately, it looks a lot like the Bates Motel, shabby and run-down, with its very own flickering sign outside.

Opening the door to our room, I'm greeted by the stench of mothballs and cigarettes.

"There's only one bed," I say, noticing the ugly jungle-print comforter.

"It's a queen. It'll fit us both."

"Uh-huh," I say, distraught over the idea of sharing a bed with lovelorn Agnes. What if she snaps and stabs me in the middle of the night?

She inspects the bathroom. The tiles are dirty, and on the wall there's a large brown stain that looks like dried blood. She opens her Goyard suitcase and takes out a bottle of Tilex and a Brillo pad, then snaps on a pair of latex gloves.

"This will only take an hour or so. Then we'll go out for dinner. I'm not really in the mood for a movie. I hope you don't mind," she says, closing the bathroom door behind her.

I pace the musty room, finally opening the sliding door to let in some air. Behind the motel is a forest, which makes me think of Hope. Shit. Is Maddy going to remember to feed her? That job is pretty much Agnes's now.

I knock on the bathroom door.

"What?" Agnes says.

"I need to borrow your phone."

"Come in."

I open the door to find Agnes crouching in the shower stall, her Brillo pad hard at work. The exhaust fan whines like a dying animal.

"Who do you need to call? Your grandmother again?"

"Ha ha. No. I wanted to remind Maddy to feed Hope."

"She'll remember. She's crazy about Hope."

"But you're the one who feeds her."

"And I'm not there, so Maddy will do it. Have some faith, Sarah. Is that all you wanted?"

"No," I say, annoyed. "You should keep the door open. It's not good to breathe in these fumes."

"It's fine. The fan's on. Close the door. I don't want the germs to escape."

"Whatever." I shut the door.

12

The Salamander is packed with couples, and Agnes and I are sitting at a corner table. There's a definite mood here: low lighting, a strolling violinist, single long-stemmed roses for sale.

"This place is trying way too hard to be romantic," I say.

Agnes looks up from her plate of shiitake mushrooms and polenta. "Well, some people actually like romance," she says, calmly stabbing a mushroom.

I ignore her snippy tone and cut into my chicken. She's obviously tortured by thoughts of Maddy and Sebastian having sex. She probably knows she's the last person Maddy is thinking of right now. It's kind of heartbreaking.

Still, I can't resist saying, "I hope Maddy's okay."

Agnes chews without blinking or saying a word. If she's worried about losing Maddy to Sebastian, she should talk to me about it; isn't that what friends are for?

"So why don't you have a boyfriend, Sarah?"

I take a sip of water. "I don't know if you've noticed, but there aren't a lot of men at Wetherly."

"There are plenty of male professors."

"Yes, but they're all married. Besides, I don't do relationships."

"Really," she says, raising an eyebrow.

"Really." I take another sip of water. "Relationships are messy and complicated and a complete waste of time. Guys are only good for one thing anyway."

She smirks. "That's very progressive of you. I guess you're kind of an expert, what with all the men you've slept with."

I ignore the insult. "What about you? What about that mystery person you lost your virginity to?"

"What about her?"

So it was a girl. I raise my napkin to my lips. "Do you still keep in touch?"

"No. It was a meaningless fling. It happened while I was in Switzerland."

"Right," I say, cheeks burning. We've avoided talking about Agnes's sex life for so long that it almost feels taboo. And way too intimate. She should really be more respectful of my intimacy issues.

I drag a piece of chicken through my mashed potatoes.

"I'm not a lesbian, though," Agnes says.

Our eyes lock. Is she trying to be funny? Then again, I guess there are a myriad of possibilities: Agnes could be bisexual, bicurious, homoflexible, heteroflexible, a LUG (lesbian until graduation), or just straight and in love with Maddy.

She takes another bite of polenta and for the next couple of minutes we avoid looking at each other. While she stares at her plate, I focus on the guy and girl sitting next to us. They're dressed identically, in jeans and black turtlenecks, and they're both eating lamb chops. They're barely talking, but every so often they'll look up at each other and smile. The heat finally leaves my face.

Our doe-eyed waitress refills my water just in time to break the grating silence. "Can I get you anything else?"

"Just the check, please," says Agnes.

"Sure thing." The waitress slinks away.

It's quiet again. I take out my wallet and check to see if the money's still there. It is. It's the largest amount of cash I've ever carried around with me. I place my wallet on the table and turn back toward the couple.

"Why do you keep staring at them?" Agnes asks.

I shrug. "They look happy."

"It's rude to stare."

"And you're Miss Polite, right?"

"I'm polite to strangers."

"Who cares? You're not polite to me."

"I'm honest with you," she says, "and that's better. A friend's job is to tell you the things you need to hear, even if you don't want to hear them."

"So then why are you still lying to me?"

Agnes wipes her mouth on her napkin. "What are you talking about?"

I shake my head.

"What am I lying about?" she asks.

The waitress returns with the check, and Agnes hands over her black American Express card.

"I wanted to treat," I say.

"Forget it." She waves me off. Then, after our waitress leaves, she asks me, "What do you want to know?"

"You're obviously upset. Talk to me."

"You want me to admit that I'm jealous of Sebastian?"

"Yeah."

"Well, I just did. I'd tell you more, but I don't think you can handle it."

"Oh, please," I say.

After a long pause, she asks, "Shall I start from the beginning?" Her eyes dart around the room and then land on mine. "When I was six years old, a strange thing happened. Maddy and I were in my room playing with our Barbies and I looked over at her and saw right into her soul. In that moment I knew we belonged together. I don't know how a six-year-old could understand something of that magnitude, but I did. It was the most profound thing I've ever experienced. Suddenly everything made sense. I literally felt an uncontrollable force pulling me toward Maddy. It wasn't sexual, or even emotional. It went beyond all that. With Maddy, it was like I was suddenly whole."

"Did she feel the same way?"

"Yes, although we didn't talk about the incident until years later. When we were twelve, I brought it up to her, and she said she'd experienced the same thing. She saw into my soul too, but was too afraid to say anything. I was astounded; I had no idea the feeling was mutual. Normally I'm skeptical about spiritual or psychic phenomena, but what we experienced was real. Maddy and I have a special bond that can't be broken by anyone."

"You mean Sebastian."

"I mean anyone," she says, eyes glinting. She folds her napkin into a neat square and places it on the table. "Have you ever felt so strongly about someone that nothing else in life mattered anymore?"

I shake my head.

"It's an incredible feeling." With a wistful look in her eyes, she says, "It's . . . otherworldly."

"Isn't that just love?"

"It's *more* than love. My whole being is tied to Maddy—and that overrides love. I don't consider myself a very sexual person, Sarah. I don't lust after people. Sex is something I could do without. But I do need to belong, to feel that I'm part of something."

"And you're sure Maddy feels the same way?" I ask her again.

Agnes nods. "She's just more hesitant than I am. Nobody likes to give up their power. But that's one of the most important lessons in life, isn't it? To let go. To trust. I know Maddy and I belong together; it's just taking her a little longer to realize it."

"She's dating Sebastian."

"Because she's afraid. She's not ready for something this powerful. It's easier to be with someone you don't really love. Then you're in control."

"She seems to be attracted to him."

"She *wants* to be attracted to him. It would make her life easier. But he's just another distraction. She's using him to put distance between us."

I give her a sidelong glance. "If you've always felt this way, then what happened in Switzerland?"

"Oh," Agnes says, looking down, "that girl only appealed to me because she resembled Maddy: tall, blond, innocent looking. Nowhere near as beautiful, of course, but she was a coquette and kept trying to get close to me. I was homesick. I lost my head. It was a mistake. I knew it even as it was happening." Flushing, she takes a sip of water. "I've never told this to anyone other than Maddy. I don't even know why I'm telling you." She takes another sip. "She's everything to me, Sarah."

"Did you ever find out what the Gypsy said to her?"

The color drains from Agnes's face. "That's no longer an issue. Maddy probably forgot all about it, so you don't need to worry about it anymore."

"How can you assume she forgot? When you first told me about it, you were so distressed."

"Just drop it, okay?" Her tone is curt.

"I don't understand." I shake my head. "Did Maddy tell you what the Gypsy said? Is that why you're—"

"I said drop it, Sarah. It was nothing. Promise me you won't ask Maddy about it."

"Why?"

"Trust me. It's for your own good."

For my own good? I shrug and decide to drop it for now. But all I can think about is how desperate Agnes seemed when she first told me about the Gypsy. And after all her talk about how friends are supposed to be honest with each other, she's lying to me now. Why? Is Maddy in trouble? Did the Gypsy tell her something horrific?

Agnes impatiently scans the room. "Where's our waitress?"

Back at the Bates Motel, I toss and turn while Agnes sleeps like a corpse. A snoring corpse.

I can't seem to turn off my brain. I think about how similar Agnes and I are; all these years I've been using sex to shield myself from pain while Agnes has been using her idealized love for Maddy. I think of Scissorhands and all the guys I've slept with, none of whom I ever got to know. Why? Because I'm terrified of love. Love makes people insane. It's made Agnes delusional, weak, and totally dependent on someone who doesn't seem to love her back. And, as smart as Agnes is, she can't see that. What would she do if Maddy's fear of dying young actually came true? How would she go on living without Maddy?

And yet there's a part of me that admires Agnes. It takes guts to love like that. I doubt there are many people in this world who have that kind of courage. Or are capable of such devotion. I'm certainly not; I'm too damaged. Or maybe that's just my excuse. Maybe I choose not to love because I don't want to suffer. Maybe beneath my zombie facade, there's a scared little coward.

Stop obsessing, Sarah. Go to sleep.

I toss and turn for another hour and then finally drift into dreamland.

We're in a forest: Maddy, Agnes, and I. We're walking in the dark, single file, with Maddy leading. Branches scrape against my face and arms. It's freezing. On the ground, dead swans line our path. *Wait*, I think, *I've been here before*. I tell Maddy this, but she ignores me. I tell her I want to get out of this place, that I have a bad feeling, but she insists that we keep walking. We come to a tunnel that we have to swim through to get to the other side. At the end of the tunnel, on a patch of dry land, is Hope, lying in a coffin.

I wake up panting, with a tremendous urge to pee.

I get out of bed and tiptoe into the bathroom, now completely sanitized, thanks to Agnes. I sit on the cold, hard toilet seat and look down.

Blood. My period. It finally came.

Sometime around dawn, Agnes's cell phone rings. She jumps out of bed, rummages through her purse, and answers it.

"What's wrong?" she asks frantically. "Okay. Wait there. Don't move. I'm coming to get you." Agnes throws her phone on the bed and hastily strips out of her Burberry pajamas.

"What happened?" I say.

"I'm not sure—Maddy was crying and there was static—but

Sebastian's obviously behind this." She flings her pajamas into her suitcase and puts on a pair of gray flannel trousers.

"Where is she?" I ask.

"At Dunkin' Donuts. She walked."

"I'll go with you." I change into yesterday's clothes and flip on the lights. Then I grab my jean jacket from the back of an armchair and shove it into my backpack.

Through gritted teeth, Agnes says, "If he did anything to her, I'll kill him."

"I know you will," I say, following her out the door.

When we pull into the parking lot of Dunkin' Donuts, I spot Maddy through the window. She's the only customer in the shop and she's facing the other way, hunched over in her ivory cashmere sweater-coat.

Relief spreads across her face when she sees us walk in. Agnes sits next to her in the plastic booth and I sit across from them. There's an empty doughnut box on the table. Maddy looks surprising well for someone who's been crying. No red puffy eyes or splotchy skin. And her new haircut really brings out her cheekbones. *My* new haircut, that is.

"He broke up with me," Maddy whimpers.

Sebastian's words come to mind: *She's the one who wanted a time-out. Not me.* My right eyelid starts to twitch.

"Why?" I ask.

Maddy shrugs and wipes her eyes. "We didn't have sex last night."

Agnes breathes a sigh of relief.

"I wanted to. I even wore this." She unties her coat to reveal a sheer black nightie. "But I just didn't feel ready. So we went to sleep and Sebastian seemed pretty understanding about the whole thing. Then, this morning, he woke me up at five. He had a boner. I told him that giving up my virginity was a big deal to me and that I'd feel better about it if I knew we had a future together. He got all quiet. I asked him what was wrong and he said he didn't want us to get too serious—that he wanted to start seeing other people. And he said it so calmly that I didn't get it right away. When it finally hit me, I was devastated." Maddy's voice cracks. "I accused him of cheating on me but, of course, he denied it. I called him a liar, and then we basically stopped talking after that. I told him to get out, but before he could get dressed, I was already out the door."

The chubby guy behind the counter leers at Maddy.

"Maybe you should cover up," says Agnes.

Ignoring her, Maddy says, "Can you believe I ate six dough-nuts? I'm going to turn into a cow. Oh well, who cares. It's not like I have a boyfriend anymore."

"So you didn't find anything out about the other girl?" I ask.

"No, and honestly, I don't care anymore. Whoever she is, I know she can't compare to me."

"That's definitely true." Agnes nods enthusiastically.

I exhale. Sebastian didn't rat me out, after all.

"Anyway," Maddy says, "if Sebastian wants to see other people, then fine. I was thinking about seeing other people myself."

Agnes sits up straighter.

"Like who?" I ask.

"I don't know. Somebody new," Maddy says, winking at me.

The wink is confusing. Who is she thinking of? One of her professors? A random townie? *Me?*

"Well, this is really for the best," says Agnes, practically beaming. "You don't need Sebastian. He wasn't worthy of you."

"You're right." Maddy sighs. "I just hope I don't die a virgin."

"You won't," Agnes chirps. "You won't."

"Can we go home now?" Maddy asks. "I really want to snuggle with Hope."

In the car, I try to process what's happened. What made Sebastian decide to end things? On the phone he sounded like he wanted to stay with Maddy. And what was all that stuff about her wanting a time-out? She asked for a time-out, which Sebastian didn't want, and then he decided to break it off? It doesn't add up.

13

flies are buzzing around her frail body. Frenzied ants are march-
ing all over her. She's curled up under the maple tree, face half
gone, as though a woodpecker had spent the morning pecking
away at it. Stark white bones peek through her ravaged flesh. I
turn away. I can't bear to see her like this—dead, rotting, infested
with vermin. She's dead. This isn't a dream. Hope is really dead.

"Nooooooo!" Maddy howls, spraying the insects with the
garden hose. "Go away, you killers."

Agnes disappears inside the house.

I stare into Hope's empty food bowls and feel sick: Maddy
forgot to feed her! I knew this would happen, I knew it! I should
have insisted on calling Maddy. This is *my* fault.

Hope. Why did Maddy have to give her that awful name?
Hope is the darkest emotion. It can kill a person.

An angry hornet buzzes near my ear. I swat at it, and miss. It
disappears and comes back. I swat at it again, this time feeling its
fuzzy body against my hand. I don't care if it stings me as long as
it dies. It's vile and disgusting; it doesn't deserve to live. I take
off my boot and swing at the hornet, again and again—sometimes

hitting it, sometimes not—until it finally collapses on the grass, flapping its wings pathetically. I put my boot back on and crush it.

"Hope," Maddy cries. "Oh, Hope."

She kneels next to Hope's wet corpse. Maddy's plaster-white skin appears shadowy and garish against the earth. For a moment I picture her dead, lying in a coffin, flawlessly made-up: two splashes of fuchsia high on her cheeks; thick, spidery lashes; pale, pale lips. Her hair is long, resting in snakelike coils around her face, and she's wearing a white silk taffeta gown. Wan and still, she looks like a dead bride.

Agnes comes out of the house with a shovel and a folded white bedsheet.

Maddy gets up, not bothering to wipe the mud off her ivory sweater-coat. She takes the sheet from Agnes. "What's this for?"

"To wrap the body in," Agnes says. "I'm going to lift her up. You slip the sheet under her."

Maddy unfolds the sheet and Agnes elevates Hope's body with the shovel, but Hope slides right off it. Agnes tries again, more aggressively this time.

"Not like that!" I snap. "You're hurting her."

"She's dead," Agnes says flatly.

"Still," I say, "there's a better way to do this."

"No, no, no," Maddy cries. "I can't. I can't." She drops the sheet and runs into the house.

"Great," Agnes says. "It was *her* pet."

"Yeah, and she's the one who fucking forgot to feed her."

"Everyone makes mistakes. And Hope wasn't well. She probably should have died the night we hit her."

"We should've taken her to a vet."

"Yeah, well, too late now." Agnes sighs. "Are you going to help me or what?"

"I'll take care of it. Just give me a minute," I say, waving her off.

"Don't take too long. It looks like it's going to rain. I'll start digging the grave."

When Agnes turns away, I exhale, roll my shoulders. I watch her walk across the backyard, stopping in front of the elm tree. I watch her take the first stab at the dirt. The shovel makes a vile sound—strangely high-pitched, like a rusty door hinge.

"Wait," I say.

"What?"

"This is where the grave should be," I say, pointing to the patch of grass beneath Hope's body. "This was her favorite spot in the garden."

"Then wrap her up so I can get to work. I still have to cook brunch."

"Who can eat at a time like this?"

"We have to," Agnes says. "We have to keep our strength up, especially for Maddy's sake."

Without saying another word, I spread the sheet out next to Hope's body. Holding my breath, I bend down to lift her up. She's unbelievably heavy. I place her damp body on the white sheet. She's grotesque and strangely beautiful at the same time: a slab of rotting flesh, a magnificent sculpture of bones.

Agnes grabs the corners of the sheet and drags Hope's body away from the grave site. Then she meticulously ties the ends of the sheet together, turning Hope's corpse into a neat little package. She comes back and points to the grave site.

"Here?" she asks.

I nod.

With the shovel, she attacks the ground, over and over with increasing vigor, not even breaking a sweat. I think of my recurring dream: the dead swans, the tunnel, Hope lying in her coffin. It was a warning. I force the images out of my mind. Meanwhile, the repetitive grating of the shovel against the ground is unbearable. It's all I can do not to lean over and vomit. When I feel the urge again, I bite down on my tongue as hard as I can.

Agnes throws down the shovel. I stare at the gaping hole in the ground: a baby grave, a vortex to the unknown. It seems to be swirling. I have to fight hard to keep from getting sucked in.

"Okay," Agnes says. "Let's do this."

I lower the white bundle into the hole. Agnes immediately starts shoveling in dirt, working fast. Soon I can only see patches of the white sheet. And then I hear Maddy wailing from inside the house. She runs out, red-faced, clutching a pink stuffed bear. Agnes keeps shoveling.

Maddy yells, "Wait! I want to give Hope something."

Agnes stops and looks at her with concerned eyes. Maddy places the bear in the grave; it's smiling.

I'm dizzy all of a sudden, hot. Something's pushing down on me. It wants me under the soil with Hope, and I'm too tired to fight it.

The next thing I know I'm upstairs in my bed. Maddy is sitting beside me, scribbling in a notebook. My head weighs a ton.

"What happened?" I ask groggily.

Maddy looks up. "Oh, you're awake! You scared us half to death, Sarah. You fainted."

"How long was I out?" I glance at the clock: 9:13 AM. I'm guessing it's the same day, but I can't be sure.

She shrugs. "Not too long."

"Did I hit my head?"

"Yeah," she says. "Does it hurt?"

I nod. "You didn't call 911?"

"No."

"So, you just left me here to die," I deadpan.

The blood drains from her face. "No!" she says, aghast. "Agnes examined you and said you were fine. There was no concussion or anything, and your breathing was normal. We didn't think you needed to go to the hospital. Do you *want* to go to the hospital?"

"I was only kidding, Maddy."

"Oh." She blinks nervously.

Why is she acting so weird?

"Do you want a Vicodin?" she asks.

I shake my head.

"It'll make you feel better."

As much as I want to dull this headache and block out all thoughts of Hope, I don't deserve relief right now. I killed Hope. I need to suffer. "No, thanks," I say. Then, changing the subject, I ask her, "How did I get up here?"

"We carried you." She touches my wrist. "Cheer up, Sarah. There's nothing we could've done."

"You forgot to feed her."

Her face darkens. "Boyfriends can be distracting sometimes. Anyway, Hope was sick. From the very beginning. She hardly ever ate. I think her death is a good omen."

My head spins. "A good omen? You adored her. You're the one who wanted to rescue her in the first place."

"Yes, but no one can escape death. It's a part of life," she says somberly.

Great. She's on her death trip again. "You're just upset about Sebastian."

"No. I'm completely over him."

"You broke up three hours ago."

Her eyelashes flutter. "It just wasn't meant to be."

"Where's Agnes?" I ask.

"In the kitchen."

"I have to talk to her," I say, sitting up.

"Don't get up," she says. "I'll go get her. Stay in bed. You need to rest up for tonight."

"Tonight?"

"We're doing a ritual."

I raise an eyebrow. "What kind of ritual?"

"You'll see."

Uh, okay.

She leaves her notebook on the chair. Once she's out of the room, I reach for it. Underneath several scratched-out lines is a corny little poem about Hope:

Hope is dead,
Our hearts are heavy with dread.
Goddess of light, we ask for relief
From sorrow and anger and painful grief.
Let us move forward in our lives—
With strength and love and open eyes.
Sisters we are, now and forever,
Heart and soul, bound together.

I return the notebook to the chair and get out of bed. I go into the closet and take out my River Phoenix poster. Unrolling it makes me feel a thousand times better. So much for wanting to suffer. I place the poster on the bed and allow myself to get lost in River's eyes.

Suddenly, I hear four rapid knocks at the door.

I admire River's long bangs for a moment, and then roll the poster back up. "Come in."

Agnes is wearing her yellow linen apron. "Maddy said you wanted to talk to me."

"Yeah." I sit on my bed. "I'm worried about her."

Agnes crosses her arms over her chest. "Why?"

"She's acting weird. Just now she was saying that death is a part of life and no one can escape it."

"Well, that's true, isn't it?"

"Yes, but she's not even upset about Hope."

"Hope was a sick animal. We prolonged her life for a little bit, but she was bound to die."

"She's not even upset about Sebastian."

"I guess Maddy finally came to her senses," Agnes says, adjusting her apron.

"It's a complete one-eighty. It's too erratic."

"That's just how Maddy is. One minute she thinks she's in love, the next minute she's over it. I told you—*I'm* the only constant in her life."

"She was crying hysterically when we buried Hope. Then, just now, she said Hope's death was a good omen. I think this has something to do with the Gypsy. We have to ask her about it."

Agnes stiffens. "I really regret telling you about that. You're blowing it out of proportion, Sarah."

"But—"

"But nothing!" She blinks wildly for a few seconds. Then, in a low voice, she says, "Maddy's fine. She's finally free of Sebastian and she has me. Everything's good now. I know she can be difficult and moody and unpredictable at times, but you're not perfect either and we put up with you. Give her a break. She's been through a lot."

I get it now: Agnes is so excited about Sebastian being out of the picture that she's not thinking clearly either. All she's thinking about is having Maddy to herself.

Agnes glances at her watch. "Are we through? I need to get back to my frittata."

"Yeah," I say.

"Don't worry so much. It'll give you wrinkles."

After she leaves, I check my skin in the mirror above my bureau and spot my first wrinkle: a worry line, thick and short, running horizontally between my eyebrows. *Fuck.*

It's midnight. We're sitting around Hope's grave, each of us holding a candle. It's windy and the air smells of mud and wet grass. Maddy stands up and, with the same shovel Agnes used to dig Hope's grave, she draws a circle around us in the dirt. Her eyes, I notice, still have that somber look.

"This is the sacred circle. Place your candles inside it." Maddy screws her long taper into the soil.

Agnes and I do the same.

"We're going to do a healing ritual," Maddy says in a low voice. "This will ease the pain of Hope's death so that we can move on. Now . . . close your eyes and concentrate."

Maddy snaps her eyes shut. I glance at Agnes, who gives me a semithreatening look before closing hers. Why, I wonder, does Agnes flip out every time I mention the Gypsy? What secret does the Gypsy hold, anyway?

Maddy begins speaking in a strange monotone. "Goddess Diana, we ask that you bless Hope and guide her on this journey into her next life. And please give us the strength to get through this difficult time. Help us to bond as sisters."

I hear the neighbor's back door open and then close.

Maddy continues, "Now, sisters, keep your eyes closed and try to imagine a white, healing light. Can you see it?"

"Uh-huh," I say, even though I can't see a damn thing.

"Agnes?" Maddy asks.

"I see it."

"Good," Maddy says. "Now try to imagine that you're bathing in the white light. The light is taking away everything that hurts in your body. It's taking it and absorbing it so you no longer feel any pain. You understand that Hope has gone to a better place."

Yeah, two feet below my ass.

"We ask the Goddess Diana to bless us and protect us—especially Sarah, because she's hurting the most, and it pains me to see my sister suffering like this. Okay, now, with your eyes still closed, let's hold hands."

I extend both of my hands. Maddy grabs the left one, and I take Agnes's.

"Now, open your eyes," Maddy says in her regular voice. "You are healed!" She lets go of my hand and I let go of Agnes's.

Two of the three candles have blown out—mine and Agnes's—but Maddy's still flickers on. Aside from the light spilling outside from the kitchen, it's dark out here.

"How do you feel?" Maddy asks, patting my knee.

Reluctantly, I say, "Okay." What's weird is that I do actually feel better.

Suddenly the kitchen phone rings, startling me.

"Ignore it," Maddy orders.

It rings seven more times before it stops.

Maddy looks to Agnes. "How do you feel?"

"Fine," Agnes says, nodding.

"Good," says Maddy. "I feel better too." She reaches inside

her bra and pulls out a piece of paper. Then she reads aloud her poem for Hope.

I glance at Agnes's placid face. When it comes to Maddy, she's an expert at hiding her impatience.

Once she's finished reading, Maddy places her poem over the flame and lets it burn. "Okay," she says, blowing out the candle and winking at me, "now let's go inside and get wasted."

14

I wake up to the smell of cinnamon sticks and wet fur. My head is throbbing. In the corner sits Hope's beige, faux-fur dog bed—large enough for a Saint Bernard—eerily empty. Why am I lying on the floor with a chenille blanket over me? I close my eyes and try to fall back to sleep, but then I remember: Hope's pale skull, the gloomy sky, the digging, the ugly brown mound.

We were drinking last night, Jack and Cokes followed by straight Jack. But we weren't drinking in here, even though Maddy wanted to. She wanted us to have a kind of wake for Hope, but I told her the idea was ridiculous—not to mention morbid—so we got drunk in the red room instead. Or maybe only I got drunk. I can't remember. I do remember single-handedly finishing the whiskey.

The alcohol made me feel good—so good that I let Maddy give me a makeover, something I never would've agreed to while sober. She plucked my eyebrows, applied pink shimmer to my lids, and covered my lips with a coat of dark red lipstick. We laughed and laughed and laughed. Then I must have passed out.

I get up, stumble toward the staircase, and stop to peek in the library: empty. Everything looks normal. I go upstairs.

Maddy's bed is made, with her forty stuffed animals on top of the pink comforter, all smiling at me. Her books on astrology, numerology, and palm reading sit in a neat stack on top of her nightstand.

I go next door and peek inside Agnes's spartan, colorless room. It's like a nun's chamber. The bed always looks untouched. The alarm clock on the nightstand reads 1:32 PM. Shit. I missed all of my morning classes. I walk toward the window and look outside. Agnes's car is still in the driveway. Since Agnes usually drives to class (even though we're just three blocks from campus), I'm guessing that she and Maddy walked today. Why didn't they wake me?

I go back to the nightstand and, on impulse, open the top drawer, half-expecting to find a Bible. Instead, I find Agnes's handgun resting on top of a pair of black leather gloves. It's small, understated, compact, just like Agnes. While running my fingers over the pebbly grip, scenes from the night we hit Hope come back into focus. Quickly, I shut the drawer.

I go back into Maddy's room and sit down on her comforter. I stare at her stuffed animals—her "children," as she calls them. Most were given to her by Sebastian, so naturally that would make him the father. That's how things work in Maddy's world, like a fairy tale. Every night, Maddy gives each of the stuffed animals a good-night kiss. One time I caught her whispering something in the purple elephant's ear, but I pretended not to notice. She's so immature. Even her room smells like cotton candy. And she's obsessed with all things Disney. Figurines of the Disney princesses sit atop her dresser. A Cinderella clock hangs from the wall. Sometimes I think she and Sebastian were made for each other. Both are like giant children, vacillating from selfish to sweet, from naive to wise, all in the blink of an eye.

I pick up one of the stuffed animals: a tiny, gray cashmere bear that fits easily in my palm. Its little face looks melancholic. Suddenly I'm overcome by a crazy impulse to take the bear. I don't know why, but I just have to have it. I know it's wrong and weird and compulsive, but I can't seem to stop myself. Besides, Maddy's got so many stuffed animals, I doubt she'll miss this one. I slip the bear into my pocket.

As I walk out of the room, I catch a glimpse of my reflection in Maddy's full-length mirror, and it stops me cold. I'm a *freak*. I've got red lipstick smeared all over my face and mascara rings around my eyes. I go closer to the mirror and shriek when I see what Maddy did to my eyebrows: they're gone! All that's left are two anorexic lines, shaped like semicircles, giving me that perpetually surprised look. Not only that, but one of my brows is a lot shorter than the other, the tail completely lopped off. I want to cry. How could Maddy do this to me? Why? On impulse I decide to burn all of her stuffed animals.

But first I have to get rid of this hangover.

I go down to the kitchen and make myself a large pot of coffee. I take four Advils and try to calm down. *They'll grow back*, I tell myself. *They're just eyebrows*. In the meantime, I'll pencil them in. People do that. Some people even like that skinny eyebrow look. Strippers, especially.

I dial Maddy's cell, but her mailbox is full. I hang up and dial Agnes's cell. It keeps ringing and ringing. I want to scream. How can you disappear after obliterating someone's eyebrows?

I look out the kitchen window. The grave. It's still there. Of course it is, and the small brown heap appears even more gruesome today. I take a deep breath and open the back door. I walk toward the grave, dragging my feet across the grass. This is it. This is what you get when you die.

I imagine myself buried next to Hope, trapped forever in the dank, cold mud, smothered by infinite darkness. *You shouldn't have left me. It's your fault I'm dead.* I feel like vomiting, but instead I fall on my knees and cry.

It's four o'clock and they're still not back. I'm sitting on my bed, waiting, waiting, waiting. I took a shower, tidied up Hope's room, drank my coffee, stole an eyebrow pencil from Maddy's makeup box (she owes me big-time for what she did), drew in some eyebrows (they don't look half-bad), and hid Maddy's little gray bear inside one of my boots, one of the few places where Agnes doesn't clean. And I feel better. The cry did me good. I didn't burn Maddy's stuffed animals, but I'm still pissed at her.

The phone rings sharply. It's them. I run downstairs and grab the kitchen receiver.

"Hello?"

"Sarah?"

Oh God, it's Sebastian. "Maddy's not here," I say. "What do you want?"

"Hey, is that the way to talk to someone who's just had his heart broken?"

"You're the one who wanted to see other people."

"Is that what she told you? Listen, *she* broke up with *me*."

Is he lying? Or is Maddy? I don't have time for this.

"Why are you calling?" I ask him.

"I want to get back together with Maddy. I'm dying without her. I left her a ton of messages, but she hasn't called me back," he whines.

I think of my eyebrows and say, "Consider yourself lucky."

"What?"

"Nothing. I'll tell Maddy you called. I have to go."

"Wait—"

I hang up, relieved that Sebastian is not the last guy I slept with. Of course, it'd be even better if I never slept with him in the first place, but it's too late now.

I tap my fingers on the kitchen counter, noticing Agnes's gardening shears sitting on top of the phone book. Suddenly I think, *Scissorhands*. Is this a sign from the universe? Am I supposed to call him or something? But I don't have his number. I don't even know his name.

But I do know where he lives.

I find Agnes's car key on the dining table, but hesitate to take it because I know how fussy she is about her things. *Oh, fuck it.* The universe wants me to see Scissorhands. So I leave a note: *Had to borrow car. Back soon.* I stick the note on the fridge under Maddy's Tinker Bell magnet and grab my jacket.

Only when I'm in the car do I realize that I don't exactly know how to get to Scissorhands's apartment. I remember that his place was close to the Hampshire campus, and I remember the willow trees and his yellow Victorian with green trim. Elm Street, I think. Or was it Pine Street? It was definitely some type of tree. I decide to start with Elm Street. I plug it into the GPS and back out of the driveway.

"In two hundred feet, turn right," barks the GPS lady.

When I get to Elm Street, I realize that the neighborhood doesn't look at all like how I remembered it. There are several yellow Victorians with green trim; any of them could be his. I circle the block, feeling more and more deflated each time. Why did I come here? It was a dumb idea.

Finally, I decide to pull over. He *does* exist. I know he does. I look across the street, and there—like magic—is Scissorhands's Victorian. Fate has intervened! I park the car and walk toward the house, not sure what I'm going to say. After all, he might not be so happy to see me.

Hi, remember me? We had sex a while ago. I know I freaked out afterward, but that's only because you were so sweet to me, which made me feel like I was falling for you, which scared the hell out of me because my parents had a totally fucked-up relationship and I promised myself I would never fall in love. But then my pet fawn died and I was home alone and there were these garden shears sitting on top of a phone book and I started thinking about you and I was wondering . . . Do you want to go out sometime?

I stop walking. I can't do this. Why am I here? It's insane. *I'm* insane.

And yet I'm still here. There's obviously something I want, even if I don't know what it is. I roll my shoulders and continue walking toward the door. I knock gently and hold my breath. No answer. I press my ear against the door. Silence.

A second later, I hear bare feet against the wood floor and then the click of the lock. I panic; my heart's jammed up in my throat; I want to run.

But I don't.

The door opens. He's wearing a black T-shirt and black shorts, and he has a big smile on his face. "Hi."

"Hi."

"I almost didn't recognize you with your short hair."

Butterflies. He's cute, cuter than I remembered. "Yeah," I say, "I just had it cut."

"It looks good on you."

"Thanks. I'm still getting used to it." I nervously touch the nape of my neck. "Is this a bad time?"

"No, not at all. I was just making pizza. You came at the right time. In five minutes, the dough will be ready."

"You're making it from scratch?"

"Uh-huh, it's easy. Come in." He grabs my sleeve and pulls me inside.

We go into the living room and sit down on the couch.

"I'm sorry for barging in on you," I say.

"No. I'm glad you came."

I look at him. "You are?"

He nods. "I went to your dorm, but they said you moved out. They wouldn't give me your address, so I started asking random people at the library about you, but apparently you're a mystery girl. Of course, I didn't have much to go on—beautiful girl, dark hair, calls herself Sarah, no last name." He tilts his head toward me slightly. "Sarah's a popular name. If your name were Henrietta, I'm pretty sure I would've found you."

"I should've given you my number. Or taken yours. I don't know why I didn't. I'm crazy."

"Well, you're here now. That's all that matters." He glances at his watch, then says, "Can I ask you something?"

I hold my breath. "Yeah."

"Do you like pizza?"

I exhale, trying to hide my relief. "Who doesn't?"

"Great." He jumps up. "Come with me."

We go into the kitchen. He washes his hands and I wash mine.

"This is the fun part," he says, sprinkling flour over the cutting board.

He places the dough on the board and, standing behind me,

takes my hands in his and together we knead the dough. Doing this should feel cheesy, but for some reason it doesn't. It feels really nice. The squishy dough, his strong hands, the way he smells—like soap and peppermint. I think this is the most intimate thing I've ever done with a guy, and I actually like it. Maybe I'm not as damaged as I thought. Maybe all it took was the right guy.

"Have you ever done this before?" he asks.

"No."

"I knew it. A virgin."

"Very funny," I say. "Hey. I'm really sorry I left in such a hurry last time."

"It was my fault. I ruined things by moving too fast. We should've spent the night talking and getting to know each other. I scared you off."

"I scared myself off."

"Sounds like we're a couple of scaredy-cats."

He kisses the back of my neck.

"But you're not a scaredy-cat," I say. "You actually went to my dorm."

"That's true. So . . . can I get a kiss for that?"

"Maybe." I smile. "You have to tell me something first."

"Anything."

"What's your name?"

"Reed," he says, laughing. "Reed Harrison."

I turn around and we kiss. And he caresses my face with his floury hands and I think, *Thank you, universe.*

A little after midnight, I pull into our driveway. The house is ablaze with light.

While I'm rummaging for my keys, Agnes opens the front door. "Where have you been?" she demands, hand on hip.

"Sorry. I lost track of time," I say, sliding past her. With her sensitivity, though, she can probably sense that I was with a guy.

I hurry up the stairs and try to ignore Agnes's rapid footsteps behind me. I dash into the bathroom, noticing that Maddy's door is closed. I shut the bathroom door behind me and lock it.

A second later, I hear a knock.

"Yeah?" I say.

"I want to talk to you," says Agnes.

"Not now." I squirt a huge glob of toothpaste on my toothbrush.

"It's important."

"Later."

"Please?" Agnes almost never begs. I'm intrigued. "I got you a present," she adds.

Now *this* is weird. I unlock the door.

She opens it and charges inside.

"Where were you today?" she asks.

"Where were *you*?"

"I took Maddy for a walk."

"For three hours?"

"You can believe what you want, but it's the truth. Maddy was upset after last night, so I suggested a walk."

"Thanks for leaving me a note."

"Sorry. I thought we'd be back before you got up."

"I called both of you."

"We left our phones at home." Agnes perches on the edge of the bathtub.

"So, Hope's death finally got to her?" I ask.

"What do you mean?"

I give her a sidelong glance.

"She's upset because of what happened with *you*."

"Huh?"

"You don't remember? You called her some terrible names."

"What are you talking about?"

"Does 'malevolent witch' ring a bell?"

"No. Why would I call her that?"

"Your eyebrows."

"Oh," I say, and though I have no recollection of calling Maddy a malevolent witch, I'm glad I did.

"You were furious. You completely overreacted."

"She demolished my eyebrows! She'd have a fucking conniption if I did that to her."

"It's not like she did it on purpose."

"I'm not so sure."

"What's that supposed to mean?"

"Nothing," I say, spitting out a mouthful of toothpaste.

"They're eyebrows. They'll grow back."

"Whatever."

"Your eyebrows *were* pretty bushy."

"Thanks," I say, and rinse. "You always take her side."

"I don't know why you're so angry. They look fine now," she says.

"That's because I penciled them in."

"Well, that's what you're supposed to do."

I sigh. "Forget it. I don't know why I even bother."

"She feels awful," Agnes continues. "She's been crying all day. She was just trying to make you look pretty. Besides, she was intoxicated."

I rinse out my toothbrush and put it in its holder.

"So, you never answered my question," she says. "Where did you go?"

"Nowhere."

"Then why did you take the car?"

I shrug.

"Don't throw away a friendship over something as trivial as eye—"

"I went to see a guy. Men, remember them? Some of us still need them."

Agnes's nostrils flare ever so slightly. "Did you have fun?"

"Yeah," I say, unable to suppress my smile.

"I'm glad. Here, this is for you." She hands me a plastic bag. "It was Maddy's idea." Inside the bag is a black iPhone. "So you can reach us," Agnes says. "Anytime."

After my shower, I tap on Maddy's door.

"Come in," she says in a weak voice.

I open the door and find her lying in bed, wedged between her stuffed animals. For a second, I worry that she noticed her gray bear was missing, but then she smiles so I relax.

"You okay?" I ask.

She frowns. "I'm sorry about your eyebrows. I didn't mean to screw them up. I shouldn't have gone anywhere near your face after all those Jack and Cokes. I'm *so* sorry. I'll make it up to you, Sarah. I'll be your personal slave or whatever you want. Please, just say you'll forgive me. Say you still want to be my friend, because I don't know what I'd do if—"

"It's fine," I say, sitting down at the edge of the bed. "Look, I penciled them in. You can hardly tell."

"I'm a jerk."

"No. I shouldn't have made such a big deal out of something so stupid. I don't even remember what I said. It was the alcohol talking."

Suddenly Maddy starts crying. I reach for the tissue box on the nightstand, and when I hand it to her, she pulls me into an unexpected hug. "Do you really forgive me?" she sobs.

"Of course."

" 'Cause I don't know what I'd do if you stayed mad at me."

"I'm not mad. Really."

"I love you, Sarah Bear," she says, giving me a kiss on the cheek.

Though I'm still annoyed, I decide to forgive her. How could I not? I just had the most incredible date of my life. I'm practically overflowing with giddiness.

Still, I do feel kind of ridiculous for comforting *her* when I'm the one without any eyebrows. I know that my brows alone aren't a big deal, but things are beginning to add up. She copied my haircut and she lies constantly. Did she or didn't she break up with Sebastian? I still don't know the answer, because her stories rarely make sense. On top of everything, she always gets what she wants. Yet I still like her for some reason. It's as though she's got some kind of voodoo hold over me.

15

Slow down," Professor Connelly orders the class. "You're all going too fast. Pretend you're an ant crawling over the surface of the figure. Follow every curve. If the line goes into the figure, draw it. If the line ends, stop. We're not trying to make a perfect picture. We're looking for idiosyncratic character."

She's circling the room, watching us sketch the male model: a tall black guy around thirty-five years old, with dreadlocks, a ton of muscles, and a big penis. The girls are all panting over him. This is what happens at a women's college. Everything gets reduced to sex.

Professor Connelly stops at my easel and stares at my drawing for an uncomfortably long time. I haven't been able to get the penis right. Is that what she's staring at? Finally, she leans in and whispers, "Nice drawing." Then she props her hand on her hip and says to the class, "Come here, everybody. Take a look at what Sarah's doing."

I steel myself before everyone crowds around my easel.

"Sarah has a very sharp eye," says Professor Connelly. "Notice the character of her lines. Notice the overlap and the effective foreshortening. It's a pretty terrific drawing, isn't it?"

The class responds with a collective unenthused, "Uh-huh." I fidget under the scrutiny of fifteen pairs of hot eyes, studying me as well as my drawing. Does the erratic quality of my lines give me away? Does it betray my fears, compulsions, or fucked-up childhood? Or does the weirdly drawn penis say more about me?

"Okay, back to work, everybody. I'll give you another five minutes. Then I want you to get out your pen and ink."

Everyone shuffles back to their seats except Professor Connelly, who is still hovering over my easel. She puts her finger on the penis. "Fix that," she says, then walks away.

I erase and start over, this time separating my mind from my body and approaching the task purely as an intellectual exercise. I take a good, hard look at the model's penis, heavy and purple, casually resting on the balls. But all I can do is bite down on my tongue and fight the urge to giggle.

After class, I take my drawing pad and art box down to the pond. Everything around me is golden, beautiful, the ground cloaked in thousands of yellow leaves. Although it's only October, the days are already getting shorter and there's a bite in the air.

I sit down and study my drawing, determined to get the penis right. I'm not going to let a dumb sex organ intimidate me.

My phone chimes with a new text message. It's from Reed. *Turn around*, it says.

I turn and there he is, standing behind me. I gasp. "What are you doing here?"

"I was driving to work and I couldn't stop thinking about you, so I decided to stop by."

I feel myself flush, first from excitement, then embarrassment. I look like crap today: no makeup, dirty jeans, my ratty old sweatshirt smothered in charcoal dust.

He sits down next to me and we kiss. Then he looks at my drawing. "You're really good."

Groaning, I say, "I can't draw the penis."

"Oh, is that a penis?" He covers his mouth. "I thought it was a small raccoon."

"Very funny." I give him a playful shove. "Maybe you should model for me."

A devilish grin appears. "Okay," he says, and starts unbuttoning his pants.

"Not *now*!"

"All right, all right. You just let me know when."

I shake my head. "You're crazy, you know that?"

For a moment I wonder about this character I'm playing, this girl who's flirting and laughing and having fun with a guy, this girl who seems like she's one half of a couple. Is she really me? I've never acted like this with anyone before, and yet it feels so natural. Was this always inside me?

My phone rings suddenly. It's Maddy. I ignore the call.

"My roommate," I explain to Reed. "I'll call her back later."

"Are you ever going to introduce us?"

"Sure. Sometime. Later on," I say, though I can't picture Reed and Maddy in the same room. What would they talk about? Of course, Agnes would have to be there too, and that would be even more awkward.

Changing the subject, I say, "Where do you work?"

"I work for my professor. I tutor his kid in geometry twice a week."

"I had no idea you were good at math."

"Well," he says, glancing at his watch, "there's a lot you don't know about me." He gives me a sexy grin.

My phone rings. Again, it's Maddy.

I look to Reed. "It's my roommate again. Maybe it's important."

"Answer it," he says. "I have to get going anyway. I'm late for work." He gets up, dusts himself off.

I answer the phone. "Hello?"

The line goes dead.

"Hmm," I say. "The call got lost."

"She'll call back," Reed says, leaning down to kiss the top of my head. "I'll call you after work, okay, cutie?"

"Okay, bye."

I watch Reed walk away, and then, while waiting for Maddy to call back, I redraw the penis. When I'm satisfied, I pack up my things and go.

The entire house smells of chocolate. Maddy is in the kitchen, braless, wearing a white tank top and hot-pink velour short-shorts.

"I called you," she says, shoving a plateful of brownies at me.

"I know. I called you back but you didn't pick up." I take one. "What's going on?"

"Nothing. I just wanted you to know that I made brownies."

I bite into it. It's terrible: dry, brittle, and slightly salty.

"How is it?"

I force a smile. "Good."

She places the plate of brownies on the counter. "So, are you going to tell me, or am I going to have to guess?"

"Tell you what?"

"Why you're smiling. Did you get an A on your psych exam or did you see that boy again?"

"What boy?"

"Agnes told me you went to see a boy the other day. Who is he?"

Part of me doesn't want to tell her because I know she won't like it, but another part of me is just too excited to keep it in.

I take another bite of the hard brownie and chew. Feeling Maddy's eyes on me, I finally say, "There's nothing to tell, really. He goes to Hampshire. I met him when you and Agnes were in Vermont. We're just hanging out." I leave my brownie on the counter, open the fridge, and pour myself a glass of milk.

"What's his name?"

"Reed," I say, taking a sip of milk before returning to the counter. "I don't know if you remember, but he was at the diner our first night here."

Maddy sits down at the dining table. "The guy with the paper dolls?"

"Yeah." Her memory is impressive.

"See, I really *am* psychic," she says with a glint in her eye. "Actually, he was the only guy under thirty in that whole place. I remember thinking he was kind of cute. You had sex with him, didn't you?"

"No," I lie. Some things are private, after all. "We just made out."

"But you *will* have sex with him eventually."

I shrug. "Probably."

"So, let's do a reading on him."

"A reading?"

"Yeah, so you can see if this is a good relationship before it gets too serious."

"That's okay," I say. Not because I don't believe in psychic phenomena; I just don't believe *Maddy* is psychic. Besides, I already know Reed's a good guy.

"Come on."

"No, I don't feel like it."

"Don't be afraid of the tarot, Sarah."

"I'm not afraid," I say. *Oh, what the hell. It's just a silly game.* "All right, let's do it." Leaving the brownie behind, I take my glass of milk and sit down at the table across from her.

She reaches for her baby-blue Marc Jacobs bag. "I don't even need to use tarot cards. I use regular playing cards 'cause I've got *the gift*." She pulls out a small deck of Tiffany playing cards and hands it to me. "Concentrate while you shuffle the cards. Try to focus all your energy on your question."

I shuffle the cards. A part of me wants to believe that Maddy *can* unlock the truth. But more than anything, I just want to hear what I already know—that Reed and I are a good match.

"Okay, ask your question," Maddy commands.

"Will Reed and I be happy together?"

"Put the cards on the table facedown."

I do as she says. Maddy takes the top three cards and lays them facedown. Then, one by one, she flips them over. The first card is a two of clubs; the second, a three of hearts; and the third, a queen of spades.

"Now, let me concentrate." Maddy places her fingers on her temples and closes her eyes. She looks so serious, it's kind of funny. Her lower lip begins to quiver. A minute passes before she opens her eyes again. "I'm sorry, sweetie," she says, shaking her head. "It's not going to work out."

My body tenses. "What?"

"He's hiding something."

"What do you mean?"

Frowning, she says, "He's got a dark secret. I don't know what it is, but you don't want to get involved with this guy. He's not a bad person, but he's not a good match for you. Eventually he'll break your heart."

"Sounds like a curse."

"I'm sorry, Sarah Bear. But the cards don't lie. The good news is you can end things now, before you get hurt."

"What else do you see?" I ask, feeling a little light-headed.

"Sure you want to know?"

I sigh. "Yes. Tell me everything."

She stares at the cards. "This guy's an artist, right?"

My head swims. "You can actually see that in the cards?"

"Of course."

I begin to panic. Can Maddy really read my mind? If so, does that mean she knows about Sebastian and me? I'm suddenly very afraid of her.

"He may be sweet now," she says, "but later you'll see his possessive side. Like a lot of artists, he's insecure and totally self-absorbed. If you date him, you'll be stressed-out and miserable." She looks up from the cards. "Good thing you didn't sleep with him, huh?"

But I *did* sleep with him. *And* I like him.

"By the way," I say, changing the subject, "I forgot to tell you Sebastian called the other day."

"He can keep calling, because I'm not calling him back. I have nothing to say to him." Maddy comes over and puts her hand on my shoulder. "You okay? You look a little pale."

"I'm fine. I barely knew the guy. And like you said, now I can end it before it gets too serious."

"That's right. And we have each other, Sarah Bear. Who needs boys, anyway?" she says, wrinkling her nose.

I do.

* * *

Later, in my room, I'm too impatient to wait for Reed to call me, so I call him first.

He answers on the third ring. "Hey, you beat me to it. I was just about to call you."

Butterflies. The sound of his voice alone does that to me. "I missed you."

"I missed you too."

"Do you want to do something tomorrow?" I ask. "During the day?"

I hear him shuffling papers in the background. "You don't have class?"

"Nope. Do you?"

"Nothing I can't skip."

"No. I don't want you to do that."

"Well, I do," says Reed. "I'll come pick you up in the morning. How's nine?"

"Perfect," I say. I can sneak out of the house before Maddy wakes. "Can you pick me up at the mail center?"

"Sure. I can't wait to see you."

"Me too. Good night."

"Sweet dreams."

I hang up, reassured that what Reed and I have is special. I don't think he has a dark secret. And I don't think Maddy is psychic, even though she knew Reed was an artist. It was a lucky guess. After all, I'm an artist. Why wouldn't I be attracted to a kindred spirit?

What's important is that Reed likes me and I like him. A silly tarot-card reading by an information-withholding roommate is not going to change that.

16

At eight o'clock I wake up to Lou Reed's "A Perfect Day." Not a bad song to wake up to—a little depressing, but depressing in a good, contemplative way. I let the song play until the end and then turn off my clock radio. Nothing can get me down today. It's Friday, I have no classes, and I'm going to see Reed in an hour.

I tiptoe into the bathroom and quietly shower, making sure to shave my legs and moisturize thoroughly. Back in my room, I put on a skirt, which I rarely do, and study my reflection in the mirror. The skirt looks decent, but I feel awkward in it, like a preteen wearing high heels for the first time. Next to the dark denim, my legs look impossibly white and cadaverous. After years of perpetual concealment, I almost forgot how weirdly shaped they are: big and flabby from the knees up, straight and skinny from the knees down. Like a couple of corndogs. Not the look I was going for. I tear off the skirt and slide into my favorite pair of Levi's, a vintage Doors T-shirt, and my brown corduroy jacket. I apply black mascara and clear lip gloss, then tiptoe downstairs.

The scent of Agnes's morning blend fills the air. I find her sitting at the dining table in her Burberry pajamas, reading the paper. She looks at me and asks, "What are you doing up so early?"

"I have a meeting with my psych professor," I lie. The last thing I need is for Maddy to know I went to see Reed.

"This early?"

"I couldn't make it to his regular office hours, so I made an appointment. I'm so behind in his class."

Agnes's face remains expressionless. "Want some coffee?"

"No, thanks. I'm late."

"Do you want to take the car?"

"No," I say. "I need the exercise. And cold weather burns more calories."

"But it's raining."

I look out the window. *Shit.* I was so busy obsessing over my outfit that I didn't even bother to look outside. "It's all right," I say. "I'll bring an umbrella."

"Suit yourself." She goes back to her paper.

The walk is dreadful. It's useless carrying an umbrella when the rain is coming down sideways. I'm getting blasted, my hair is attaching itself to my lip gloss, and my feet feel soggy. By the time I arrive at the student mail center, I feel about as sexy as a wet poodle. And then I catch my reflection in the window: I look like a stalker. Why didn't I think to wear *waterproof* mascara? It's a good thing Reed already likes me.

I take a seat in the middle of the barren room, pull my hair back into a ponytail, and do the best that I can to wipe off my lip gloss and smeared mascara. Then I smooth on some vanilla-scented lip balm. Lip gloss isn't very kissable, anyway—too sticky. I glance at my watch: nine o'clock. He must be running late. I get up to check my mailbox. I open the little metal door and a bundle of letters leaps onto the floor. Bills, bills, bills, junk, and . . . *Holy shit!* A letter from Nana. I tear it open:

Dear Sarah,

I hope you are enjoying your time at Wetherly. I suspect that you are keeping up with your studies and, more important, learning how to be a lady. I look forward to witnessing your transformation in the summer. Until then, you should probably stay on the East Coast. I'm sure you've made many new friends, so perhaps you'd like to spend the holidays with them rather than flying back to California. Thanksgiving is too short, and I won't be here during Christmas. I'm going to Australia with Bowie, a man I met at church. Bowie has a beautiful home in Brentwood, and we've been spending a lot of time there. I haven't been this happy since your grandfather was alive. I suppose this is my reward for taking care of you all of these years.

I am enclosing a check for $1,500, which should cover your expenses until summer. If not, I suggest you look for a job. You are an adult now and need to learn how to support yourself. I do hope you've been attending church regularly. As I recall, there's a lovely chapel not far from Haven House.

God bless you,
Nana

I can't believe it. A boyfriend at her age? And ditching me for a guy named Howie? I wasn't planning on going home for the holidays, but I never anticipated not having the option. And what about my birthday? Did she forget? It's kind of impossible—I've got the same birthday as Jesus, for Christ's sake! Plus, it's my eighteenth. Shouldn't I at least get a cake?

The good news is that Nana's not dead, which actually crossed my mind a few times. I pictured her lying on the floor, injured, hearing the phone ring when I called, but not being able to answer it. But Nana's fine. She's just been busy playing house with Howie, not thinking about me at all. If she had called me even once she would've learned that I'm no longer living at Haven House. Whoever's living in my old room would have told her that. But obviously she doesn't care.

Yet I'm relieved to have the money. My credit card balance has been growing exponentially, and I was just beginning to understand why a college student would consider stripping her way through school, especially now that I have a monthly iPhone bill to deal with. But how is $1,500 going to last me till summer when it's only mid-October? Nana is obviously not all there. Does she know it's not the fifties anymore? When she was a student at Wetherly, girls were taught how to become good wives. Now we're being taught how to become our own husbands. Why did Nana even send me to such an expensive school just to make me worry about money, when I could have gone to UCLA and saved her a bundle? Is she demented or cruel? Maybe both.

When I see Reed's ancient, rusty Nissan Sentra pull up, I stuff Nana's letter into my backpack and walk into the pouring rain. This is not the time to be upset. It's all about Reed now.

* * *

We go to his apartment and sit on his black couch for a while. We look at each other and smile and hold hands. It feels strangely natural not talking, like we don't need words. I'm tempted to tell him about Maddy's reading, but decide not to kill the mood.

I let go of Reed's hand and run my fingers over his knee and, in no time at all, we end up in his bed. The sex is intense. At the same time, I feel safe with him. This is where I want to be, feeling everything, savoring each detail.

Afterward, he spoons me and we listen to the rain.

"Sarah, Sarah, Sarah," he says. "I'm going to tell you something, and I don't want you to freak out, okay?"

I freeze. Is this where he tells me his dark secret? *Shit*. Without turning around, I mumble, "Okay."

He kisses my shoulder. "I love you."

"*What?*"

"I love you."

My heart literally does a dance. No one has ever said those words to me before. Ever. I'm so stunned, so happy, I don't know what to do. So I turn around and look at him. God, he's adorable and so sweet. And he's mine. Is this what Agnes was talking about? This feeling that nothing else in the world matters except this person and the way I feel about him?

He pulls me closer. "You don't have to say it back to me right now. Say it when it's true for you."

I can't stop grinning.

"Wait. Don't move," he says, getting out of bed. He leaves the room and comes back with a pen and a sketchbook. He sits on the edge of the bed and peels back the sheets. I'm naked underneath. He starts drawing.

"Don't!" I grab for the sheets.

"Come on." He takes my hand, holding it for a moment before bringing it to his lips. "You're radiant."

Radiant? I feel myself relax a bit. Reed draws and I don't stop him. His hands quickly scrape out lines and tones and soon I see a serious-looking girl with moody eyes staring back at me. She's lying on her side with one arm not-so-casually positioned in front of her stomach. She doesn't have any limbs missing and she has tiny hips. He made them smaller than they are in real life; he must really love me.

He puts down his sketchbook, and we have sex again. It's even better this time, more relaxed, more meaningful. His touch is tender and loving, and the way he looks at me—like I'm the only girl in the world—is intoxicating. He *loves* me. And I . . . I . . .

"Reed," I say suddenly.

"Yeah?" He opens his eyes.

"I love you too."

His eyes light up.

It's the first time I've said those three words to anyone, much less to a guy I actually love. I feel buoyant and hopeful, not sick to my stomach like I thought I would. People *can* change, I feel like telling Nana and the rest of the world. History does not have to repeat itself.

At four o'clock reality hits: I've been gone for an entire day! My phone's been ringing nonstop, and I have a ton of new messages from Maddy and Agnes—none of which I've listened to yet. As much as I want to stay and snuggle with Reed, I ask him to drive me home.

In the car, I start to feel anxious. I think about Maddy's predictions. What if Reed breaks my heart? It'd be possible now; I'm completely vulnerable. He could hurt me more than anyone. And what if he does have a dark secret?

"Hey," Reed says. "What are you thinking about?"

I smile weakly. "Nothing."

We don't speak until we get to Wetherly. Then I ask Reed to drop me off a block away from the house, explaining that my roommates are nosy.

"I'll call you," I say, leaning over to kiss him.

"What are you doing this weekend?" he asks.

"I'm not sure yet."

"Let's do something. We could go to Boston, spend the night there. Or whatever. I just want to see you." He's already getting clingy. What happened to that strong, independent guy I was so intrigued by? Is this the insecurity that Maddy was talking about?

When I don't answer, Reed asks, "What's wrong?"

"Nothing. I'm just thinking." But what I'm really doing is obsessing. Will he end up hurting me? Will he make me miserable? I don't want any more pain. My life so far already feels like one giant heartbreak. So I avert my eyes and lie to Reed. "I'll check with my roommates," I say. "I think they wanted to do something this weekend."

"Okay," he says, patting my knee. "Well, let me know." He sounds a little hurt, and now it's awkward.

Why do I have to ruin everything? I'm such a bitch. "I'll call you," I say, forcing a smile. Then I step out of the car and sprint down the street.

The house is dark when I enter, quiet except for the sound of the dripping faucet. I flip on the hall lights and walk toward the kitchen, toward the drips.

"Maddy? Agnes? Anybody home?"

I place my backpack on the floor next to the dining table. A sliver of light shines from under the basement door. Agnes is home.

Pressing my ear to the door, I hear her talking on the phone. I can't tell who she's talking to, but her voice is strained. I knock on the door. After all this time, I've never gone down to the basement. Agnes hasn't exactly invited me, and she keeps the door locked when she's not at home. What, I wonder, is she hiding down there? I've imagined all kinds of sick things: slabs of dissected animals, shrunken heads in Mason jars, a closet full of S and M gear. A dead body.

Knocking one more time, I call out, "Agnes? It's Sarah. Everything okay?"

I hear a soft shuffling and then a barely audible "Come in."

Bracing myself, I open the door and go down the dark, creaky stairs. Agnes is sitting at her desk with her back to me. A naked bulb lights the room. The air smells of lemongrass candles on top of Raid. Boxes clutter the floor—surprising, since clutter is not in Agnes's vernacular. Even I find it stifling and my OCD is nowhere near as bad as hers. I scan the room, and what I discover is not at all what I expected.

It's much, much worse.

Dolls. Hundreds of them, like some little-girl fantasy gone wrong. Two huge walnut cabinets with glass doors hold the bulk of them. The dolls in the first cabinet are made of porcelain or wood and they all have similar faces: round, cherubic, powdery white, with big bulgy eyes and pouty lips. The second cabinet holds Barbies swathed in shimmering, lollipop-colored gossamers. My eyes land on one that's dressed as Marie Antoinette. She looks slightly different from the other Barbies, her face smaller, slimmer, more delicate. She's wearing a pale blue, corseted ball gown trimmed with gold lace, and a hat with real feathers. As much as I hate dolls, I have to admit this one is pretty exquisite. She's not as wholesome-looking as the other Barbies, but she's regal, with albino skin and a slightly wicked smile. The more I look at her, the more sinister she appears, and then I realize who she reminds me of: Maddy. She has the same disturbingly immaculate beauty and vacant eyes.

Agnes swivels around in her chair, her eyes bloodshot, tired.

"What's going on?" I ask her.

"My mother called. She's trying to set me up with the son of one of my father's business associates. A Harvard brat. She wants me engaged by the end of the year." Agnes sighs. "As if that's ever going to happen."

"*Engaged?*"

"She can't wait to plan my wedding. I told her I have midterms coming up, but she could care less." Agnes rolls her neck, then starts cracking her knuckles.

"So, she doesn't know?" I ask.

"Know what?"

"That you're . . . you know . . . *gay?*"

"I'm not gay," she snaps.

"Oh," I say, feeling stupid.

She gives me a weird look, like it's my fault I don't understand that she's asexual, hates men, desperately loves Maddy, but is *not* a lesbian. When did sexual identity get so complicated? I guess that's a dumb question.

I decide to change the subject. "So, what are you going to do about the guy?"

"I told my mom I was busy, which means she'll try again in an hour. I really don't know how I'm going to get out of this one."

"Can't you just tell her you're . . . you know . . . not interested in dating anyone right now?"

Agnes throws me a glare. "No."

I don't say anything. Then I wave my hand in front of the cabinets. "Uh, I'm sorry, but . . . what's with the dolls?"

"My mother started this collection for me when I was five. She's been buying them for me ever since, even though I hate dolls." Agnes gets up and opens the first cabinet, removing a wooden doll in a floral cotton dress and a funny-looking hat. "This one was made in France in 1875, and is worth a mere thirty-five thousand dollars."

I gasp. *Thirty-five thousand dollars? I could live off that for a long, long time.* "I didn't know dolls could cost that much," I say.

"Oh, they can." She rubs the back of her neck. "If you're willing and have the money, there are always ridiculous things to buy. And the more money you have, the more absurd the purchases. That's why wealthy people have so many silly collections. What else are they going to do with their money?"

I glance at the Marie Antoinette doll again.

Noticing, Agnes says, "That's the only one I like. It reminds me of Maddy." Carefully removing Marie Antoinette from the cabinet, she adds, "But Maddy's much more beautiful, of course."

Much more harmful too.

A smile creeps onto Agnes's face while she adjusts Marie Antoinette's hat. She then puts the doll back into the cabinet and, with her foot, nudges aside a pile of boxes. "I should probably rent a storage unit."

"Why can't you just tell your mom you've outgrown dolls?"

"Impossible." Her face darkens. "It's a hobby we're supposed to be bonding over. Besides, she's never been interested in hearing the truth. She's fragile, nervous, and prone to depression—you know the type. The last thing I want is to upset her, especially when I didn't exactly turn out the way she wanted."

"What do you mean?"

"I wouldn't let my mother give me a cotillion. She had plans for me: a future filled with shopping, sailing, charity balls, and, of course, procreation. She almost had a stroke when I told her I wanted to study medicine." Agnes resumes cracking her knuckles. "The dolls are a compromise. I pretend to love them and she continues to buy them for me. It's the little game we play so she won't regret not being able to have children of her own, or feel she adopted the wrong kid."

"I'm sure she'd never think that." It's what you're supposed to say in a situation like this, but what do I know? Her mother could have regrets just like mine did. I'm living proof that not all mothers are maternal. I feel bad for Agnes. It must be awful worrying that your mother regrets adopting you. I know my parents regret *having* me, but that's different. They didn't choose me, whereas Agnes's parents specifically picked her to join their family.

"My mother and I are complete opposites," she says. Wow. Once you get Agnes talking, she doesn't stop. "And my father— all he and I ever talk about is the stock market. That is, he talks and I listen to him regurgitate the *Wall Street Journal*— Oh, shoot! I forgot to call Maddy." She reaches for the receiver on her desk. "She's on campus, looking for you." I notice the antique typewriter next to the phone. Another collectible, I'm sure. "I was supposed to call her when you got home. She was really worried. Where did you go, anyway?"

"I told you, I . . . uh, had to talk to my professor." Not very smooth. I blame it on the sex. It's my personal belief that too much sex kills brain cells.

Agnes says, "I would've looked for you myself, but my mother called. You were gone for quite a while." She raises an eyebrow.

"I went to town. I had a lot of errands to run. And then I . . . um, I went to look for a job."

"A job? Why?"

"It's complicated. My grandmother is temporarily cutting me off. She's trying to teach me the value of money or something," I explain. Although I do feel close to Agnes right now, this isn't the time to tell her the truth about Nana or my childhood. And luckily, Agnes is smart enough not to ask.

She raises her hand and says, "Hold on." In her tender, just-for-Maddy voice, she coos into the phone, "Finally. It kept ringing. Why didn't you pick up sooner?" She pauses, bites her lip. "Well, Sarah's back. Where are you? Do you want me to come pick you up? Okay. We'll talk when you get home. Bye." She hangs up and looks me squarely in the eye. "I could lend you the money. Then you wouldn't have to get a job. And you could pay me back whenever."

I'm touched by her offer. "Thanks, but I'll manage."

"I would give you a job myself, if you'd feel more comfortable."

"Doing what? Cataloging your dolls?" I snicker.

For a moment Agnes looks contemplative. "What if I hired you to be my household assistant? You could help me around the house and with the grocery shopping. It'd be like having a real job, except your hours would be much more flexible."

"I should be helping you out with those things anyway. And paying rent."

"I would never make a friend pay rent. Really, Sarah, let me help you. Besides, you'd be doing me a favor. I was thinking about hiring a housekeeper anyway, but with your assistance, I wouldn't have to." She rummages around her desk until she finds her checkbook. "How does five hundred a week sound?"

Insane. "I appreciate it, Agnes. I really do. But I'll figure something out. I'm going to take a shower now. Are you going to be okay?"

She nods.

I turn and climb the basement stairs. When I get to the top, Agnes says, "Sarah?"

"Yeah?" I turn around.

"Thanks."

"For what?"

"Listening."

"No problem." I smile and walk out the door.

After my shower, Maddy pounds on my bedroom door. "Knock knock," she singsongs. I'm so not in the mood to deal with her. She shouldn't have told me my relationship with Reed was doomed. Even if she thought she saw it in the cards, she shouldn't have told me, because now I can't stop worrying about it.

"Sarah, can I come in?" she asks, and then opens the door before I can respond. "Hi," she says, plopping down next to me on my bed. She bounces up and down, a bubblegum-pink blur. Her hair is tied into two perfect Princess Leia buns. How did she get her short hair to do that? Is it a wig? She notices me staring at her hair. "Extensions," she says. "I got them today. I was *so* sick of having short hair, so I went to Sally Jo's. They didn't do a good job, though. They're totally pinching me." Maddy finally stops bouncing. "So, where did you go today?"

"To town. Didn't Agnes tell you?"

"She said you were looking for a job—something about your grandma cutting you off—but I thought she was kidding."

"No." Who would joke about something like that?

"So, really? A job? But you're in college. You don't have time to work. Why is your grandma being so mean?" She scrunches up her nose. "Work sucks."

This little act—the scrunching up of her nose—annoys me more than anything. I feel a rush of anger. What does Maddy know about work? Has she ever had to work? I doubt she ever had to spend an entire summer working in a Hot Dog on a Stick booth while wearing a hideous polyester uniform and explaining to dumb customers the difference between the cheddar-cheese stick and the pepper-jack-cheese stick. And I doubt she ever had to work as a shoe gopher during a Nordstrom's Anniversary Sale, scavenging for women's size-eleven shoes in a dark, sweltering storage room. *Work sucks*. I feel like slapping her.

"Yoo-hoo, earth to Sarah. You're zoning out."

I wonder if I look as furious as I feel. If so, Maddy doesn't seem to notice.

"I called you a million times today," she grumbles. "Why didn't you call me back?"

"My battery died."

"I really needed to talk to you."

"Why?"

"Sebastian and I talked, finally."

My blood quivers. "Oh."

"Yeah, it's kind of a long story." Maddy gets comfortable on my bed. "He sent me a dozen roses today." She makes a face. "Of course, I threw them away and that made me feel a little better, but then he started calling and leaving me messages and that made me really mad, so Agnes took me out to lunch to get my mind off things. Then we went to get my extensions. The whole time, I kept calling you, but you never picked up, and by the time we got home, I was still upset, so I broke down and called him. I didn't tell Agnes because I didn't want her to get all overprotective. Anyway, I called, and a girl picked up."

My palms get sweaty. "Really?"

"Yeah. I hung up on her. Then I did a reading and the tarot cards said she's not the girl he cheated with. It was someone else. I have to find out who she is."

"Why can't you just let it go? You don't want Sebastian back anyway, right?"

"The truth has to come out, Sarah. Otherwise I'm going to be tortured forever. If he hadn't cheated on me in the first place, I wouldn't have broken up with him."

"Wait," I say. "I thought *he* broke up with *you*."

"Not technically. That weekend he came to visit, he actually came clean about sleeping with someone else, just like I suspected."

"He did?" I squeak.

"Yeah. He said it was just a one-time thing, back in September, with a girl he didn't even like. He said he was lonely and she was there and she basically threw herself at him, so . . ."

But I didn't throw myself at Sebastian.

She goes on. "The fact that he could have sex with someone else . . . I mean, I thought he was *the one*. How could I spend the rest of my life with someone who betrayed me? I had to end it. But it's still his fault because if he hadn't cheated on me, we'd still be together. And that's the same thing as saying he broke up with me."

It is? Why didn't she tell us this in the first place? I remember her distinctly telling Agnes and me that Sebastian broke up with her, not the other way around. She made herself sound like the victim. Why?

I take a deep breath. "Did he tell you who the girl was?"

She looks away. "No."

I try to hide my relief.

"You don't keep things from me, do you, Sarah?"

"What?" We lock eyes.

"You've never lied to me, have you?"

Fuck. Does she want me to confess? Is that what she wants? I'm so tired of this bullshit. I'm sick of feeling paranoid every time she utters Sebastian's name. If I don't get this off my chest, I'll implode.

"You know, don't you?" I finally say.

She pauses, then says, "Well, yeah. It's kind of obvious."

The words flood out of me. "I'm really sorry. It was a horrible thing to do. I don't even know why I did it. I wasn't thinking, it just happened and I know that's not an excuse, but I don't know what else to say other than I'm sorry, and I feel awful and I'll do whatever it takes to make it up to you."

"You slept with him?"

"Yeah," I say, confused.

"Today?"

"No, not today." What the hell is she thinking?

"Then when? I mean, you were gone all day, so I figured you went to see him. You did see Reed today, didn't you? You can tell me; I won't get mad. I'm your best friend."

Oops. I avert my eyes and say, "Yes, I went to see him today."

"And you slept with him."

I nod.

"Even though I told you he would break your heart? Why would you put yourself through that? Wake up and smell the testosterone, Sarah. You don't understand boys the way I do. You've never had a boyfriend. I mean, you've slept with a lot of guys, but relationships are different. They're a lot more complicated than just sex."

I ignore her condescending tone because I really do feel bad. After all this time, I still can't believe I fucked Sebastian. I need to get this off my chest. I have to tell her the truth.

"Maddy," I say, "I have a confession to make."

"Don't tell me you didn't use a condom."

I should do it fast, like ripping off a Band-Aid. Looking her in the eye, I say, "I slept with Sebastian."

She just stares at me. Not the reaction I was expecting. She doesn't look angry or shocked or hurt at all; she looks simply . . . blank. A moment later, she covers her face with her hands and says in a monotone, "What?"

"I'm so sorry. It was a shitty thing to do and I feel really awful about it."

She looks at me. "*You* feel awful? You had sex with the man *I* was supposed to marry, the love of my life, and *you* feel awful?" She gets up off the bed, crosses her arms over her chest, and says, "How could you?"

"I never wanted to hurt you. It was a stupid, stupid thing to do. I don't know what I was thinking."

"You obviously *weren't* thinking," she scoffs. "When did it happen?"

"Early in the semester, when I didn't know you very well."

"Be more specific."

"It was that day you went with Agnes to look at the house—you know, the day Sebastian came by to surprise you. It was just that one time. It never happened again."

She begins pacing. "So, let me get this straight. All this time, you and Sebastian have been hiding this from me? You let me worry and cry about that other girl when all along you were the slut who fucked my boyfriend?" Her lips twist into an ugly scowl. "Well, *fuck you*, Sarah!"

I keep my eyes on the floor. As bad as I feel, I can't get over the fact that she just said *fuck*. Twice. She never says *fuck*. Curse words really are more powerful when they're uttered by people who don't normally swear. "I wanted to tell you," I mumble, "but I just couldn't."

"You know, it's so fucking ironic too. Here I was, thinking of *you*, worrying that Reed would break your heart the way Sebastian broke mine, praying that he wouldn't, without even the slightest clue that you were the evil whore who fucked up my relationship. All this time I was hating *you*, and didn't even know it. I feel so foolish. After everything I've done for you, Sarah, this is how you repay me? No wonder you don't have any fucking friends."

Damn. That was a little mean. I decide to let it slide, but I know I'm on the verge of exploding.

Maddy wipes her eyes with her fingertips and then resumes pacing. "You know, someone should sew your legs shut. You'd sleep with anyone, wouldn't you?"

"Depends how big his penis is," I blurt out. "And, by the way, Sebastian is nowhere near eight inches."

"I guess you'd know," she hisses.

"Like you don't."

Maddy stops pacing and snarls, "At least I'm still a virgin."

"They don't give out awards for that, Maddy," I snap back. "I don't think you're as innocent as you pretend to be. And I don't think you ever really loved Sebastian. How could you? You only care about yourself. And even though you know Agnes is in love with you, you act oblivious. That way you can keep using her."

There's more I want to say, but something stops me. It's like I subconsciously know that if I continue I might end up betraying Agnes, who, unlike Maddy, deserves my loyalty.

Maddy pivots and heads for the door, turning around to look at me one last time. She waves her index finger at me. "I'd be careful if I were you. You might catch a nasty, incurable STD." She opens the door and pauses. With her back to me, she says, "You might want to check if our old room at Haven House is still available, because Agnes isn't going to be happy when I tell her what you did."

A chill runs up my spine.

She just stands there with her back to me, as if she's waiting for me to say something really ugly, really regrettable. There are a million cruel words at the tip of my tongue, the most accessible of which are *Go to hell* and *Die now, bitch*—appropriate, but totally unoriginal. But it's hard not to speak or even think in clichés when you're this furious. I want nothing more than to unleash all my hatred and fear on Maddy right now, but something holds me back. I don't know what it is. I want to hurt her, I really do, but for some reason . . . I can't. And then I think, Maybe she really *will* die young. I hope so, because I don't think I'll be able to take much more of this. Who needs her? Life would be infinitely more peaceful if she were dead.

When I don't say anything, she walks out, slamming the door behind her.

My first impulse is to get out of the house before Maddy tells Agnes and Agnes subsequently murders me.

I shove my feet into my Chucks, snatch my jean jacket, and bolt down the stairs. The house is dead quiet. They're probably in the basement. I open the front door, gasp in the cold air, and let the night swallow me whole.

17

I don't know where I'm going. I just know that I can't stop walking. Hot tears sputter out of me. I keep going—down the path I take to class every day and past the dean's house. When I get to the pond, I stop and stare into its ebony surface, and wait for clarity to come to me.

Things were good and then I had to go and fuck them up. What if Agnes kicks me out? I can't go back to Haven House. I don't belong there anymore. Then again, do I still belong with Maddy and Agnes? Even if the answer is no, I can't leave them, and I won't unless they force me to. I can't leave anyone I care about. That's the theme of my life. I'm the leavee, never the leaver. Because I'm weak.

What now? I have nothing with me, not even my wallet or my phone. If I had my cell, I would call Reed. Maybe I should sneak back into the house and get it, call Reed, and stay over at his place.

Yes, that's what I'll do.

* * *

I go in through the still-unlocked front door and creep toward the stairs. The basement door is closed with just that sliver of light shining from underneath.

As I take my first step up the staircase, a board creaks loudly, and I freeze. Just as I'm about to take my next step, a voice calls out from the kitchen, "Sarah, is that you?"

It's Maddy. I have two options: turn and lunge for the door, or face her. I decide to face her.

She's sitting at the table with a giant ball of Kleenex in her hand. She looks terrible—her face red and blotchy, her eyes raw, swollen. Seeing her like this chips away at my anger. A little.

"You came back," she gurgles.

"I had to get my phone."

"You're going to leave again?"

I nod.

"Please don't, Sarah. I want you to stay." She gets up and hugs me, nearly knocking me over.

I don't hug her back.

She pulls me in tighter. "I'm so sorry." Her face is hot and damp and her grasp childlike and needy.

Suddenly I start crying.

"It's okay," Maddy says. "Don't cry. I forgive you."

"I didn't mean all those things I said."

"I know, Sarah Bear. Neither did I. Here, come sit."

We sit down at the table and she hands me a tissue and watches me blot my face. Then she smiles weakly and says, "He's a guy and he needs sex. I couldn't give him that. But it's not my fault. I didn't do anything wrong."

"I know."

"He loved me; he was just horny. And you were there and willing. It's perfectly understandable."

Ouch. I don't want to kill this mood of forgiveness and reconciliation, but did she just insult me?

"Where's Agnes?" I ask, dabbing at my eyes.

"In the basement. Her mom called again."

"Did you tell her what happened?"

"No. She's been down there this whole time. But I wasn't going to tell her anyway. This is between us, Sarah. It's our little secret."

Our little secret? I shudder. Isn't that what child molesters say?

"So, I was thinking," she continues. "You know how you said you would do anything to make this up to me?"

Reluctantly, I nod.

"I thought of a way." She looks down at her hands, picks at her chipped violet nail polish for a moment, then meets my eyes. Her lips curl into a smile. "Break up with Reed."

"What?" I say, stunned.

"It's only fair. You took my boyfriend, so you should give me yours in return."

"You want to date *Reed*?"

"No, I just want you to stop seeing him. I want you to prove that our friendship means something, that nothing will ever come between us again. Especially not a boy. If you gave him up, I would know that you really cared about me and then I could trust you again."

"But that's crazy, Maddy."

"You need someone who's secure anyway. Especially since you aren't."

I stare at her in disbelief.

"Your parents abandoned you—that's enough to make a person insecure. I mean, don't you ever secretly think you're unlovable, because if your parents didn't want you, then . . ."

I keep staring at her. Is she insane, or just evil?

"What? Why are you looking at me like that?" she asks innocently.

I shake my head and scowl. "Do you ever listen to yourself?"

She touches my hand. "Don't take it the wrong way. I wasn't trying to say you're unlovable, because you aren't. What I meant was, maybe you don't know *how* to love. Because no one ever taught you."

I rub my eyes. "God, Maddy. Did it ever occur to you that I might actually *like* Reed? I mean, what if I can't just give him up?"

"I never said it was going to be easy, but if you really cared about our friendship . . ." She trails off.

What a manipulative bitch.

"Look," she says. "This is exactly what you did to *me*, except you did it behind my back. At least I'm being open about it. I'm not going to talk to Reed, much less have sex with him. I just want you to give him up like I had to give up Sebastian."

"Two wrongs don't make a right."

"But you barely know the guy. I mean, you just met him. He can't possibly mean as much to you as I do, or as much as Sebastian meant to me before this whole mess. I promise you, Sarah, if you do this for me, everything will go back to normal. We'll be friends again. Everything will be perfect. I won't tell Agnes. But if you don't, then I don't know what will happen . . ."

I hear noise coming from the basement.

Emboldened, Maddy looks me in the eye and says, "I'm not asking too much, am I?"

I feel like an old toy in the hands of a bratty child. When I hear Agnes's approaching footsteps, I mutter, "Okay."

I'll just have to hide my relationship with Reed. There's no way I'm going to stop seeing him because of Maddy.

"Thank you, Sarah. I knew you'd understand." She claps giddily. "You are the best friend in the whole wide world, you know that?"

The basement door opens and Agnes appears in the doorway. "What's going on?"

"Oh," Maddy says, grabbing a fresh tissue, "I was just thinking about Sebastian again."

"You need to stop torturing yourself, M. You're better off without him."

"I know," Maddy says, winking at me. "I know that now."

Agnes goes into the kitchen and puts the kettle on. Then she sighs and says, "So, do you two want to go to Boston tomorrow? My mother won the battle—I'm going to meet that Harvard half-wit after all."

18

It's eight o'clock. We're in Boston, killing time at a Starbucks before Agnes's blind date with Hoyt. Little does Hoyt know that Agnes will be bringing two additional girls on their date. I have a feeling he won't be pleased.

Boston is so-so. The weather is dark and damp, with the threat of a major storm, but there's definitely more to do here than at Wetherly. Yet all we did today was shop: Newbury Street, Copley Place, CambridgeSide Galleria. Though I didn't buy anything, I'm exhausted from following Maddy and Agnes around and supplying endless opinions on the various outfits they tried on. I didn't want to come to Boston in the first place, but Maddy refused to come without me, and Agnes wasn't about to come to Boston alone even though it was *her* blind date. Together they convinced me that we'd have a blast shopping, eating, and exploring the city. But it hasn't been a blast, because I miss Reed.

I've been thinking about him nonstop, as well as about Maddy's ultimatum. How dare she ask me to give him up, as though he were a bad habit, like smoking or nail-biting. As if she has the right to ask me to stop seeing a guy I love. She must think she's queen of the world. Well, her plan backfired. It only made me love Reed more.

Last night, right before bed, I called him. It went straight to voice mail, so I left him a message saying I wanted to spend all day Sunday with him. When I woke up this morning, there was a voice mail from him saying he would meet me in town at nine on Sunday morning. And then he said he couldn't wait to get together and that he loved me. *See?* I felt like telling Maddy. *I'm not unlovable.*

Agnes takes one last sip of her coffee and gets up to throw away the rest. "Let's get this over with."

When Agnes returns to our table, Maddy pats her on the back. "You're a good daughter. We all have to make sacrifices for the ones we love." Maddy doesn't look at me when she says this, but I know she's saying it for my benefit. Every time she opens her mouth, she finds some way to remind me of our agreement.

I take my Caramel Macchiato with me as we make our way back to the car. The air outside smells of mold and wet asphalt.

In the car, just as Agnes is about to pull away from the curb, Maddy says, "Wait. I need to get something from the trunk."

"Hurry," Agnes says, "I told Hoyt I'd be there at eight."

I look at my watch. "It's already eight twenty."

"I know," Agnes says, irritated.

"Shouldn't you let him know you're running late?" I ask.

"He goes to Harvard. He'll figure it out." Agnes starts cracking her knuckles.

Maddy gets out of the car, opens the trunk, and returns with two large shopping bags. She climbs into the backseat next to me, and places one of the bags on my lap. "This one's for you."

Agnes starts the car.

I look at the large brown bag emblazoned with the words LOUIS VUITTON. "What is this?"

"A present, silly. From the both of us," says Maddy. "But it was my idea and I picked it out." That means Agnes paid for it. One picks, the other pays. They're the perfect shopping team.

I squirm under the brown bag. Expensive gifts make me uncomfortable. The iPhone was bad enough, but now Louis Vuitton? I don't even like Louis Vuitton. It's one thing to accept a gift I like and then owe Agnes and Maddy my life, but to accept a gift I don't like and then still owe them my life—well, that's just lame. Why am I getting a present, anyway?

"My birthday's not till December," I say, stalling.

Maddy says, "Think of this as a prebirthday present. Or whatever. It's a gift! Open it."

I do as she says. Inside the bag is a box, and inside the box is a cloth bag, which predictably contains a purse. The purse is small and drum-shaped with an extra-long strap. It's hyperfeminine and not me at all. It's Maddy's kind of purse. "Wow," I say, dumbstruck.

"Say cheese," Maddy says, and I look up just in time for Maddy to get a shot of me with her iPhone. "Do you like it?" she asks, her voice giddy. "When I saw it in the store, I thought of you. Isn't it cute? I got the same one so we could match. We'll be purse twins!"

Purse twins. Now there's a concept. "Thanks," I say, "but I can't accept this."

"Of course you can," Agnes says, meeting my eyes in the rearview mirror.

Maddy touches my arm. "You can use it tonight. Here, I'll help you transfer your stuff." She seizes my backpack and starts loading up the purse. She hands me my phone. "Looks like you have a missed call."

Shit. It's probably from Reed. Everyone else who calls me is in this car. I hold my breath while I glance down at the screen. It's a number I don't recognize. Thank God. And there's a voice mail too. Maybe Reed was calling from a pay phone.

"Who was it?" Maddy asks. She's so fucking nosy.

"I don't know," I say.

Maddy gives me a dubious look. "Were you expecting *someone* to call?"

Bitch. "Well, this girl in my psych class said she was going to call about my notes," I lie. "It's probably her."

"Maybe she *likes* you," Maddy says, winking at me.

I ignore her.

Maddy pulls out an identical purse from the other shopping bag and squeals, "Look! Purse twins!"

I force a smile.

Agnes fishtails through the traffic and steadily cranks up the Mozart.

"When did you guys go to Louis Vuitton?" I ask.

Maddy says, "While you were at the bookstore. Pretty sneaky, huh?"

"Yeah," I say, suspiciously eyeing my new bag. "Pretty sneaky."

Cheesy as it is to say, walking through the Harvard gates feels like a rite of passage. It's Harvard, after all. But the campus looks like any other New England college campus: old, grand, with proud, crumbling buildings, lush trees, and abundant ivy. The air is invigorating, as if laced with speed.

A guy in a camel-colored corduroy jacket walks by.

Agnes calls out to him. "Hey. Where's Massachusetts Hall?"

The guy turns around.

"Yeah, you," Agnes says. "Do you know where Massachusetts Hall is?"

The guy waves his arm in the general direction of nowhere.

"Thanks," Agnes says, and then mutters, "for nothing."

While we wander around Harvard Yard, I can't stop obsessing over the fact that my new purse clashes with my grungy, thrift-store Army jacket. I'm a walking fashion faux pas, whereas Maddy looks stylish and cute in her leopard-print coat and brown knee-high boots, which match her purse perfectly.

Agnes takes out her phone and calls Hoyt. "I can't believe I'm doing this," she says to us, tucking a loosened lock of hair behind her ear. "Hoyt. It's Agnes. I can't find your dorm, so could you please come outside? Thanks." She hangs up.

A second later, a cute blond guy wearing jeans and a black peacoat emerges from the building in front of us. "Agnes?" he says, looking at Maddy.

Nope.

"Over here," Agnes says, snapping her fingers. "I'm Agnes. These are my friends. They're coming with us. I hope you don't mind."

"The more the merrier," says Hoyt, looking a little confused. His eyes dart around frantically, then land on Maddy. "Welcome to Cambridge."

His eyes, oddly enough, are a Louis Vuitton brown, and he's kind of on the short side, around five feet seven, but perfect for Agnes, considering she's barely over five feet tall and never wears anything higher than a kitten heel.

Maddy extends her hand. "I'm Madison. And this is Sarah."

Hoyt takes Maddy's hand and says, "Nice to meet you." He seems unable to tear his eyes away from her.

"Hi," I say, waving to get his attention. Hoyt finally looks at me and smiles.

"So, what do you ladies feel like doing tonight?" he asks. "I thought Agnes was coming alone, so I made reservations for two at a French restaurant. I could change the reservation, or we could go somewhere else . . ." He scratches his head.

"We already ate," Agnes lies. We haven't eaten since lunch.

Hoyt looks disappointed. "Maybe we could grab a drink somewhere."

"We can't drink," says Agnes. "We're underage."

"Oh, right. You're freshmen?"

"First-years," Agnes corrects him. "We don't use words that contain *men*."

"Right," Hoyt says, looking flustered. "Well, what would you like to do?"

Agnes shrugs.

Hoyt tugs on his ear. "Let's see. They're having an eighties party at Thayer Hall."

Maddy claps excitedly. "I love the eighties!"

Agnes hesitates. "Why don't we just go to a movie?" She tries to make eye contact with Maddy, but Maddy avoids her glance.

"A movie's no fun." Maddy pouts. "Besides, how are we supposed to get to know Hoyt in a dark movie theater?"

Hoyt blushes. How cute is it that he blushes? Then again, it's not like he can help it. He *is* pretty fair-skinned.

We end up in a dark, sweaty room that smells of beer and dirty socks. Duran Duran's "Wild Boys" is pulsating through the air.

I get a disturbing flashback of that Yale party I went to with Keiko and Amber and that gross guy I made out with. I'm just glad nobody here is naked.

The music switches to New Order's "Bizarre Love Triangle" and a guy in the corner starts miming to the music. Everyone looks sort of generic, not really Harvard-y. Just regular college kids of all ethnicities and in all states of drunkenness.

Hoyt turns to Agnes and shouts above the music, "Can I talk to you?"

Agnes looks at us briefly, a look that says she's annoyed (as if we couldn't tell) and also taken aback. She thought she could scare Hoyt away, but he's quite persistent. "Fine," she says, biting her lip.

"Excuse us, ladies." Hoyt nods politely at Maddy and me before following Agnes out into the hallway.

"I wonder what that's all about," I say to Maddy.

"Who cares? I'm gonna lose my virginity tonight."

"*What?*"

"I said, I'm gonna lose my virginity tonight!" Maddy scans the room with that same hungry look she got earlier when she was eyeing Louboutins on sale.

"No, I heard you . . . but why tonight?" I ask.

"Because I feel like it."

"I thought you were waiting."

"I was, but now I want to get it over with. I've been waiting my whole life. I thought it was going to be with Sebastian, but since that's never going to happen, I might as well just do it with a Harvard guy. I know the first time's supposed to be special and all, but, whatever. The next hot guy I see will be the one. Hey, how about him?" She points at a dark-haired guy who eerily resembles Sebastian, except that he's wearing glasses and a white

Miami Vice blazer that Sebastian wouldn't be caught dead in. "What do you think?"

"I don't think so, Maddy."

"Why? What's wrong with him?"

"Nothing, it's just that . . ." I trail off.

"What?"

I pause. "Nothing," I say. What *can* I say? If I tell her not to lose her virginity tonight, she'll never let me live down the Sebastian incident. Besides, it's her virginity; she can do whatever she wants with it. And since the guy she's ogling looks a lot like Sebastian, it'll kind of be like she's doing it with him. After all, any guy—even a Sebastian look-alike—would be better than the real thing. And who knows? Maybe Maddy will become nicer after she gets laid.

She smiles coyly at the Sebastian twin and twirls her extensions around her index finger. After a few minutes of this, the guy finally notices her. He gives her a stiff smile, then turns away and starts talking to a guy in acid-washed jeans who's standing next to him. Maddy continues to stare at him, but he doesn't look back. For some bizarre reason, all the guys here are ignoring Maddy and I can't figure out why. Is her beauty too intimidating? Or can they smell her desperation?

"Wanna dance?" asks a chubby guy dressed as Billy Idol. It takes me a second to realize he's talking to me.

"No, thanks," I say. The guy looks a little disappointed, and I start to feel bad. And then I feel pissed for feeling bad. It's the Hunchback of Notre Dame syndrome—the assumption that all chubby, unattractive guys have hearts of gold—and I'm a sucker for it, even though I know it isn't true.

"I'll dance with you," Maddy says to Billy Idol. She clutches his hand and whisks him off to the dance floor. They disappear into the crowd.

I stand by myself for what feels like twenty minutes, shifting my weight from my left leg to my right leg and back again. I check my phone to see if it was Reed who left me that voice mail, but no, the message is in Spanish and it's for a guy named Paco. Soon a slow song comes on—Crowded House's "Don't Dream It's Over"—and people start scurrying away from the dance floor.

Maddy comes back with a big smile on her face. "Whew," she says, fanning her cheeks with her hand, "that was fun. You should've danced with him. He was sweet."

I just nod and hope he's not the guy she's chosen for her deflowering.

Agnes and Hoyt come back inside and head straight for the dance floor. Then they start dancing. I turn toward Maddy, whose eyes are bugging out.

There are only a handful of couples on the dance floor. Agnes avoids looking at us. There's a constipated expression on her face, but it seems like Hoyt is enjoying himself.

"I can't watch this," I say. "It's too painful. Let's get out of here."

Maddy and I find the restroom, where I wash my hands three times.

Minutes later, Agnes joins us. "I was looking all over for you guys."

"How was the dance?" I ask.

"He touched me," she says, wincing.

"You were slow dancing," I say. "He's supposed to touch you."

"I mean, inappropriately."

"Where?" asks Maddy.

171

"I'd rather not say."

"You're the one who brought it up," I point out.

"Tell us," says Maddy.

"I don't want to talk about it," Agnes insists. "It was somewhere intimate."

"Your breasts?" I say.

"No."

"Your butt?" asks Maddy.

"No!" Agnes replies. "The small of my back."

"And?" I ask.

"And I didn't like it. He shouldn't have been so presumptuous," says Agnes. "That's an intimate spot on a woman. Some would say the *most* intimate spot."

Maddy and I ponder this for a moment.

"I don't know," I say. "I can think of another spot that's way more intimate."

Agnes scoffs, "The obvious spot, no doubt. Trust me, you're not supposed to touch the small of a woman's back—or her feet—unless you're her lover. Hoyt should've known that."

"Maybe he wants to be your lover." Maddy giggles.

"Maybe he was just trying to work his way down to your ass," I say.

"Don't be vile," says Agnes.

Maddy asks, "So, where *is* Hoyt?"

"He went back to his dorm."

"Without saying good-bye?" I say.

"I told him to go. I said I'd dance with him once, and then we would go home. That was the agreement."

"What did you guys talk about when you were outside?" I ask.

"Nothing much. Our families. School. He told me to tell you he enjoyed meeting both of you."

"That's nice," Maddy says.

"Whatever." Agnes rolls her eyes. "Let's get out of here."

"Fine by me," Maddy says. "No one wants to de-virginize me anyway."

"*What?*" asks Agnes.

"Nothing," Maddy says, winking at me. "Let's go."

19

Can we stop at McDonald's?" Maddy whines, fifteen minutes into our two-hour drive home. "I'm so hungry."

Agnes turns down the radio. "You can't keep eating junk food, Maddy. We have a cassoulet waiting for us at home."

Maddy makes a face. "But we're still hours away."

"I'll get us back in forty—"

Suddenly Maddy squeals.

"What is it?" I ask her.

She frantically rummages inside her purse. "I lost my wallet."

"Are you sure?" asks Agnes.

"I can't find it anywhere."

I say, "Maybe it's in your other purse."

"No, that bag's empty."

Agnes exits the highway and turns back toward Boston. "All right, let's retrace our steps. When did you last take out your wallet?"

"At Starbucks," answers Maddy.

"Okay," Agnes says, "we'll go back there."

Ten minutes later, we pull up in front of Starbucks. We go in. The acrid smell of coffee burns the inside of my nose. We scour every inch of the place but don't find the wallet. Agnes interrogates the employees. "Sorry," they say, one after the other.

We walk back to the car, taking the back alley just in case the wallet somehow ended up outside. A silver Lexus is parked next to the garbage bins and a prostitute in a black leather mini-skirt, pink tights, and a white faux-fur jacket is leaning over the passenger-side window, chatting up the driver. A moment later, she opens the car door and the dome light comes on, exposing the driver's face. He's fortyish with thinning brown hair, a pinched nose, and glasses. He motions for the hooker to get in. This alone really depresses me. She climbs into the car and shuts the door. I watch as the dome light dims. The man looks back at me for a second and I feel a jolt of panic. His expression is not only desperate, but angry. It's the same look Maddy sometimes gets. She had it earlier tonight. Maybe that's why none of the Harvard guys approached her. They were afraid.

When we get back to Agnes's car, there it is: Maddy's patent-leather Louis Vuitton wallet, lying in the gutter next to the car. It's a surreal image, the hot-pink wallet resting on top of a withering banana peel. We stare at it. Was the wallet here the whole time? Why didn't anyone take it? The screaming fuchsia is kind of hard to ignore.

"My wallet!" Maddy shrieks. "It must've fallen out of my bag before we left for Harvard." She then points to a McDonald's across the street. "Perfect. Now we can go eat."

I roll my eyes at Agnes, but, of course, she would never doubt Maddy. It's hard for me to believe the wallet was here this whole time, conveniently lying next to the car and also across the street from McDonald's. She must have orchestrated this. But why? Just to get her way? Is McDonald's really that important to her?

Maybe not, but Maddy always gets what she wants.

After McDonald's, we head back toward the highway. I'm relieved to be going home. I feel gross and tired and disgusted with Maddy, and I really want to talk to Reed before the night is over.

Just as we're about to enter the highway, we hear a loud bang, followed by a force so strong that the car spins out of control. My body slams forward into the driver's seat; I feel as though I'm somersaulting through the air.

Everything goes still.

I hear Agnes and Maddy in the distance calling my name, but for some reason I can't answer them. I'm not in the car; I don't know where I am. They keep calling me, but I can't respond. I think my spirit got shocked out of my body. I try to wave my arms and kick my legs but nothing happens. And then I realize where my spirit is: above the car, suspended in the air. I try to get down, back into my body, but I don't know how. Meanwhile, Maddy keeps calling me.

And then, suddenly, I snap back in.

"Sarah, can you hear me?" Agnes asks, sounding close now. "We were in an accident. Are you hurt? Say something, wiggle your fingers—anything to let us know you can hear me."

I hear Maddy whimpering in the background.

"I'm okay," I say, slowly lifting my head. "I'm okay."

Maddy reaches for my hand. "Oh, Sarah, I'm so glad you're all right. I couldn't bear it if you were hurt."

"You scared us half to death," says Agnes.

"What happened?" I ask.

"It was a hit-and-run," Agnes says. "Some lowlife in a black sedan crashed into us and then took off."

"Did you see his plates?"

Agnes shakes her head. "He was going too fast. Plus, we were spinning so it was hard to see anything."

Maddy adds, "It was an American car. A Buick, maybe?"

"We have to call the police," I say.

"That's the last thing on my mind," Agnes says. "We need to get you to a hospital."

"I'm fine." Looking down at my body, I see no broken bones, no blood. If I'd worn my seat belt, I might have been able to avert the whole out-of-body nightmare. "How long did it take for me to respond?" I ask.

"About a minute," says Agnes.

So, for a minute I was technically dead, floating in the air! But I decide not to tell Maddy and Agnes about that.

"I'm fine," I repeat. "I don't need to go to the hospital."

"You sure?" Maddy asks.

I nod and look out the window. We're smack in the middle of a deserted intersection. The ground, slick with oily puddles, is a fun-house mirror, reflecting light in distorted shapes. I see shrieking faces, decaying corpses, giant sticky insects. Maybe I *should* go to the hospital.

Agnes gets out of the car. I follow her out, making sure to avert my eyes from the fiendish puddles.

The back passenger side of the Mercedes is wrecked. Steam rises from the engine and there's a horrible burning smell.

Agnes kicks the side of the car. "Piece of junk. The air bags didn't even activate. They sold my father a defective vehicle. Wait till he hears about this." She kicks the car again. "I'll call us a cab."

Just as Agnes whips out her phone, a mysterious white Honda with tinted windows pulls up next to us. The window rolls down to reveal a dorky blond guy in his midtwenties. "Are you ladies all right? Do you need a lift?"

"No," Agnes says coldly.

"Actually, yes," says Maddy. And, in a single breath, she relates the events of the evening, including the Harvard party and the missing wallet, ending with, "Our friend needs to get to a hospital."

"No," I insist.

"We need to make sure you're okay," says Agnes.

The guy gets out of his car. He's wearing the yuppie uniform: a baby-blue button-down shirt, chinos, and brown loafers. "Give me your keys," he says to Agnes.

"Why?"

"I'm going to move your car. You can't just leave it in the middle of the intersection."

"I'll move it myself."

Maddy gives Agnes a look, and Agnes reluctantly hands the guy her keys.

"I'm Brian, by the way," he says. "I'm a computer consultant."

Maddy says, "Nice to meet you, Brian. I'm Madison, and this is Sarah and Agnes. We're college students."

"Wellesley?" he asks.

"No, Wetherly." Maddy bats her lashes.

He grins and, in a borderline superhero voice, says, "Don't worry, ladies. I'll handle this. First I'll move the car, and then I'll take you to the hospital."

"We don't need to go to the hospital," I say.

"Please, Sarah?" Maddy sobs. "We just want to make sure you're okay."

"Fine," I say. Those damn tears will be the death of me.

It's three in the morning when I'm finally released from the hospital. I'm surprised to find Brian in the waiting room, chatting up Maddy while Agnes bites her nails.

Maddy runs over to me. "What did the doctor say?"

"I'm going to live."

"Wonderful," Agnes says, getting up to pat me on the back.

Brian grins at us. "Ready?"

"Brian's driving us home," Maddy explains.

"All the way back to Wetherly?" I ask.

"Yeah," says Maddy. "Isn't that nice of him?"

"Are you cold?" Brian asks Maddy, once we're in the car.

Maddy is sitting up front, and Agnes and I are in the back.

"I'll turn on the heat if you are," he says.

Maddy nods and Brian obediently adjusts the temperature. He's been plying her with compliments, as if he actually believes he has a chance with her, and Maddy is loving every minute of it. The worst part is, ever since Brian arrived, she's been using her cutesy voice nonstop.

I glance at Agnes, who is looking out the window. I close my eyes and think about what they told me at the hospital: that I could've died. Or at least sustained a spinal injury from not wearing my seat belt. When the ER doctor first told me that, it didn't register. She kept repeating it to get a reaction out of me. "I don't care!" I finally yelled back.

But I do care. I don't want to die. Before Wetherly, I might not have cared so much, but things are different now. I have friends who accept me, flaws and all, and who—despite our disagreements—want me to stay alive. Fate brought us together for a reason. I'm not sure what that reason is yet, but being with them has definitely changed me. They've opened me up, and if it weren't for them, I doubt that I would even have the guts to love Reed.

I died for a minute, didn't I, when I was suspended in the air? And it was Maddy's voice I heard, Maddy who brought me back to life.

20

the next morning I wake up with a paralyzed neck. I've had kinks before, but never like this. I can't turn toward the clock radio. All I can do is stare up at the ceiling. And then I realize: I'm not alone. Someone is lying next to me. *Please, God, not Brian.*

The stranger moans, a moan which I distinctly recognize as Maddy's, and I breathe a sigh of relief. She rolls over, shaking the entire bed, and begins to make little smacking sounds. I place my hand under my head and manually lift myself up.

It's 10:17. I can smell Agnes's coffee percolating downstairs. I slide into my blue flip-flops and hobble down to the kitchen.

Agnes, dressed and aproned, is leaning over a sputtering skillet.

"Hey," I say.

She turns around. "Morning. How are you feeling?"

"I can't move my neck."

"That's whiplash." She turns back toward the skillet, and I watch as she ever so carefully flips over a batch of silver-dollar pancakes.

I pour myself a cup of coffee and sit down at the dining table. Agnes slides a coaster under my mug and says, "I'll get the heating pad out for you after I finish up here."

"I'm sure I'll be fine after a hot shower."

She grabs a plate from the cupboard and fills it with pancakes. "Whiplash is serious. It can't be left untreated. Otherwise it'll come back and haunt you."

She sets the plate of pancakes in front of me. "Thanks," I say.

"*Bon appétit.*" After handing me a set of utensils, she goes back to glopping more batter into the skillet. "He's still here, you know."

I look up. "Who?"

"Brian. He's sleeping in Maddy's room," she says with a grimace. "He didn't even shower before he went to bed."

"You let him stay over?"

"I had to. Maddy insisted. I wanted to get him a room at the Wetherly Inn, but Maddy said that would be rude. I knew he was too tired to drive back, but I really didn't want him staying here."

"Where was I when all this was happening?"

"In your room. You went straight to bed after we got home. After you went upstairs, Maddy got Brian settled in her room. At first I thought she was going to share her bed with him, but then she came back and slept with me. I couldn't sleep a wink. I kept worrying that Brian would rob us. I mean, we don't know a thing about him. He could be a serial killer. Or worse."

"What's worse than a serial killer?"

"Let's just say I wouldn't be too thrilled if Maddy decided to fall in love with this guy."

I snicker, but the stern look on Agnes's face tells me she's not joking. "Don't worry. He's not her type," I say. "Maddy could never like a guy that dull."

"Sebastian wasn't particularly interesting."

"No, but he was hot." My face suddenly heats up. I wish I could take back those words.

Agnes smiles deviously. "I didn't know you thought Sebastian was hot."

"I don't." My ears burn. "I'm just saying he's better looking than Brian. I mean, at least Sebastian dresses well, even though he *is* kind of typical looking. But, personally, I think Sebastian's lack of brain cells makes him almost grotesque, don't you?"

Agnes just stares at me. My face must be covered in hives. I look down at the floor and try to will them away.

"Interesting," she finally says.

"What is?"

She doesn't answer, and begins chopping potatoes.

I dig into my stack of pancakes. Desperate to change the subject, I say, "So, how did Maddy end up in *my* room?"

"Well, I couldn't sleep. I kept tossing and turning, until finally I just flipped on the light and worked on some problem sets. Maddy woke right up and said she was going to sleep in your room. Is she still sleeping?"

I nod, mouth full.

"I wish Brian would just hurry up and leave."

"Why don't we bang some pots and pans outside his door?" I suggest.

"We don't want to wake Maddy." While tossing the chopped potatoes into the frying pan, she explains, "I already feel bad that I kept her up half the night."

"But you have to admit it was pretty nice of Brian to drive us back."

"He had ulterior motives. He took one look at Maddy and that was it." She sounds both proud and jealous.

If she starts talking about how gorgeous Maddy is again, I'll definitely heave. Yes, she's beautiful on the outside—we all know that—but it's her insides I'm not so sure about. Then again, it was Maddy's voice I heard when I was having my out-of-body experience. Maddy, in her own way, saved my life.

"There aren't many true Good Samaritans out there," Agnes adds.

I shrug and take another bite while watching Agnes push the potatoes around with her spatula. "So, what are you going to do about your car?"

"Get a new one."

"The damage wasn't that bad, was it?"

"No, but I don't want to drive a car that's been in an accident. It's bad luck."

"But aren't the odds *against* you getting into another accident?"

"The laws of probability were designed for ordinary people with ordinary minds, Sarah. I believe in the extraordinary." She walks toward me with the skillet. "Want some home fries?"

"Sure."

She scoops some potatoes onto my plate, and sets a bottle of Heinz in front of me. I drown my home fries in ketchup and take a bite: crispy on the outside, soft on the inside. "You know what's really extraordinary?" I say to Agnes.

She turns to me. "What?"

"These home fries."

Agnes gives me a sheepish smile and then turns away.

Forty minutes later, Maddy comes downstairs. I'm sitting at the dining table with a heating pad draped over my shoulders. Barefoot and glowing, Maddy is wearing a silk-and-ostrich-feather robe.

"Good morning, ladies," she chirps. "Isn't today just the most beautiful day ever?"

"It's overcast," Agnes says matter-of-factly, then continues wiping down the counter.

"But it's still beautiful." Noticing the heating pad, Maddy gives me a curious look.

"It's for Sarah's whiplash," Agnes explains, pouring Maddy a cup of coffee.

"Hmm . . . I think I might have a little whiplash too."

Agnes hands her the cup. "Want me to rub your neck?" she asks, a little too eagerly.

Maddy scowls. "No! I was just kidding, Agnes."

Embarrassed, Agnes quickly removes her apron and folds it into a perfect square. Without taking her eyes off the apron, she asks, "Did you sleep well?"

"I sure did," Maddy says, plopping down at the table. "Yum, pancakes. I just love the smell of pancakes. Don't you think it's the best smell in the world?"

Okay, what is with her today?

"I'll fix you a plate," Agnes says.

"Later. I want to shower first." Maddy looks at me quizzically. "Are you feeling all right? You were talking in your sleep last night."

"I was?"

"Yup, you were telling me all your secrets."

"I don't have any secrets," I say with a shrug, and then begin to worry. Did I say something about Reed?

"I'm joking. You were talking gibberish. Though I did hear you say 'Reed' once or twice."

Crap. Reed. I totally forgot about our date today, and I didn't even call him last night. I must have brain fog from the accident.

185

He probably thinks I stood him up. We were supposed to meet at nine and now it's already eleven thirty. *Shit.*

"Who's Reed?" Agnes begins wiping the stove with a sponge.

"He's the guy Sarah had a crush on," says Maddy. "But it's over now—right, Sarah?"

"Right," I say bitterly. I wish she would stop taunting me.

Agnes asks, "Is he the guy you told me about?"

"Yeah," I say. "It's nothing. I just thought he was cute." I turn to Maddy. "Weren't you going to take a shower?"

"Uh-huh." She gets up. "I'll make it quick."

When Maddy leaves, I tell Agnes I'll be right back. I run up to my room and grab my phone out of my purse. There are five missed calls from Reed. I call him back but he doesn't pick up, so I leave him a message telling him I was in a car accident but that I'm fine and that I'll call him later. Then I go back downstairs and pour myself another cup of coffee.

Agnes fixes herself a plate and sits down next to me at the dining table. "Where's the ketchup?"

"I don't know. It was right here."

"That's odd. Maybe I put it away." She gets up and rummages through the cupboards. "I don't know where I could've put it," she says, sitting back down. "I'll look for it later."

"So, why do you think Maddy is in such a good mood?"

Agnes finishes chewing, then says, "You know how people get after car accidents. It's a frightening experience. But we survived. Maddy's just a little euphoric."

"Hmm," I say. But I'm not so sure.

When Brian finally wakes up, he doesn't take a shower, skips breakfast (if you don't count the banana he grabs on the way out), and leaves with a hurried and awkward good-bye. He looks different in the daylight—less geeky, more creepy.

After he leaves, Maddy pulls me aside. "Come upstairs," she whispers. "I want to show you something."

I look over at Agnes, who's busy scrubbing the greasy breakfast dishes, and follow Maddy upstairs. Clutching my hand, she leads me into her bedroom and peels back the covers, revealing a huge bloodstain in the center of the bed: scarlet, thick, lumpy.

"What happened?" I say. "Did he get his period?"

"It wasn't him, Sarah. It was me. I bled. Because it was my first time."

"You had sex with him?" I shriek.

Maddy covers my mouth with her hand. "Shhh . . ."

A shiver passes through me.

"Yes," whispers Maddy.

"Eww."

She gives me a playful shove. "Don't say that."

I can't help staring at the blood. I didn't know you could bleed that much the first time. I didn't my first time. Of course, my experience was strange and awful. A dark bedroom with framed Vargas prints on the wall. He was nineteen, a high school dropout who lived with his dad in Nana's building. I was fifteen. I had seen him in the lobby once or twice and thought he wasn't bad looking. One day he invited me up to his apartment while his dad was at work. We sat on his couch, and he told me I would be pretty when I grew up. Then we went into his bedroom and did it. It was quick and it hurt a lot. I didn't tell him I was a virgin and he never bothered to ask. Later that night, I couldn't stop staring at myself in the bathroom mirror. I felt different and was looking for some kind of visible change. But, in the mirror, I looked exactly the same.

"Why him?" I ask Maddy.

"I told you last night I was going to lose my virginity. I couldn't get a Harvard guy to do it, but at least I got an M.I.T. grad."

"Your point was to lose your virginity to someone smart? Trust me, your hymen can't tell the difference."

"Sarah, don't make fun of me. I wanted to. And he wasn't that bad."

"When did this happen?"

"A little while ago. After you got up, I snuck back into my room and seduced him. He seemed surprised. He had an instant boner. It didn't hurt too much, and now . . . I'm a woman!" she says, beaming with pride.

"Did he know it was your first time?"

"Not until he saw the blood. But by then it was already over. Then he got all nervous and said he had to go. That's why he left so abruptly."

"Your virginity scared him off?"

"Well, yeah . . . that and the fact that he couldn't face you guys. I told him my friends were very protective of me, especially Agnes. Not like he couldn't tell. It would've been awkward sitting at the dining table with Agnes all stone-faced." She pauses. "Promise me you won't tell her, Sarah. She'll kill me."

"Okay."

"Cross your heart and hope to die?"

"Yes."

"Say it."

Are we in kindergarten? Reluctantly, I say, "Cross my heart and hope to die."

Maddy looks relieved.

"Did you use a condom?"

"Uh-huh," she says, flipping her hair.

"He had one?"

"Yeah." She nods.

What a louse. The guy carries a condom in his wallet while driving around looking for car-accident victims?

"I'm so happy, Sarah Bear. And relieved too. I feel more worldly now. And wiser." She looks at me. "What was your first time like?"

"Bad," I say. I don't elaborate. "We'd better go back downstairs before Agnes comes up."

"You go down first," she says. "Stall for me. I have to get this stain out of my sheets before Agnes comes up to get the laundry. You know how she is about strangers' germs."

It's bizarre to me how happy Maddy is about having lost her virginity, especially since she lost it to a guy who means nothing to her. When I lost mine, I remember thinking that I would never be a virgin again. I could never go back to being a kid. I was instantly an adult, and from then on, I would always be having sex. The thought depressed me for weeks.

Obviously, Maddy doesn't feel the same way. Or maybe it just hasn't hit her yet. Then again, she doesn't have much depth. Once a thought enters her mind, it leaves just as easily, never to be pondered again. So maybe her behavior isn't unusual.

I go downstairs to find Agnes Swiffering the kitchen floor.

"Need some help?" I ask.

"No. Where's Maddy?"

"She's taking a shower."

"I have to wash her sheets. Or maybe I should just throw them away and buy new ones." She's serious.

"Isn't that a little drastic?" I say. But all I'm thinking is: how can I keep her from going upstairs? I rack my brain. And then I get an idea. "Hey, can I borrow your face for a few minutes?"

Agnes gives me a quizzical look.

"I have to do a drawing assignment for tomorrow and I'm getting really tired of drawing myself."

"Well, I suppose," she says reluctantly. "But I really want to wash those sheets first."

"I want to draw you now, if that's okay. It's best for me to draw when I'm inspired, because who knows how I'll feel later?" I glance toward the staircase. "It won't take long. Stay here. I'm just going to get my drawing stuff."

Agnes squints at me like she's confused, and I take the opportunity to run upstairs. Why am I working so hard to protect Maddy? So what if Agnes finds out she lost her virginity? It's not like Agnes will stop being friends with her. Of course, I'm grateful that Maddy didn't tell Agnes I had sex with Sebastian, and, in a way, I feel flattered that Maddy would tell me a secret she'd never tell Agnes, but this whole scenario feels a little odd. Still, I remind myself, Maddy saved my life last night. At least, her voice did. I kind of owe her for that.

I knock on the bathroom door.

"Yes?" Maddy says, sounding distressed.

"It's Sarah."

"Oh, come in."

I open the door just a crack. Maddy is leaning over the sink, vigorously rubbing a bar of soap across the stained sheet.

"You'd better hurry," I tell her. "Agnes wants to wash your sheets."

"I'm almost done. I'll sneak these down to the washing machine."

"You know, you could just tell her you got your period."

"Yeah, except I didn't sleep in my bed last night."

"Oh, right."

"Plus, she knows my cycle."

That's kind of sick. How would Agnes know? Does she inspect the garbage for Maddy's used maxi pads? Or maybe they're on the same cycle? I've heard that women's menstrual cycles tend to sync up when they're living together, but that's not a topic the three of us have discussed. Maybe they never brought it up because they're in sync and I'm not, and they didn't want to hurt my feelings.

Now I'm being paranoid. Why should I care if they're on the same menstrual cycle? I have more important things to worry about.

Still, I have to ask. "Are you guys on the same cycle?"

"What?"

"You and Agnes. Are your cycles synced up?"

"No, silly. Agnes doesn't get her period."

"She doesn't?"

"No. Agnes can't have kids. She was born that way."

"Oh." *Agnes can't have kids?* Why didn't I know this earlier? I want to know more, but this isn't the right time to ask.

Agnes calls me from downstairs, "Ready, Sarah?"

"Go," Maddy whispers.

I close the bathroom door and grab my drawing supplies from my room. The idea of drawing Agnes scares me a little. Why? Because she's Agnes. I'm halfway down the stairs when I think of the condom. Where would Maddy have thrown it? In her wastebasket, of course. And since Agnes is the one who empties all of our wastebaskets, she's going to be the one to find it. I have to warn Maddy.

I run back upstairs and knock on the bathroom door. "Maddy?"

"I'll be right out."

I wait and I wait.

"Sarah!" Agnes calls out to me.

"Coming!" I yell back.

I decide to help Maddy and empty her trash before Agnes finds the condom and goes ballistic. It's disgusting, but someone's got to do it. I go into Maddy's room and lean over her wastebasket. No condom. In fact, the wastebasket is empty. Strange. I guess Maddy already emptied it.

I turn to leave and that's when I see it: the Heinz bottle on Maddy's dresser, hiding behind a framed photograph of the three of us. Why would the ketchup be *here*? My heart leaps when the realization hits me: she used ketchup! That's why the blood looked so lumpy and fake. That's why there's no condom. Suddenly it all makes sense. She lied to me about losing her virginity. What a crazy bitch.

I feel like confronting her right here, right now, but something tells me it won't make me feel better. It'll just bring more drama and chaos to this already chaotic day. What I need is time to think about this.

I leave the ketchup bottle where it is and head back downstairs.

21

My portrait of Agnes is taped to my bedroom wall. I'm completely mesmerized by it. It's as if the portrait is trying to say something to me, but the message keeps getting lost in the translation. An hour goes by and I'm no closer to understanding.

The portrait looks nothing like Agnes. Half of the face is sinister, a distorted fun-house image. The other half is open, innocent, childlike. While I was drawing, my leaky pen left splotches all over the sinister half, giving the skin a diseased, rotting effect. I didn't intend for the drawing to turn out this frightening, but drawing with my left hand—Professor Connelly had told us to practice drawing with our nondominant hand—must have unleashed something. I didn't have control of the pen, and felt as though I were drawing directly from my subconscious. As soon as I started the drawing, I knew it would turn out the way *it* wanted and not how I wanted. I was just the conduit.

Surprisingly, Agnes was a good model—maybe even too good. She didn't fidget, talk, or even blink, sitting as still as a mannequin. I thought I would be uncomfortable staring at her for so long, but once my subconscious took over, I was in another dimension: calm, free, safe. The next thing I knew we were both staring at my diabolical drawing. Grimacing, Agnes said, "My skin is not that bad." I explained that I was temporarily possessed, that the drawing wasn't really of her, that it had nothing to do with her. I tried to blame the outcome on my poor drawing skills, my whiplash, even my leaky pen, but Agnes still ended up sulking the rest of the day.

Is it possible that what I was drawing was Maddy's tortured soul? After all, I had just discovered the ketchup bottle in her room and I was still confused and angry about all of her lies. I know Maddy has a dark soul. What I can't understand is why I'm so drawn to it. She's got some kind of power over me. And I know it can't just be her beauty. Sometimes she really frightens me. Sometimes I want nothing more than to get away from her.

But I need her. Without her, I'm nothing. Without her, I don't have Agnes, and without Agnes and Maddy, I don't have anything that resembles a family. Yes, I have Reed. But ever since Boston, things with him have been a little shaky. Not only did I completely forget about our date but I didn't even return his panicked phone calls until hours later. He was hurt that I didn't call him right after the accident. He said it proved I don't really love him. Which isn't true. But I couldn't tell him the deal I made with Maddy, or how she saved my life, or how complicated things have become; he'd think we were a bunch of freaks.

Maybe I'm making a big deal out of nothing. So Maddy lies. It's not like I don't do it. I lie all the time. In fact, I might be just as pathological as Maddy.

Then again, Maddy's lies are much more demented than mine. Lying to me about losing her virginity to Brian, then "proving" it with ketchup—now that's twisted. What's even sicker is that a part of me is actually flattered by the effort. She must have really wanted to impress me, and I'm no stranger to the idea of wanting to impress people. I'm sure she and Agnes figured out that my family is fucked up, yet they never ask me about it. Because that's what friends do. They don't care about your past. They accept you and support you no matter what. And they forgive your mistakes.

Surely I can forgive Maddy, can't I?

After psych class, I go down to the lobby of the science building to see what jobs are posted on the bulletin board. There are lots of requests for dog walkers and babysitters, but I'm looking for something more mellow. And then I find it: "Retired psych professor seeks part-time assistant." I copy down the number and go outside to make the call.

A man picks up. "This is Dr. Shelby."

"Hi, I'm calling about the assistant position."

"Yes. Are you available this evening for an interview?"

"Uh, sure," I say.

"Excellent."

He gives me his address and tells me to be there at seven o'clock sharp. I can just imagine what Agnes is going to say: *What kind of interview takes place at night? You're not doing anything unsavory, are you, Sarah?*

I decide not to tell Agnes until after the interview.

22

Dr. Shelby has beady, bloodshot eyes, wild gray hair, a whiny voice, and the worst OCD I've ever witnessed. I've been working for him for the past two weeks. He keeps the thermostat at eighty, wears cotton booties around the house (and makes me wear them too), and has this annoying habit of clearing his throat every two seconds. But it's easy work, mainly just loading and emptying the dishwasher, and the pay is twenty dollars an hour. There are specific rules I have to follow, though: no plastics must ever touch metals, I must wear rubber gloves while handling the dishes, and if my gloves ever come into contact with anything "dirty" like my clothes or my face, I have to replace them with a fresh pair.

The good thing about working for Dr. Shelby is that there's lots of downtime. He has a ton of magazines, and although the job is weird, it beats working at Starbucks or being Agnes's personal slave. On the other hand, the job also gives me a lot of time to think—which is not good—and less time for Reed. We've seen each other only three times since I got back from Boston, but things feel a little more solid now. But no matter how much time we spend together, it still doesn't feel like enough. We both want more. It's like we're addicted to each other or something. But between my job and Maddy's ultimatum, seeing Reed is tricky. I don't know what to do. Part of me wants to quit work, but the thought of quitting for Reed—or for any man, no matter how lame the job—makes me feel unempowered. I can't help it; feminism is contagious at Wetherly. Plus, a part of me worries that Maddy is right: I *am* unlovable, and eventually Reed will figure this out.

I wait for the dishwasher to complete its cycle, put away the dishes, and then go home.

Agnes greets me with a sour look. "You don't have to work. I'll lend you the money," she says.

Then she takes me down to the basement and shows me where she keeps her cash—under her desk in a Prada shoebox. Opening the lid, she reveals stacks of rubber-banded bills. The bills are hundreds and they look brand-new.

"It's not just the money. There's something gratifying about working," I say.

Agnes sighs and throws up her hands. "I'll never understand you, Sarah."

It's Wednesday night and I'm standing outside Dr. Shelby's house, waiting for Maddy and Agnes. Ever since I started working, they've been meeting me afterward, once a week, for dinner at O'Malley's, a noisy restaurant-slash-pub in town.

Maddy shows up in a velvet swing coat and jeans, and Agnes has on a long military-style coat.

"Hey, working girl," Maddy quips.

"Thank God you're here," I say. "I'm starving."

"How was work?" Agnes asks, looking preoccupied.

"Okay," I say as we start walking toward town. "Today I got in trouble for touching the clean dishes with my bare hands. So I had to rewash them."

Maddy wrinkles her nose. "Huh?"

"My boss is a major germophobe," I explain.

"Oh," Maddy says, nodding.

Still a million miles away, Agnes says, "So, we were thinking of going somewhere different tonight, like the Wetherly Inn."

"Really?" I say, disappointed. "I was kind of looking forward to having a burger at O'Malley's."

"Well, it's quieter at the inn—I have a slight headache—and I've got something important to discuss with you."

My body tenses. "What do you want to discuss?"

"I'll tell you at the restaurant."

Am I going to get busted for something? Agnes doesn't look upset. Maybe it's nothing. Maddy grins at me.

The minute we enter the formal lobby of the Wetherly Inn, I feel out of place, as though I shouldn't be here unless accompanied by a well-heeled adult. The hotel staff seems to agree. That is, until they see Agnes, whose aura reeks of money and privilege. Soon we're whisked off to a private table in the deserted dining room.

Once we're seated, I turn to Agnes. "So, what did you want to talk to me about?"

"Why don't we order first? I thought you were starving."

I open the menu. No burgers. But there is a New York strip steak for fifty-five dollars. There goes my paycheck.

After we've placed our orders and been appropriately fussed over by our waiter, Agnes turns to me and says, "Thanksgiving is in two weeks. What are your plans?"

Thanksgiving is what she wanted to talk to me about? I'm so relieved I could cry. "I'm staying in town," I say.

"Why don't you come to New York and spend Thanksgiving with my family? They'd love to meet you." Agnes sounds like she really means it.

"Yeah," Maddy chimes in. "It'd be so much fun. I could meet you guys in the city and we could go shopping and stuff."

Agnes adds, "We'd only have to spend Thanksgiving Day with my parents. The rest of the time we'd be free to do whatever we want."

"Thanks," I say, "but I have a lot of reading to catch up on. Plus, I have to work."

"On a holiday weekend?" Agnes scoffs. "Tell your boss it's Thanksgiving. Remind him that you're an American."

Though I'm curious about Agnes's parents—their apartment, their collections, their relationship with Agnes—satisfying that curiosity would never outweigh all the anxiety I'd have to endure just to make them like me. I'd have to buy a whole new wardrobe and prepare a life story that would be bland enough to make them think I come from a semidecent family. Plus, I'd have to be witty and charming and respectful. In other words, I'd have to be someone else. This kind of visit would take over a month to prepare for. Besides, I already made plans to spend the weekend with Reed, and I've been looking forward to spending every minute of it with him. Not only that, but I need the time with him. The more I see him, the less I'm haunted by Maddy's words: *It's not going to work out . . . You don't know* how *to love. Because no one taught you.*

"I can't," I say firmly. "But thanks for the invitation."

"Well, if you change your mind . . ." Agnes trails off. "I wish I could skip Thanksgiving, but my parents would never allow it."

Maddy sighs. "It's just four days." She glances at me. "I'm sure you'll be fine by yourself."

"But she won't have turkey," says Agnes. "How can you not have turkey on Thanksgiving?"

"You don't eat meat," I remind her.

"Yes, but my parents still make me eat turkey on Thanksgiving. It's tradition."

"Don't they know you're a vegetarian?" I ask.

Agnes nods. "But tradition is everything at my house."

Poor Agnes. Her parents sound like dictators. No wonder she's so uptight.

23

Agnes drags her Goyard suitcase down the stairs and leaves it by the front door next to Maddy's Prada overnight bag. It's morning, the day before Thanksgiving, and Maddy and Agnes are going home. With one more midterm left, I'm standing in the foyer, chewing on a bagel and watching Agnes secure her luggage tag. I feel like a child waiting for her parents to leave so she can have the house to herself.

Agnes shouts up the stairs, "Maddy, the cab's going to be here any minute!"

Maddy yells back, "Relax! I'm almost ready!"

"Late. Always late," Agnes mutters.

The phone rings, and Agnes dashes into the kitchen to answer it. A minute later, she comes back and calls out to Maddy, "The cab's here!"

"Okay," Maddy singsongs.

Agnes looks at me. "Last chance. Sure you don't want to come?"

"Yeah. I have a lot of work to do. I'm behind in all my classes."

"Yes, you've mentioned that. Several times. Well, if you change your mind, call me."

Maddy comes running down. "I can't wait to get out of here." She pulls me into a hug. "I'm gonna miss you, Sarah Bear. What are you gonna do all by yourself?"

"Don't worry about me," I say.

"But what'll you eat? You'll starve to death."

"There's plenty of food in the fridge," Agnes says, buttoning up her long black coat.

Then Agnes does something completely out of character. Without warning, she reaches over and hugs me. It's an awkward, cold embrace, like being hugged without even being touched. "Good luck on your midterm," she says, pulling away. "We'll be back on Sunday night."

"Call me if you get bored," Maddy says. "Or if you get lonely, I could try to come back early."

"I'll be fine," I say.

Agnes opens the front door and she and Maddy walk toward the cab.

I close the door. Suddenly the house feels chilly.

I go into the kitchen and pour myself a cup of coffee. Then it occurs to me that I can do whatever I want now. My heart quickens. *Whatever I want.* I can crank up the stereo, sing and dance around the house naked, watch TV all day, sleep in, eat in bed, paint.

I sip my coffee, all the while feeling strangely optimistic about everything.

Why the hell can't optimism last? I think I failed my econ midterm and I feel like shit. I should have studied more; I should have memorized my notes. The whole exam was based on the lectures, but I didn't even glance at my notes (which weren't very good anyway). Instead, I studied the stupid textbook and ended up not knowing how to draw the appropriate graphs for half of the questions on the exam.

I walk to the pond to let off some steam. I spot a girl from Haven House whom Agnes and I nicknamed Rah-Rah for her annoying peppiness. I don't even know her real name. Rah-Rah walks toward Haven House, and since I have nothing better to do, I follow her. I stop when she gets to the quad. Standing under the arch, I stare at my old house. I see Amber and Keiko standing outside next to their oversize suitcases. A shuttle van arrives and picks them up. What would've happened had I stayed at Haven House? Would I be climbing into that shuttle van too? Probably not; Nana would have ditched me either way.

I decide it's pointless to dwell on these things. It's time to go home, even though I dread going back to an empty house.

The house is even quieter than before. I turn on the TV and all the lights downstairs, and make myself a peanut butter and jelly sandwich. I feel a little off-balance, which is totally ridiculous. I'm an only child; I should be okay with being alone. Yet I have the urge to call somebody. The first person that comes to mind is Reed, but I don't want him to think I'm a baby. Besides, I'm going to see him on Friday and we're going to spend the whole weekend together. Suddenly it occurs to me that, despite being an only child, I've never really been alone like this. I've never had an entire house to myself. Nana—a social butterfly at heart but a homebody in action—was always in the other room.

I take my sandwich into the den and lie on the couch. I channel surf until I stumble upon Hitchcock's *Psycho* on AMC. We had to watch this in my film class. Even though we dissected the shower scene, and I know there's no actual knife-on-skin contact, the movie still spooks me. I mute the sound, and right before the shower scene, I close my eyes.

The doorbell rings. My eyes flip open. Did Reed decide to skip Thanksgiving with his family, after all? I didn't bother to check my messages after my midterm. Maybe he called to tell me he was staying in town.

It rings again. I creep toward the door and look through the peephole, but I can't see anything because it's completely dark out.

Another ring. It can't be Reed; he still doesn't know where I live. I always make him drop me off a block away. Slowly, I back away from the door.

The kitchen phone rings, making me jump. Now would be a good time to have an answering machine, but since we don't, the only way I'm going to find out who's calling is if I pick up the phone. Maybe it's somebody who can rescue me from the intruder outside. Or maybe it's the intruder himself! My hands tremble as I lift the receiver.

"Hello?" I whisper.

"Hey, it's me," says Maddy. "I'm outside. Open the door already."

"You scared the hell out of me. Why didn't you use your keys?"

"I left them in my room. Hurry! I'm freezing my butt off."

I hang up and go to open the door. Maddy's cheeks are whipped pink from the cold.

"What are you doing here?" I ask.

"I decided not to go home." She throws her overnight bag on the floor.

"Why?"

"Well, I was thinking your idea sounded pretty good—you

know, staying in and studying. I think it's about time I got serious about school. Or serious about something." She slips out of her orange bomber jacket and closes the door.

Is she avoiding her aunt and uncle, or is she up to something?

"Besides," she says, locking the door, "Thanksgiving just hasn't been the same ever since my parents died."

"I'm sorry," I say reflexively. I never know what else to say when this comes up.

"It's okay. Nobody's life is perfect, right?"

We go into the kitchen, where Maddy perches on a bar stool. "So, what are we going to have for dinner? Wanna order pizza?"

"I just made myself a sandwich, but sure, let's order pizza." The thought of ordering Domino's feels illicit. If Agnes were here, she'd insist on making her own special cheeseless pizza.

I pick up the receiver and dial Domino's.

"I'm so glad I came back," Maddy says. "I really didn't want to see my aunt and uncle. My aunt actually sounded relieved when I told her I was going to stay at school. I guess she was hoping I'd drop out and marry Sebastian, so she wouldn't have to take care of me anymore. No chance of that happening now."

I flush at the mention of Sebastian. "So, what happened? You changed your mind at the airport?"

"No. I actually flew into JFK with Agnes, and then I took a flight back."

"I'm surprised Agnes let you come back alone. She didn't try to convince you to go to *her* house?"

"Well, I didn't exactly tell her I was coming back. I didn't want her to worry."

"Oh," I say. We both know that Agnes never would have let her come back to Wetherly alone. "How did you pull that off? Didn't Agnes see you going back inside the terminal?"

"She had a car waiting for her. I told her my uncle was just two minutes away. She wanted to wait with me, but I insisted that she go. I mean, I'll tell her when she gets back, but right now, I just want to veg."

So I'm not the only person Maddy lies to.

Later, as we're sitting on the couch scarfing down pizza, I start to feel annoyed. Reed is planning to come back the day after tomorrow. This weekend was supposed to be about *us*, and now everything is ruined. Did Maddy sense that I was planning to see Reed? Is she here to sabotage my relationship? Again? I could kick myself. I should've just gone with Reed to his parents' house when he invited me, but, stupidly, I told him we'd have more fun here.

I go upstairs and call Reed's cell. I get his voice mail. He's probably in New Jersey already, asleep after the long drive. I wait for the beep and say, "Hey, sweetie. It's me. I've got some bad news. It looks like I won't be able to hang out this weekend, after all. I'm really sorry. It's kind of an emergency, but don't worry, everything's fine. So, just stay in New Jersey with your family, okay? I'm really sorry, but we'll see each other next week. I love you. Bye."

As soon as I hang up, Maddy knocks on my door. "Sarah?"

"I'm changing."

"I don't mind," she says. "We're both girls, right?" She flings open the door. "Hey, you're not changing."

"I was about to; I just didn't know what I wanted to change into."

"Well, pajamas are pajamas, right? Unless you were thinking of going out tonight."

"No."

She sits on my bed. "Is everything okay? You seem kind of down. Is it Reed? Do you miss him?"

Maybe she really *is* psychic.

"Breakups are tough, but this is really for the best, Sarah. He wasn't good for our friendship. Don't worry; you'll meet your soul mate. I know there's someone out there who's thinking of you at this very moment."

"Want to watch a DVD?" I ask, desperate to end this conversation.

"Okay." Her eyes brighten. *"Beauty and the Beast*? Or *The Little Mermaid*?"

Just kill me now. "Whatever you want." I'll never understand Maddy's Disney fetish.

"No, you pick one," she whines.

I shrug. *"Beauty and the Beast."*

"You read my mind!"

"I'll make the popcorn," I say.

Maddy jumps up and claps. "Goody!"

It's going to be a long night.

24

I wake up to the smell of butter. It's in my hair, my breath, my pores. It's in the air around me, thick and impossible to breathe.

We binged last night, and now I feel fat and disgusting, like I gained my freshman fifteen overnight. I reach down and feel my ass. Yup, definitely bigger. I look over at Maddy, who's asleep on the loveseat, a softly heaving ball of quilt.

It's close to six o'clock. I wonder if Reed called me back last night. Forcing myself off the couch, I go upstairs. My phone is on the bed where I left it, but there are no new messages or missed calls. I get under the covers and dial Reed's cell. It rings four times before going to voice mail. I decide not to leave him another message. I'll call back later, at a more decent hour.

At eight thirty, my cell phone rings sharply, jarring me awake.

I reach for the phone. It's Reed. "Hey," I say.

"Hey." He sounds happy. "I'm five minutes away. Give me your address so I can come over."

"You're *here*?"

"Yeah, I missed you too much. I told my parents I had to come back and spend Thanksgiving with you."

"But didn't you get my message?" I ask.

"What message?"

"The one I left you last night."

"I didn't get any messages."

"But I left you one. I wish you'd called me earlier, because now you drove all this way for nothing."

He pauses. "What do you mean?"

"Don't be mad. Something came up, and I can't get together this weekend after all."

"What?" he says sharply.

"Yeah, I know. I'm really sorry. I want to see you and everything, but I can't leave the house."

"We can stay in," he says, perking up.

"No."

"Why not?" he asks.

"I can't really get into it right now."

"Are you serious? Don't you think you owe me an explanation? I drove all the way from New Jersey on Thanksgiving Day just to see you, and now you're telling me I can't see you, and you won't even tell me why?"

What can I say? That I fucked my roommate's boyfriend and then stupidly confessed, and then my roommate got angry and blamed me for losing the so-called love of her life—whom I don't think she ever really loved—but, in return for the mess I made, I promised to give up *my* boyfriend to prove to my roommate how much she means to me? The truth is fucking ridiculous.

"I'm coming down with something," I say. "The flu, I think."

"The flu?" he says, exhaling. "Why didn't you say so? I'll come take care of you."

"No. It's really bad." I fake a cough. "I don't want you to catch it."

"I don't care if I catch it."

"It's not just that. My roommate decided to stay in town at the last minute, so I don't even have the house to myself anymore."

"And you're not worried about infecting your roommate?"

"She got the flu shot. Anyway," I say, trying to sound hopeful, "I'm sure I'll be better by Monday, or maybe even Sunday night. So we'll see each other in a few days."

Silence.

"Sarah," he finally says, "I don't care if you give me the flu. We can be sick together. Don't you get it? I just want to see you. I *need* to see you."

"I want to see you too . . . but I can't."

"I was looking forward to spending the whole weekend with you. You're my girlfriend. It's fucking Thanksgiving. What am I supposed to do by myself on Thanksgiving?"

I let the question hang in the air.

"Sarah . . . do you even love me?"

Sighing, I say, "Of course I love you. I love you so much. Why would I be with you if I didn't?"

"I don't know. But it doesn't seem like you do anymore. You hide me from your roommates, and, after all this time, I still haven't seen your room. I don't even know where you live, for Christ's sake. I mean, call me crazy, but don't you think that's a little weird?"

Weird? I no longer know the meaning of weird. Things have been weird ever since I arrived at Wetherly. Everything is so weird that it's starting to feel normal.

When I don't respond, Reed says sourly, "I gave you my Thanksgiving."

And the way he says it, the way he whines it, makes me hate him for a second. He's a big whiny baby.

"I didn't ask you to give me your Thanksgiving," I say coldly. "And I didn't ask you to come back a day early. *You* made that decision. *You* should've checked with me first. That's what phones are for. So don't blame *me*."

"You're right. Excuse me for trying to surprise my girlfriend."

"Some surprise," I snap. It stuns me how cruel I sound. Cold and bitter.

"I don't think this is working," he says.

"Fine," I say. "Why don't we talk later, when we're both calmer?"

"No, I mean *we're* not working, Sarah."

My heart drops.

"Maybe we should just end this before it gets ugly," he says.

My heart drops another inch. I want to say: *No, we can work this out. Don't give up. I love you. Don't leave me.* But instead, I say nothing.

A minute passes. I steel myself. "You're right," I say. "This isn't going to work." It stuns me that I've just used Maddy's words on him. Well, maybe she was right. My parents never taught me how to love, so how could I have a normal relationship? Because of my fucked-up childhood, Reed and I were doomed from the start.

"Anyway, we tried, right?" He pauses. "Things just didn't work out for us."

"I have to go," I say, and hang up quickly.

I tent myself under the sheets and let the tears drain out of me. This is all Maddy's fault. She did this. I hate, hate, *hate her*! Why did she have to come back and ruin my plans? She had no right to tell me to break up with Reed. Who does she think she is? She's nobody, nothing. If she hadn't asked me to break up with him, I wouldn't have had to sneak around behind her back, and I'd still have a boyfriend right now. If she hadn't done that stupid reading on me and told me I was unlovable, I would have had more faith in myself and in Reed. If she hadn't come home, I would be with him this very minute, in his bed, in his arms. I should have told her to fuck off.

I sneak into Maddy's room, open the top drawer of her bureau, and steal a couple of Valiums. They'd better take away this pain; otherwise, I'll have to kill her.

Sometime around noon, Maddy comes knocking on my door.

When I don't answer, she goes ahead and opens it. I hear her skip toward my bed. "Wake up, sleepyhead," she says. "Time to rise and shine!"

I bury my head under the pillow. I may be groggy and tired, but I'm still furious. I try to will her out of my room.

It doesn't work.

She sits down on my bed and starts to bounce, gradually working up her speed. Yes, she's going to annoy me to death. I keep my head under the pillow. The last thing I want is to see that dumb face of hers.

She laughs. "Hey, wake up. I want to go to the mall."

Go away.

She tugs the pillow off my head.

"You awake yet?"

"No," I groan.

"Want to go to the mall?"

"It's Thanksgiving."

"So?"

"The mall's closed on Thanksgiving." *Dumb ass.*

"Oh. Well, let's do Thanksgiving then. Let's go buy a huge turkey and some yams and stuffing and cook it all up."

"I'm sick."

"Oh, no." Her voice rises an octave. "Can I get you anything? Some Advil or echinacea or chamomile tea?"

"Just let me sleep."

"Sure you don't need anything?"

"Positive."

"At least now you have an excuse for your boss."

I open my eyes. "What?"

"You were supposed to work this weekend, right? Now you can call him and tell him you're sick."

"Oh," I say. I'd forgotten about that lie. "Right."

"Or do you want me to call him?"

"No, I'll do it. Later."

"Okay. I'm gonna cook us a fabulous Thanksgiving dinner all by myself."

"You don't cook," I say.

"All I have to do is follow the directions. Go back to sleep. I'll check on you when I get back from Stop & Shop."

After Maddy leaves, I reach for my phone, hoping Reed called me back to say he changed his mind and that he still loves me. I try to keep the fantasy going, despite the fact that my phone hasn't rung once since our fight and there are no new messages. I decide to swallow my pride and be the first to call.

I dial his cell and wait. He doesn't pick up. I call his house. It rings and rings. I hang up, wait ten minutes and try his cell again. Still nothing. Ten, twenty, thirty minutes go by. He doesn't call back. Maybe he went back to New Jersey. Or maybe he's sitting at home, ignoring my calls, trying to drive me crazy. Maybe he just hates me and never wants to speak to me again. I doubt he ever really loved me. He was probably in love with the idea of love. *Asshole*. And it's true: he broke my heart just as Maddy predicted. It's good that I didn't sacrifice my friendship with Maddy for him. He's a jerk, a jerk in sheep's clothing.

But there were times when I actually felt that he loved me. His presence made me feel safe and immune to pain. Or maybe I'm the one who was in love with love. Maybe I tricked myself into thinking I loved him because I liked the idea of someone being in love with me. Maddy's right; he wasn't good for me. Artists. They're so fickle and insecure and self-absorbed. They make the worst boyfriends.

Through the foggy haze of Valium, I see a hand coming toward me. It lands on my forehead, soft and cool.

"No fever," Maddy says. "Feel better?"

Nope, still feel like shit. Despite nearly convincing myself that Reed wasn't right for me, I still miss him like crazy. I feel like I'm missing an arm or a kidney.

"I brought you medicine," Maddy says. "Here, sit up."

I do as she says. When I see the concern in her eyes, my hatred for her lessens. She hands me a glass of water and two orange pills and I swallow them without asking what they are. I may not have the flu, but I am in pain. I'd down a bottle of bleach if it would take away this horrible, sinking feeling.

"Come downstairs," she says. "Dinner's ready."

She grabs my arm and pulls me out of bed.

25

the table is draped in heavy white linen and covered with votive candles surrounding a centerpiece of dried flowers, berries, and gourds. Maddy did this for me. I'm kind of touched.

She points to the blackened carcass sitting on the kitchen counter, still steaming, smoking up the room. "I burned it."

"That's okay," I tell her.

She cracks open the kitchen window and sits down at the dining table. "Cooking is a lot trickier than I thought. The bird was all wiggly. It wouldn't cooperate." She points her chin toward the three large bowls on the table containing cranberry sauce, stuffing, and creamed corn. "So this is dinner."

"It looks good," I say, trying to sound optimistic. Maddy frowns. "Really," I insist. I look back at the counter, at the mess of empty cans and boxes. Except for the burning turkey, the scene is a lot like Thanksgiving at Nana's: just the two of us and all this prepackaged food.

I sit down and load up my plate, though the last thing I feel like doing is eating. I force down a bite of stuffing. "Pretty good," I say, and mean it.

"Really?" A smile appears on her lips.

"Yeah."

"We have dessert too. Pumpkin pie. Don't worry—I didn't make it."

I laugh and continue chewing, not really tasting anything. The chewing is good, it calms me and keeps me from thinking about Reed. I chew myself into a trance and barely hear Maddy when she begins sharing the latest gossip on Justin Timberlake.

After dinner, we blow out the candles and leave the kitchen as it is: a big, black, smoky mess.

The next morning, I wake up with a sore throat. I'm hot and I'm shivering and my whole body's shaking. Unbelievable. Thanks to my incredible psychosomatic powers, I've actually given myself the flu! But I'm not going to let it get me down or use it as an excuse to spend another day wallowing over Reed. I'll take two DayQuils and be just fine.

I shower, get dressed, and go with Maddy to the Hampstead Mall, also known as the "dead mall" for its lack of people and any decent stores. We take the bus and arrive at the mall twenty minutes later. There are at least fifty cars parked in front of JCPenney alone—which is amazing for the Hampstead. We go inside. Ignoring the grabby-handed Christmas shoppers, we head straight to Friendly's and share a banana split and fries. I miss Reed so much my ribs hurt. I miss his hair, his voice, his sexy half smile, his body, his brain, even his beat-up Nissan Sentra. So I eat and eat until I feel absolutely nothing.

* * *

For dinner, we order chicken tikka masala and saag paneer from India Palace, and eat it right out of the containers. Afterward, I lie on the couch. Maddy turns on the TV and plops down on the floor.

"There's nothing to do in this town," she complains.

"We could go to Amherst. See if there are any cute guys."

Maddy wrinkles her nose. "We don't need boys to have fun. We can have a lot more fun by ourselves."

"Maybe we should try to get some work done," I say.

"Oh, don't be good. Be bad with me."

"I thought you wanted to get serious about school."

"I do, but it's only Friday. We still have the whole weekend." She sits up. There's a gleam in her eye. "Have you ever played with a Ouija board?"

"No."

"Want to try it?"

I raise an eyebrow. "You actually have one?"

"Yeah."

"Aren't they supposed to be kind of . . . evil?" My Lutheran teachers successfully brainwashed me into fearing Ouija boards.

"Depends what you ask them," she says, giggling. "Just kidding. No, they're not evil." She turns off the TV. "Be right back."

While she's upstairs, I tell myself I have nothing to fear.

Maddy comes back downstairs with the Ouija board and a notebook. She removes the votive candles from the dining table and takes them to the red room, where she places them on the rug in a circle, large enough to surround both of us and the Ouija board, and, one by one, she lights them. Then she gets up to close the curtains, all but one. The moon, I notice, is theatrically bright tonight, outshining our candles.

While opening the window, Maddy says, "Let me know if you get too cold, but we need to keep this open to facilitate communication with the spirits."

I roll my eyes and sit down next to her inside the circle.

She places the Ouija board between us. "Do you have a specific question you want to ask?"

I shrug. "No." But there *is* something I want to ask. I want to ask if Reed still loves me, but I could never say this in front of Maddy. Besides, after her ominous tarot-card reading, I could definitely use a break from her psychic interventions.

"Well, think about it," Maddy says. "I'll start."

Suddenly I remember my teachers saying that disturbed people tend to attract disturbed spirits. With all the weird energy Maddy has, I can't help but worry about the kinds of spirits she'd attract. Bipolar spirits? Pathologically lying spirits? Are there such things? If so, Maddy would attract the craziest of them all.

"I'm going to make you a believer." She puts her fingertips on the indicator and tells me to do the same. "Very lightly now, you barely want to touch it. Close your eyes and concentrate."

I close my eyes and try to concentrate, not sure what I'm supposed to be concentrating on. After a few minutes, I still don't feel anything.

"I don't think I'm doing it right," I tell her.

"It's not rocket science, Sarah. Relax."

I take a deep breath and exhale.

"Okay, open your eyes. Let us begin. Spirit, tell us your name."

Nothing happens. A minute passes. I yawn. Maddy keeps staring at the board.

And then, suddenly, the indicator moves. I can't believe it.

It's actually moving! My hands tremble. Is Maddy guiding it? It doesn't feel like she is, but I can't really tell. All I know is that I'm not; I'm barely touching the thing.

The indicator moves to the letter K. Then A. And then X. Maddy writes the letters down in her notebook.

"Kax," Maddy says. "That's a funny name. How old were you when you died, Kax?"

The indicator moves around in small, seemingly aimless circles, then stops on the number five. I still can't believe this is happening.

"Five? That's so sad. I'm sorry, Kax. How did you die?"

The indicator spells KAX again, then moves to I, D, E, N, and stops on T. Kaxident? Sounds like a brand of pain reliever or denture cleanser. Not so scary after all.

"Kaxident. Kaxident?" Maddy says, staring at the board. "What does that mean?"

She looks at me and I shrug.

"Wait. Ka axident. *Car accident.* Could that be it? Maybe she has a Boston accent," Maddy says, her eyes glowing. "Kax died when she was five. That's why she can't spell. Is that right, Kax?"

The indicator moves to YES. I don't know what to feel, think, say. This is impossible. We can't actually be communicating with the spirit of a dead child. Yet it appears that we are. I feel a chill between my shoulder blades.

"Okay," Maddy says quietly, "Sarah, you can ask a question now."

A gust of wind blows through the window and half of the candles go out. My heart pounds. Maddy gets up to close the window, and I don't know why I do it, but I relight the candles. I'm scared shitless. I have the urge to run upstairs and dive under my covers. But I don't move.

Maddy comes back and puts her fingertips on the indicator. "Okay, go."

I decide to test Maddy, to ask a trick question—a question that only *I* would know the answer to—so that I can find out if she's controlling the indicator. I place my fingertips on the indicator and say, "Kax, how old was I when I had the chicken pox?"

"You can't ask that kind of question," says Maddy, looking a little nervous.

"Why not?"

"You're supposed to ask about the future, not the past."

"Who says? I should be able to ask whatever I want. Kax, how old was I when I had the chicken pox?"

The indicator starts to move. It goes from N to V to R. NVR.

"Never," Maddy says. "Is that true? You've never had the chicken pox?"

I nod, speechless. There's no way Maddy could have guessed the answer. Either she's truly psychic, or Kax is real. Could Kax be real?

"Now, for a serious question," Maddy says. "Kax, when will I die?"

"Don't ask that." I try to pull Maddy's hands off the board, but she pushes me away.

"I need to know. Tell me, Kax, when will I die?"

The indicator moves around quickly in wild circles. Only Maddy's fingers are touching the indicator now.

The indicator spells DI. My heart quickens.

"When?" Maddy repeats.

The indicator spells DI, again and again.

My whole body shakes. "Maddy, stop!"

"When, Kax? *When?*"

The indicator spells SUNE.

Soon?

Maddy doesn't move. Her whole body is still except for her eyes, which are shifting wildly across the board.

I jump up and flip on the lights. Maddy hugs her chest. With her back to me, she looks small and fragile. She's crying. I steel myself and walk toward her. I kneel down and gently rub her back.

"Don't leave me, Sarah," she says. "Please don't leave me."

"I'm not going anywhere. It was a stupid game. You can't take it seriously," I say, though I'm not convinced.

"Spirits are real. They know things. Kax said 'Soon.' I'm going to die soon." She covers her face with her hands. "All this time I hoped my intuition was wrong. But I *am* going to die. You saw it—*die, die, die.*"

"We're all going to die someday," I say weakly. "That's probably what she meant, not that you're going to die young."

"She said soon."

"Maddy, listen to me. You're going to have a long, healthy life. You are. You just have to believe it."

"Do *you* believe it?"

"Yes."

"I mean, do you believe in Ouija boards," she says, her voice dropping to a whisper.

"I don't know," I mumble. "Maybe. I mean, I've never experienced anything like that before. We couldn't have imagined it, right? But maybe it's not what we think it is. Maybe we wanted so badly to see something that we made it happen."

"Don't rationalize, Sarah. You saw what I saw. It was real." She wipes her eyes on her sleeve. "There's something I have to tell you. It's something I've never told anyone, not even Agnes, and I'm only sharing it with you because I know I can trust you." She meets my gaze; her eyes are solemn. "But first, you have to promise never to tell anyone. *Ever*. And you have to promise you won't think I'm crazy after I tell you."

But I already think she's crazy. Would it be disingenuous of me to make a promise I've already broken?

"I promise," I say.

Her jaw relaxes. "Remember when Agnes and I went to Vermont?"

I nod, and wonder if she's finally going to tell me about the Gypsy.

"Well, something strange happened on that trip, while we were in New York." She looks away, then back. "I met a Gypsy lady in Chinatown. It was at night, right after dinner. Agnes and I were looking for a cab to take us back to the hotel, and I accidentally bumped into this Gypsy and knocked her bag off her shoulder."

Yup, I know where this is going.

Maddy then repeats the story Agnes told me back in September. When she gets to the part about the reading, my ears perk up.

She lowers her voice. "The Gypsy took us back to her apartment and made me a cup of tea. I followed her into the den while Agnes waited for me in the living room. The den was dark and smelled like patchouli oil. After we sat down, she asked me to hold the cup in my hands and concentrate. Then she told me to drink the tea, leaving a few drops behind. When I was finished, she took the cup from me and swirled it around three times. I watched her dump the leaves into a saucer and study the remaining leaves that were stuck to the cup. She said she saw some unlucky things in my life, but that my parents were fine. They miss me, but I don't need to worry about them."

"Did she tell you where they are?" I ask, feeling goose pimply all over.

Maddy considers this. "No. But she said they were in a safe place, and they were watching over me. Then she told me something really strange. She said the number twenty-one was a bad number for me. She said she saw a circle, which meant I was coming to the end of a cycle. And there was another circle, she said, a smaller one, which represented a circle of friends. One friend was new and the other was old."

"She actually said that?"

"Yes." Maddy pauses. "And then she warned me that one of my friends was insanely jealous, and one day she would turn against me."

I cover my mouth.

"I know. It's crazy. I was totally shocked. I asked the Gypsy if there was anything I could do to prevent that friend from betraying me. She said no, that it was meant to happen. But she told me to be cautious anyway, to protect myself, and to ask my other friend for help. That's you, Sarah . . . get it? Agnes is going to turn against me and you're my only ally."

"But Agnes would never betray you. You're all she cares about."

"That's the problem! She cares too much. Her intensity is frightening. Who knows what she'd do if she were pushed to the edge."

I rub my temple. "You really believe Agnes would betray you?"

"If I ever got closer to someone else," Maddy says. "Agnes hated Sebastian. And she's always reminding me that *she's* my best friend, not you. She's so jealous of you. Anyway, there's more." She exhales. "At the end of the reading, the Gypsy said I could ask her one question. So I asked her if I was going to die young. She got this pained look on her face, but she wouldn't answer me. She said she didn't know anything, but that even if she did, it was against the rules to say. But her expression said it all. Plus, she didn't tell me the opposite . . . She didn't tell me I was going to live to be ninety, which is what most fortune-tellers do, at least that's what I've heard. So, to me, that's just like saying yes."

"You're reading too much into it."

"I don't think I am, because after I asked her that question, she said the reading was over. I think she saw something terrible in my future, and she knew I was aware of it. If she'd seen good things, she would've said something nice. Anyway, I insisted on asking another question since she didn't answer my first one, and I guess she felt sorry for me because she said okay."

"What did you ask?"

Maddy bites her lip. "I asked her if there was anything a person could do to extend her life, if she was certain she was going to die young and wanted to change her destiny."

"You mean, like, cheat death?"

"No, not cheat it, but maybe . . . delay it for a bit."

Maddy's words hang in the air. I don't know what she's up to, but her obsession with death seems way out of control. Maybe this is what Agnes originally wanted me to ask Maddy about. But then why did Agnes change her mind?

"So, what did the Gypsy say?" I ask Maddy.

"She said yes and even told me how to do it, but warned me not to. Not like it matters," Maddy says. "I was never going to do it. I don't believe in tampering with destiny; I was just curious is all."

"So there's actually a way to extend a person's life?"

She nods.

"How?"

"That's not important, Sarah. I'm not going to do it."

"I know you're not. I'm just curious."

"We shouldn't even be talking about it. Besides, I don't remember exactly what she said. It's been so long."

I study Maddy's face. There's something fixed and unnatural about it, like she's in a trance. A moment later, she snaps out of it.

"To be honest, I'm more afraid of Agnes," she says. "Ever since the night of the reading, I've been trying to make sense of what the Gypsy said. Then, on the way to the airport, it suddenly became clear to me. The number twenty-one, the end of a cycle, a circle of friends, a betrayal—what all of this means is that I'm going to die before December twenty-first, my birthday, and Agnes is going to be my murderer."

"That's ridiculous, Maddy. Please tell me you're not serious." I don't know what to think. Is this another one of her tricks, or has she gone completely mental?

She's staring at her palm, retracing her truncated lifeline.

"Look," I say. "You can't trust that Gypsy. Or your palm, or any of that stuff. The truth is nobody knows what's going to happen. The Gypsy was unethical. She was probably trying to scare you. She saw you and Agnes, a couple of college girls, no threat to her whatsoever, so she had some fun with you. And she got paid handsomely for it too."

Maddy shakes her head and continues staring at her palm.

"Okay," I say. "Let's just say for the sake of argument that the Gypsy actually *could* see the future. She was never specific enough about anything for you to come to any conclusions. She never said you were going to die young. She never said Agnes was going to kill you. Think about it: a circle and another circle and a friend who's going to betray you? For all we know, she could have been talking about *me*! I betrayed you with Sebastian."

"No, because you made it up to me by giving up Reed. Right?"

"Maddy," I say, rubbing my eyes, suddenly very tired, "it's late. Why don't we try and get some sleep. I'm sure this will all make more sense in the morning."

Maddy stands up. "You're right. It *is* late and I *am* kind of tired." Noticing the candles, she bends down to blow them out, then points at the Ouija board. "We'll clean this up tomorrow."

"Good idea," I say, hitting the lights.

26

I toss and turn in bed, tortured by thoughts of Kax, the Gypsy, and Agnes as a potential murderer.

Months ago when Agnes first told me the Gypsy story, I was intrigued but also skeptical. Deep down, I thought the story was a ploy to get me to move in with them, but I guess I was wrong.

Maddy is a bottomless pit of personalities and she seems to be getting weirder all the time. It was strange enough when she thought she was going to die young, but now she believes Agnes is going to murder her? I have to talk to Agnes about this. But what will I say? *Maddy thinks you're going to kill her?* It's too outrageous.

And what about the Ouija board? After seeing what I saw, how can I pretend I don't believe in the supernatural? The indicator moved. And Kax knew that I never had the chicken pox, and there's no neat and logical explanation for that.

I feel someone staring at me. Slowly I turn toward the wall. It's the portrait I drew of Agnes, staring right at me! I get out of bed and stumble toward it. As I get closer, I realize it looks different from before. I don't know if it's the darkness or my mind playing tricks on me, but the portrait looks a little like me now. My pulse quickens. Those are definitely my eyes, and that's definitely my mouth—except I look completely deranged. How could my drawing have changed? Who tampered with it? I must be hallucinating. I tear the drawing off the wall and shove it in the trash. The last thing I need right now is to be terrorized by my own creation.

I climb back into bed, but freeze when I hear the toilet flush. I wait for the bathroom door to open. It opens, and then the floorboards creak as Maddy walks back to her room. When I hear her door shut, I exhale.

Then I hear a tapping at my door. I bury my head under the covers.

"Sarah? Are you asleep?"

No, no, no. Stay away from me.

She opens the door. I feel her hesitating in the doorway while her crème brûlée lotion wafts into the room. With my head still under the covers, I picture her standing there in her silk-and-ostrich-feather robe and bare feet. I will her to go away. I picture a barbed-wire fence around my bed, a moat, a dozen crucifixes.

But she doesn't budge.

A minute passes and then she comes in. She walks to the vacant side of my bed and peels back the covers. I keep my eyes closed. Cold air stabs me in the back while she climbs in. Then it's warm again. She's so close I can smell her mouthwash. For several minutes I don't move, don't breathe, don't think. Eventually, I hear her snore.

Something is jabbing me in the upper arm. I ignore it. Another jab, and then another. I force my eyes open, startled to see Agnes standing over me with a scowl on her face.

"What?" I say.

She points toward my chest.

"What?" I repeat. I look down at my chest, and nearly jump when I see Maddy's hand resting on my breast. I brush her hand away and sit up.

"What exactly have you two been doing?" Agnes asks.

"Nothing. What are you doing home so early?"

"Do I need a reason to come back to my own house?" She looks me in the eye. "What happened last night?"

"Nothing." I look away. "Maddy must've come in after I fell asleep. She was probably afraid to sleep alone."

"Uh-huh. Then why was she fondling your breast?"

"Fondling my breast? God, Agnes, what is wrong with you?"

"So you weren't fooling around?" she asks, raising an eyebrow.

"Fooling around? Please." I reach for my robe.

"Okay, don't get angry. I believe you." She lowers her voice. "I was worried, that's all. I left Maddy several messages but she never called me back. Finally, I called her aunt, who told me Maddy had decided to stay at school to catch up on her studies. And since that sounded completely ludicrous, I assumed something terrible had happened. So when I rushed back here and found the two of you in bed together . . . naturally, I overreacted. I'm sorry."

"You should be," Maddy says.

Agnes and I both freeze.

"Did we wake you?" Agnes says sheepishly.

"Yes, you did." Maddy waves a finger at Agnes. "I never knew you had such a dirty mind."

Agnes turns crimson. "Why didn't you tell me you were coming home?"

"Do I have to tell you everything?"

Agnes looks down at the floor.

Maddy climbs out of bed, naked. God. Why is she naked? She walks across the room, puts on her robe, and then walks out the door.

"I bought doughnuts!" Agnes calls after her.

"I'm not hungry." Maddy comes back into the room. "Sarah, come downstairs with me."

I look to Agnes, but she avoids my gaze. Maddy grabs my hand and pulls me toward the stairs. At the last minute, when I'm almost out the door, I snatch Agnes's hand and drag her along with us. At the bottom of the stairs, Maddy drops my hand and I let go of Agnes's.

In the kitchen, Agnes busies herself with making coffee and setting out plates and napkins. I catch her sneaking glimpses at Maddy, but Maddy ignores her, and despite saying she wasn't hungry, she scarfs down two chocolate doughnuts. Maybe Maddy's bad mood is just a cover for her newfound fear of Agnes.

I think the Lutherans were right: Ouija boards are evil. And so are fortune-telling Gypsies.

After breakfast, I help Agnes with the dishes. She washes, I dry. Maddy wanders into the den to watch Saturday morning cartoons, which she's rarely awake for. The minute she's gone, Agnes pulls me aside.

"I need to ask you a favor," she says.

I hesitate. "What?"

"Could you leave Maddy and me alone for a little while?"

"Sure," I say, relieved that the favor is so minor. "I'll go upstairs."

"No. I need you to leave the house."

I scratch my head. "For how long?"

"Just a few hours."

"A few hours? All the libraries are closed today. And it's too cold to sit out by the pond."

"Go to the mall. Or wherever. Here, take the car," she says, shoving her key into my palm.

"You got your car fixed?"

"No, I bought a new one. Go ahead, take it."

"Okay," I say, both puzzled and annoyed that she's so eager to get rid of me. Is she punishing me for having spent two days alone with Maddy? Is she *that* jealous?

The Gypsy seemed to think so.

I look down at my makeshift pajamas—a white tank and red sweatpants. "I need to change first."

"All right, but hurry," she says, not-so-gently nudging me toward the stairs.

Upstairs, while changing, I start to panic. What if Agnes does something to Maddy? What if Maddy is in danger?

No, I reassure myself. Agnes would never hurt her. If only the Gypsy understood how much Agnes cares for Maddy.

I lock the front door and walk toward the driveway, wondering how Agnes is going to explain my sudden disappearance.

In the driveway sits a shiny new black Mercedes S500—a clone of the car Agnes had before the accident. The fact that Agnes bought the exact same car doesn't surprise me a bit. She could have bought any car, but when Agnes likes something she likes it to death.

I open the door, slide into the buttery seat, and inhale the intoxicating new-car scent. I flip through the CDs in the side pocket of the door, hoping to find something other than opera or classical music. I find nothing, and decide to go back into the house for my CDs.

I walk stealthily into the house. Maddy's cartoons are still on full blast. I poke my head into the den and what I see literally makes me jump back. Maddy is lying on her back on the couch with her feet in Agnes's lap, and Agnes is giving her a foot massage. An actual foot massage.

Didn't Agnes once say that a woman's feet and the small of her back were areas meant for lovers only? They certainly look like lovers right now. It's the most intimate I've ever seen two people interact outside of intercourse.

But why is Maddy even letting her do it? Especially after last night. I thought Agnes was supposed to be the enemy. I don't get it. Normally Maddy won't tolerate even the slightest display of affection from Agnes, and now they're acting like a couple. Maybe they're secret lovers. Maybe they've been playing musical beds behind my back all this time. How could I have been so naive?

"Not so soft. You're tickling me," Maddy coos, the same way she used to coo for Sebastian.

"How's that?" Agnes asks in a low voice.

"Too hard," Maddy whines. She's trying to be cute. "There. That's good. Keep doing that."

I tear my eyes away and tiptoe upstairs. I riffle through a pile of CDs next to my bed. Grabbing Nico, I bolt out of the house.

I get in the car and drive, and before I know it, I'm parked outside of Reed's apartment. Forcing myself out of the car, I walk toward his door and knock on it. No answer. I'm such an idiot. I had someone who loved me, and I totally fucked things up. If only I knew some of Reed's friends. Then I could call them up and ask where he is. But I've never met any of them. Maybe I should stay in the car and wait until he comes back.

I walk back to the car and turn up the stereo. Depressing Nico is perfect for depressing times like this. I listen for a while, then climb into the backseat and close my eyes.

27

When I open my eyes, the sky is a cool black. An entire day napped away. I smooth my hair and climb out of the car. Then I walk toward Reed's apartment again and knock on the door, firmly, calmly.

There's no answer.

I wait a few more minutes before heading back to the car. And then I drive, dreading what's waiting for me at home.

Maddy and Agnes are sitting at the dining table looking surprisingly normal, not all lovey-dovey like before. Agnes is stabbing a salad with her fork, and Maddy is picking at what looks like a microwaved potpie. I guess Agnes was too "busy" to cook dinner. They didn't even wait for me.

"We called you," Agnes says. Is she gloating? There's color in her cheeks and an actual gleam in her eyes. "We called you, Sarah," she repeats.

"I didn't have my phone with me," I mutter.

"How was work?" Maddy asks, and then Agnes gives me a look that says I should play along.

"It was . . . okay," I say.

"You left so suddenly," says Maddy. "I thought you were going to tell your boss you were sick."

"Oh," I say, "I forgot to call him, and anyway, I felt better today."

Maddy smiles at me, but there's something artificial about it. I look away. When I turn back I catch her glowering at me, though her lips are still upturned. She's mad at me? Why?

"So, what did you guys do today?" I ask.

Canoodled, of course. An awkward silence follows. Agnes avoids my gaze and says, "Nothing much. Come eat."

"I'm not feeling very well." I place Agnes's car key on the counter. "I'm going to go lie down."

Agnes looks up at me. "I'll check on you later."

"Get some rest, Sarah Bear," Maddy chirps.

I go to my room, close the door, and crawl into bed. I'm not tired at all. In fact, I'm so overly rested that I have a headache. So I get up, fluff my pillow, and toss the pillow Maddy used last night onto the floor. Then I go to the window and open it. I lean over the sill. What if I jumped? I could do it; I could end it all. If things ever got that bad. Of course, two stories isn't exactly high enough.

I close the window and scold myself for being so melodramatic. I don't want to die. Even if I did, I certainly wouldn't choose a dramatic death. Pills maybe, or gas like Sylvia Plath, but nothing gory, ugly, or painful. Death should be beautiful, even if life isn't.

Still antsy, I pace my room. Part of me wants to go downstairs and confront them, demand the truth. The other part just wants to go downstairs and be with them and pretend that everything's normal. Why are they shutting me out? If they truly are lovers now, then I'll be the third wheel and this living arrangement will never work. Things will only get more complicated and strange.

I need to start focusing on classes again, preparing for finals, not spending all of my time consumed with Maddy and Agnes. Maybe I should move out—not now, but next semester. First, I'll fly to California for Christmas. I've saved enough money from my job to buy a plane ticket, and even if Nana doesn't want me there on my own, there's nothing she can do to stop me. I have a key and she still is my legal guardian. After the holiday, I'll make a new start. I'll move back into Haven House and try to make new friends. I'll see Maddy and Agnes less and less, and talk to them less and less. Gradually I'll be free.

But why does the thought of moving out fill me with dread? Why do I get the feeling that *I* will be the one who can't let go?

There's a knock at my door. I stash my back issue of *Star* under the bed and pull the covers up to my chin.

"Come in," I say.

The door opens brusquely and Agnes, wearing her granny glasses, enters my room with a bowl of chicken soup on a tray. She sets the tray on my nightstand.

"How are you feeling?" she asks.

"Better," I say. "Where's Maddy?"

"She went to bed."

Agnes motions for me to sit up, and I watch as she transfers the tray to my lap.

The steam from the soup ignites my appetite.

She sits down at the foot of the bed and turns toward me. "I hope you don't mind that I told Maddy you went to work today."

"No," I say, taking a spoonful of soup, "but why did you say work?"

"I didn't know what else to say. I didn't want her to call your cell a million times. And I had no idea you were sick."

I nod.

"So, where did you go?" she asks.

"Does it matter?"

She shrugs. "You were gone a long time."

I take another spoonful. "What were you and Maddy doing that was so private?"

She looks away. "I just wanted to talk to her. Alone. We had an argument the day before Thanksgiving, on our way to the airport."

"She never told me."

"That's probably because . . . it was about you."

"Me?" I say, slightly rattled. "What did *I* do?"

"You didn't do anything. It was a misunderstanding." Agnes lowers her eyes and begins picking at her cuticles. "I thought Maddy was ignoring me. I thought she didn't want to be my best friend anymore. I'm ashamed to say this, but I was jealous of all the time *you* were spending with her."

Our eyes lock. She's out of her mind. When have I ever spent time alone with Maddy? I can't think of a single time before this weekend.

"But everything's fine now. Maddy reassured me that she still wants to be my best friend. You're our friend too, of course, but Maddy and I have history."

Agnes slides off the bed and begins to pace. So she really *is* jealous. Maybe the Gypsy was right. Maybe she *is* dangerous.

"I'm not trying to take Maddy away from you," I say.

Agnes looks at me like she's amused. "I know."

"You're Maddy's best friend and I'm totally fine with that. I'm not trying to replace you or come between you guys or—"

"I know, Sarah," she says, more insistent this time.

"Are you sure? Because it's important to me that you understand that."

"Yes, I get it. You don't have to keep saying it. Let's change the subject, okay?"

"I just have one more question," I say. Agnes meets my eyes. "Are you sure what you feel for Maddy isn't more than friendship?"

She swallows visibly. "What are you implying?"

I muster the courage to bring up the foot massage. "I saw you guys earlier. On the couch. I came back to get a CD and I saw you."

"And?"

"And I know what's going on," I say, aware of the nervous edge that's crept into my voice.

"And what's that?" she asks.

"Come on, Agnes. Don't pretend you don't know what I'm talking about."

"But I *don't* know what you're talking about."

"You want me to say it out loud?"

"It would certainly help."

"I saw you giving Maddy a foot massage." Now, suddenly, *I* feel ridiculous.

"And?"

"And, I want to know if you and Maddy are . . . in love. I live here, so I think I have a right to know if you guys are a couple now."

"A couple?" Agnes laughs. "You're very funny, Sarah. I wasn't giving Maddy a foot massage. She had a cramp in her foot. I was helping her to get it out. In love? *Please.*" She laughs again, more condescendingly this time. "You really have a vivid imagination."

I look away. Why, why, why does she always make me feel like I'm overreacting? And why does she have a logical explanation for everything? I know what I saw and yet she's making me doubt myself. I don't know whether to hate her or admire her for it.

"Well, I guess I'll say good night." She walks toward the door, stops halfway, and turns around. "Unless you have any other theories you'd like to share with me."

I roll my eyes.

"Okay, then, see you in the morning," she says, closing the door behind her.

28

On Wednesday, Dr. Shelby comes to the door wearing a gas mask.

"Flu season," he explains in a warbled voice.

I guess a regular surgical mask just wouldn't cut it. But I'm used to all of Dr. Shelby's eccentricities by now.

"I have three loads for you today," he says excitedly.

He leads me into the kitchen, where I wash my hands, put on a pair of gloves, and start loading the dishwasher. I feel his beady eyes creep up my back and down my thighs. I remind myself that I'm getting paid twenty dollars an hour to tolerate this.

The phone rings, and Dr. Shelby disappears into his office.

When I finish loading the dishwasher, I go into the living room and crack open my microeconomics textbook. I got a D on my midterm and I'm afraid I'm going to fail the class. I flip to page one: the law of supply and demand. Something I happen to know a lot about, living with Maddy and Agnes. The more available I make myself to them, the less they want my friendship. From now on, I should limit their time with me—be mysteriously absent once in a while—and see if it increases their demand for me.

As I contemplate this, Dr. Shelby appears in the doorway, still wearing his gas mask.

"I'm letting you go," he says.

"What?" I say, caught off guard.

"Please leave."

"Did I do something wrong?" I ask. "Did I mix the plastics with the metals again?"

"No, but your services are no longer required. Please go."

"But—"

"You're fired," he insists.

I throw up my hands. "Whatever." I grab my book and backpack and get up to leave. Dr. Shelby springs to the front door. As I walk toward him, I take a good hard look at his freaky face, which I'll never have to see again. He hands me a white envelope, and I take it and walk out the door.

"Sarah?"

I stop, but don't turn around.

"Choose abstinence."

What a freak. I continue walking. *Choose abstinence?* From what? Sex, drugs, or alcohol? Or does he want me to be like him and abstain from life?

When I get to the end of the block, I open the envelope. Three hundred dollars. Not bad for ten minutes of work. I decide to reward myself with a slice of pizza from the pizzeria next to the mail center, so I head toward Lemon Street.

Inside my mailbox is a letter from Nana. Strangely, the envelope is typed and looks like it was done on a typewriter. Why so official? More important, when did Nana acquire a typewriter? I shove the letter into my backpack. As I'm walking out, I spot a girl from my econ class, and it occurs to me that I could ask to borrow her notes. She might say no—people are pretty cutthroat here—but it wouldn't hurt to ask. And it sure beats my other option, which is to fail economics.

The girl has Bettie Page bangs and a high, tight ponytail.

I clear my throat. "Bettie?"

"Betsey," she corrects me.

"Right. Betsey." I don't tell her I got temporarily confused by her bangs. "I'm Sarah. I'm in your econ class."

"Micro or macro?"

"Micro."

She stares hard at my face. "I don't think I've seen you in class before."

"Yeah, I've missed a lot of classes. I was actually wondering if I could borrow your notes."

She looks me up and down—at my hands and my cargo pants and my dirty combat boots—as though trying to assess whether I'm worthy of her precious notes.

"I don't usually lend them out, but I guess it would be okay as long as you returned them to me within an hour. I don't like to be without them for too long. You can photocopy them."

"Thanks. I'll be quick."

"Well, I don't have them with me. They're in my room and I won't be home till six." She pauses, then smiles. "Why don't you come to my house for dinner?"

Why is she being so nice all of sudden? Actually, who cares? I need those notes. "Sure," I say. "That sounds great."

"I live in Tyler, right next to Bass Hall." She wiggles three fingers at me and glides out of the mail center.

And then I realize what I've just agreed to: dinner in a dorm. Being in a dorm again will be awkward. For a moment, I consider not going, but the fear of failing economics urges me on.

At the pizza place, I buy a large Diet Coke and skip the pizza. I sit down and tear open Nana's letter. Inside, wrapped in a sheet of lined notebook paper, is a round-trip ticket to LA. Unbelievable. There is no enclosed letter, no card, not even a Post-it—but Nana actually *wants* me to come home. Did she and Howie break up? I can't stop smiling. I never thought I'd be looking forward to seeing her, but I am. The day after finals, I'll be back in California.

Of course, thinking about going home also makes me miss Reed. For a moment, I consider inviting him to Nana's for Christmas. He'd probably think I was nuts. But he invited me to his house for Thanksgiving, so why not reciprocate? It's the polite thing to do. And who knows? Maybe we'd have a better shot in California, without Maddy's interference.

I decide to call Reed before I lose my nerve. I take my phone out of my backpack and call his cell. It rings a few times and then I hear a recording: "I'm sorry. The number you have dialed is no longer in service. Please check the number and try your call again." I call his home phone and get the same recording.

He changed his numbers? Not because of me? Without thinking, I send him an e-mail from my phone. I type: *How are you?* But I don't expect a response. I want to cry but I'm too stunned. I think of his sandpapery Adam's apple; his dark eyes; his pale, pale skin. His beautiful, grotesque drawings and his apartment, which always smelled of turpentine. He was my first real boy-friend and I'm not ready to let go.

But I guess I have no choice. It's really over now.

At six o'clock, I arrive at Tyler House. I take a deep breath before ringing the doorbell.

A girl with pigtails lets me in. She telephones up to Betsey's room and, a minute later, Betsey trots downstairs swinging her big ponytail from side to side. Together we walk into the crowded dining hall. We fill our plates with lasagna, garlic bread, and salad. I can already imagine what the food will taste like, and I know it will pale in comparison to Agnes's cooking. Betsey grabs a stack of chocolate chip cookies leftover from lunch and we scan the dining room. Since there are no empty tables, she suggests eating in her room.

I follow her out of the dining hall and up to the third floor, which smells like a locker room. At first I'm relieved to be out of the claustrophobic dining room, but then I experience a different kind of anxiety: eating in Betsey's room will be uncomfortable. I feel so removed from dorm life. How will I explain my bizarre living situation? How will I ward off Betsey's questions?

Her room is typical, with Matisse and Dalí posters on the walls and empty Coke cans adorning the windowsill. One of the beds is unmade, and its burgundy sheets look a little dirty. I get a sudden flashback of life at Haven House: music blasting from across the hall, the communal bathrooms, the disgusting hair-balls. I can't imagine moving back there.

We sit down on Betsey's purple chenille rug.

"Much better. It gets so loud in there sometimes," Betsey says. "Which house do you live in?"

"I live off campus."

"That's cool. Do you live alone?"

"No, I live with two other girls."

"Do they go to Wetherly?"

"Yeah, but you probably don't know them."

"What are their names?"

Excuse me, but is this an interrogation? I think Betsey just broke some kind of record: four questions in less than two seconds.

I force a smile and say, "Agnes Pierce and Madison Snow."

"You're kidding."

I raise an eyebrow. "No. Why?"

"Well, everyone knows them—or at least knows *of* them."

"Really?" I wonder if it's because they're wealthy. I bite into a cherry tomato and the seeds go squirting out of my mouth. To my horror, they land on Betsey's arm. "Oh my God. I'm so sorry."

Betsey stares at her arm. My eyes dart frantically around the room, searching for a paper towel or a box of tissues.

"Sorry," I say again.

"Don't worry about it." She reaches under her bed, pulls out a roll of toilet paper, and wipes her arm. "Actually, I've seen you on campus with Agnes and Madison. I wasn't sure it was you, but now you just confirmed it. So . . . what's it like living with them?"

I shrug. "Pretty normal, I guess." So that's why Betsey invited me over; she wanted to grill me about Maddy and Agnes.

She grins at me. "But aren't they sort of . . . odd?"

"No," I lie, feeling suddenly protective of them. Then, out of curiosity, I ask, "What do you mean by *odd*?"

"I heard they were like Siamese twins—you never see one without the other. Supposedly they're so close they can communicate telepathically."

245

Betsey looks like she's waiting for a response, so I laugh and say, "I think I've heard them talk once or twice."

She doesn't laugh, and her expression is heavy. "I heard that Madison tried to kill herself once."

I nearly choke on my garlic bread. "What?"

"Yeah. Supposedly she's pretty screwed up. She took a bunch of sleeping pills. I guess they found her in time and pumped her stomach."

Shrugging, I say, "I never knew that."

"But you do know that Agnes is very controlling of Madison."

I try to hide my surprise at the statement. "I haven't really noticed," I lie.

"Well," she says, still chewing, "one time Agnes flew into a jealous rage when she caught Madison talking to some girl in her class."

"I'm sure that's not true—"

"No, this girl in my house—Susie Rosenberg—she saw the whole thing. She said Agnes went ballistic. She grabbed Madison by the hair and called her a slut in front of everybody. No one could believe it. So much drama, you know? I mean, hello, we're in college, not junior high. Besides, poor Madison is mentally ill. You'd think Agnes would be gentler with her." Betsey gives me a curious look. "You really haven't witnessed any of this stuff at home?"

"No," I say, averting my eyes.

"You're not that close to them, then?"

"Not really."

"You should probably keep it that way. At least, don't get too close to Madison. Agnes might come after you."

A nervous laugh escapes me.

"I'm not joking."

"When did that incident happen?" I ask.

She shrugs. "A month ago, maybe."

"That doesn't sound like Agnes. She doesn't even use words like *slut*."

"You're right. She didn't call her a slut. She called her something else, something more subtle. I can't remember what it was . . ." Betsey tears off a piece of garlic bread and shoves it into her mouth. "*Coquette*!" she exclaims, mouth full. "She called her a coquette."

I don't know what to say. Despite Agnes's jealousy, it's hard to believe she would fly into a rage in public. She's too proud, too controlled. Besides, why would she react so insanely to something as harmless as Maddy talking to another girl in class? I can understand why Agnes thinks *I'm* a threat, but not some random stranger.

And yet, the word *coquette* does lend Betsey's story some credibility. It's exactly the kind of funny word Agnes would use. Her kind of insult. But if the story is true, Maddy would have been mortified and definitely would have told me about it, right? Then again, she didn't tell me about her most recent argument with Agnes.

I don't know what to think anymore. Who are these people, my so-called best friends? Do I even know them?

29

When I get home from Betsey's, the house is dark and Maddy and Agnes are MIA. So much for my supply and demand experiment; they didn't call me once today. On the counter there's a note written in Maddy's hand:

> *S,*
> *We went to see a movie. Back late.*
> *M & A*

After what Betsey told me tonight, I'm relieved they're not home.

At eleven thirty, when I'm lying in bed awake, I hear the front door click open. Maddy and Agnes's muffled voices float up the stairs.

"I won't do it," says Agnes.

"You owe me after what you pulled tonight," Maddy says in an agitated tone.

After a long pause, Agnes says, "I didn't do anything. I'm sorry you misunderstood."

"So, you're saying I'm stupid now?" Maddy shrills.

"Lower your voice." Another pause. "Of course I'm not saying that."

"You send mixed messages."

Silence.

Maddy says, "A true friend would help me."

"What you're asking is absurd. It's inconceivable. I can't, M. The answer is still no."

"Fine. Forget it. I'll never bring it up again."

"Try to understand."

"Don't touch me!"

"I'm sorry."

Maddy says, "Just leave me alone." She comes up the stairs. Her feet shuffle outside my door and, a moment later, a slow, deliberate knock penetrates the stillness of my room.

"Sarah?" she whispers. "Are you awake?"

Though I'm intrigued by the snippet of conversation I just heard, I don't want to deal with suicidal Maddy right now, so I ignore her. Eventually she goes away.

It's the middle of the night when I wake to a light tapping on my shoulder.

"Sarah."

I turn toward the voice and find Maddy sitting in my bed, eyes flickering in the dark.

"Help me," she whispers. She's trembling.

"What happened? Did you have a nightmare?"

She shakes her head.

I reach for the switch on my bedside lamp, but Maddy grabs my arm. "No! She'll see the light."

"What's going on?" I sit up, now fully awake.

She curls up into a ball, resting her chin on her kneecaps. "We didn't go to a movie tonight. We went to the Wetherly Inn." Her voice quavers for a moment and then she regains control. "Agnes said she wanted to talk. She's been really aggressive about our friendship lately, demanding more and more of me, making me promise that we'll be best friends forever. When we got to the hotel, she told me she had booked a room. She said it'd be quieter up there than in the dining room, so I said fine and we went up to the fourth floor. When she opened the door to the suite, I knew something was up." Maddy makes a face. "There were flower petals on the bed, chocolate-covered strawberries on the night-stand . . . I asked Agnes what she thought she was doing. She just smiled and told me to check out the bathroom. So I did, and there was a Jacuzzi tub filled with warm water and more flower petals. Again, I asked her what she thought she was doing, and she smiled and told me it was *for us*."

My head starts to throb.

"She wanted us to take a bath together. I told her I thought it was inappropriate and that I wanted to go home. But she got so angry she started punching the wall. I told her to stop, but she said she wouldn't unless I agreed to stay a little while longer. I had no choice—she's the one who drove—so I said okay, and I sat down on the bed and ate a chocolate-covered strawberry."

I scratch my head and wonder if Agnes is having a break-down.

"After she cooled off," says Maddy, "she offered me a glass of champagne. When I refused to drink it, she threw the glass against the wall. Then she went into the bathroom and drained the tub. When she came back, she sat down on the opposite side of the bed, not saying anything for a while, and then out of nowhere she pushed me down on the bed and . . ." Maddy swallows.

"What?"

"She . . . she . . . forced herself on me."

For a moment I can't speak. Agnes forced herself on Maddy? What does that mean exactly? I want to ask Maddy but when I turn toward her, I see that her face is broken, gray, sapped. I can almost see the energy trickling out of her, so I tell myself the details aren't important.

Clutching Maddy's limp hand, I ask, "Did she hurt you? I mean, physically?"

"I'm okay." She turns away and begins to sob.

"I . . . I just can't believe it," I stammer.

"Me neither." She covers her face. "I feel so dirty and disgusting. And ashamed. Afterward, she kept apologizing, but it was too late. She said she didn't know what came over her, that she loves me so much it's literally driving her insane. She even broke down and cried—it was the first time I'd ever seen her cry. I just don't understand anything anymore, Sarah. If she really loves me, why would she do something like that?"

"I don't know. Maybe she's having a mental breakdown."

Who *is* Agnes, anyway? I don't doubt that there's a dangerous, unstable side to her—a side that apparently even Betsey knows about—but is Agnes really capable of rape? Is rape what Maddy is accusing Agnes of? It just doesn't sound right. And yet Maddy can't be lying. Who, other than a complete sociopath, would lie about something like this? Maddy is troubled, and maybe she really did attempt suicide once, but deep down she's not a bad person. I know this. It's intuition. Or faith. She might not have the best track record for truth telling, but she is genuinely upset right now—that much I can see—and she's not such a magnificent actress that she'd be able to fake this.

I put my arm around Maddy's shoulder and hug her while she cries some more.

After a long silence, I ask, "What are you going to do?"

She pulls away. "What do you mean? There's nothing I *can* do."

"You can report her."

Maddy wipes her eyes on her sleeve. "No! She's my oldest friend. I could never do that. Besides, I feel sorry for her."

"She *raped* you. That's what you're saying, isn't it, Maddy?"

"Yes. But I can't report her. Then *I'd* be humiliated." She pauses. "Things would be different if I were attracted to her, but I'm not. I'm not gay, and even if I were, I'd never want to have sex with *her*; she's like my *sister*. It's sick! She thinks that just because I'm a virgin—well, not after tonight, I guess—but just because of that, she thinks there's a chance I'm a closet lesbian."

"But you're not a virgin," I remind her. "You lost your virginity to Brian."

She covers her face with her hands. "No, actually, that was a lie. I made the whole thing up because I wanted to impress you. I wanted you to think I was experienced and worldly like you, not the boring old virgin that I am—or *was*. I was going to tell you the truth eventually, but I guess I forgot." She looks at me. "I'm not like you, Sarah. You're special. You've got something . . . something that makes people gravitate toward you. Sebastian saw it. Reed saw it. And I see it."

"I have no idea what you're talking about."

"And that makes you even more charming."

Charming? Me?

She chews on her pinkie nail. "I'm scared, Sarah. I think the psychic's predictions are coming true. I don't know what Agnes is going to do next. She's dangerous. Something bad is going to happen; I can feel it."

"Don't say that."

"It's true. Agnes is going to kill me. She'd rather see me dead than with someone else."

"You have to report her—"

"I can't!"

"Then you have to stop being friends with her."

She inhales. "If only it were that easy. She'll never let me go."

And I know she's right. Agnes is the exact definition of relentless. She'd never give up on Maddy. Maddy is her life.

"Sarah," Maddy says, staring into the wall, "what if she . . . attacks me again?"

Before I can shake my head, Maddy murmurs, "You don't know her like I do. She has this other side. A dangerous, sexual side."

"Then why did she tell me she was asexual?" I say.

"She likes to think she is, but she's not. She thinks she's superior, superhuman, beyond the flesh. But she's just repressed." Maddy turns to me and clenches her jaw. There's fear in her eyes. "Rape isn't about sex, anyway, right?" she says. "Agnes was trying to show me who's boss. She sensed me pulling away and this was her way of telling me she's never going to let me go."

My chest tightens. "Do you want me to talk to her?"

"No! Promise me you won't say anything, Sarah. Please. I'll figure something out. But, for now, let's try and get some sleep."

"Who can sleep?"

"We have to try. Let's talk tomorrow. Meet me at Norton Center at noon." She leans over and kisses my cheek. "I love you, Sarah Bear. You're my one true best friend."

I say nothing and wonder what Agnes would do if she heard that. Die, I conclude, that's what she would do.

253

After Maddy leaves, sleep is impossible. I replay her story over and over in my mind, and what sounded valid in the moment now sounds outrageous. Agnes isn't a rapist. I may not know her as well as Maddy does, but I know she's no monster. I've never seen Agnes being sexually violent, so doesn't she deserve the benefit of the doubt? She has never lied to me, whereas Maddy has told countless lies. And didn't Betsey say Maddy was screwed up? She doesn't even know Maddy, but apparently that's the rumor. What if this is just another one of Maddy's tricks, like the ketchup incident? What if she really *is* a great actress and this is her performance of a lifetime? Maybe she's trying to get me to hate Agnes. Though if she actually got me to hate Agnes, what could she possibly gain from it?

Then again, Agnes *is* excessively uptight and anal, and people like that eventually snap. In the beginning, I didn't even like Agnes, yet I allowed her to woo me with her money. I practically put myself on a shelf and let her buy me—with the free rent and food and gifts—all the while thinking Maddy was the problem. I blamed Maddy for everything. But maybe Maddy wasn't the problem. Maybe it was Agnes all along.

30

It's noon and I'm sitting at a table in Norton Center, where the stench of beef fat and fried onions overpowers. I didn't sleep at all last night. I lay in the dark, anxious, confused. Finally, at dawn, I slipped out of the house and went for a walk.

I tried to poke a hole in Maddy's story. Female rapists are rare to begin with; female-on-female rapists even rarer. All I needed was one inconsistency to Maddy's story, one overlooked detail. I'm not sure if I wanted to find it for Agnes's sake or for my own. Maybe both: to give Agnes the benefit of the doubt and also to protect myself from the ugliness of Maddy's accusation. After all, I never asked to know about Agnes's savage side. I wanted the three of us to be happy again. Finding a flaw in Maddy's story, I thought, would get us back there.

"Hey," Maddy says, sitting down across from me. Her eyes are clear, bright, and amazingly bagless. "Did you order?"

"No. I thought we'd go home for lunch."

"I'm not going home. But you probably should. We don't want Agnes to get suspicious."

Maddy tugs on a hangnail. "Sorry about the bomb I dropped

on you last night." She stops tugging. "But I had to tell you. You're my best friend, my *true* best friend."

My cheeks burn and I hate myself for it. I know I'm betraying Agnes, but I'm strangely flattered to know that Maddy likes me best.

"So what do we do now?" I ask.

She shrugs.

Time to challenge her story. I clear my throat and say, "Remember how I had to leave for work all of a sudden on Saturday?"

"Yeah."

"Well, I didn't actually go to work. I left because Agnes asked me to leave you two alone."

She frowns.

"Agnes said you guys had a fight on the way to the airport, and she wanted to talk to you in private."

Maddy rolls her eyes.

"Anyway, I went back into the house to get my CDs and I saw Agnes giving you a foot massage."

She stiffens. "It's not what you think, Sarah. I had a cramp—"

"That's what Agnes said. But to me, it looked like . . . like I was interrupting something."

"Gross." Maddy makes a face. "You weren't interrupting anything. I had a cramp, that's all. Agnes just takes every opportunity to make things sexual. Don't you see? She set it up so we'd be alone, so she could make a move on me."

"But my point is, you guys looked happy. And *you* looked like you were enjoying it."

"I was repulsed! Look, here's what happened. I had a cramp in my foot. Agnes offered to get it out for me. I didn't want her touching my foot, but before I could say no, she had it in her lap.

256

She tickled me. I started laughing. That's probably when you came in. But you didn't see what happened afterward. The massage started to get kinky. I could tell Agnes was enjoying it too much, so I pulled away. She got mad and tried to grab my foot back. I told her to stop, but she wouldn't, so I ran up to my room and locked the door. Then she followed me upstairs and started screaming at me. She accused me of being a coquette. I tried calling you, but you didn't have your phone with you that day."

I shake my head. "But why haven't *I* ever seen this side of Agnes?"

Maddy shrugs. "She doesn't want you to see it."

"You guys seemed fine when I got home."

"That's because Agnes finally calmed down and apologized to me like she always does after an episode. It's her pattern. She doesn't stay mad for long; she's just so repressed that she blows up and ugly things come out of her. But afterward she's always sorry. She spent the rest of the afternoon reorganizing my closet. I know I have to get away from her, but a part of me knows she'll never let me go, so why even bother trying? But I can't go on like this. She's like a jealous boyfriend. And she's wearing me down." Maddy covers her eyes and groans. "I don't even know why she's so obsessed with me. This school is full of lesbians. Why can't she like one of them?"

"Because they're not you," I say. "You can't choose who you love."

Maddy touches my hand. "You're so wise."

I can't help but notice the way she's looking at me, sort of admiringly. It's embarrassing. I look away and, before I can censor myself, blurt, "Maybe it's not all Agnes's fault. Maybe you led her on. I mean, why else would she call you a coquette?"

Maddy's eyes tear up. "It's not my fault she's in love with me. There's nothing I could have done to prevent that. I didn't lead her on."

"You could've discouraged her."

"I did. I dated Sebastian, didn't I? She raped me, Sarah. How can you take her side?"

I look down for a moment then back at her. "You're right. I'm sorry." But then I remember the conversation from last night and Maddy's chilling words: *You owe me after what you pulled tonight.*

Maddy was trying to blackmail Agnes. Why? And with what? The rape? It makes no sense.

"What's wrong?" Maddy asks suddenly.

"Nothing."

"No, something's bothering you. I can tell. What is it?"

I shrug. "I heard you guys talking last night."

"When?"

"When you got home. You were trying to get Agnes to do something, but she refused. You said she owed you after what she did to you."

Maddy chews on her hangnail for a moment, then puts her hand in her lap. "Well, I didn't want to be the one to tell you this, but you should know that Agnes got you fired."

"What?"

"She called your boss and told him you had herpes."

I laugh uneasily. "*What?*"

"I'm not kidding."

"She told Dr. Shelby I had herpes?"

"She knew it would scare him enough to make him fire you."

"Why the fuck would she do something like that?" I say, my voice rising. "Who *does* that?"

"She doesn't want you working. You know that."

"But why?"

"She wants you around so she can keep an eye on you."

"So she called my boss and told him a vicious lie about me?"

"She's trying to control you," says Maddy. "*Both* of us."

"No wonder Dr. Shelby told me to 'choose abstinence.' I can't believe Agnes did that! I'm going to call her right now and—"

"You can't. I promised her I wouldn't tell you. And I asked her to find you another job. That's what you heard us talking about."

"And she refused, right?"

"She's jealous of you, Sarah. You're her enemy now."

"*Enemy?*"

Maddy's face darkens. "Don't worry, we'll get her back. But direct confrontation is not the way to go. Just give me some time to think about this."

Not knowing what else to say, I mumble, "Okay," but the menacing look on Maddy's face makes me worry.

After my classes, I decide to go home instead of avoiding Agnes. *She's* the one who got me fired. She should be avoiding *me,* not the other way around.

When I open the front door, Agnes pokes her head out of the kitchen and asks, "Where's Maddy?"

"I don't know," I grumble. I close the door and yank off my gloves. I'm ready to let her have it, but I repress the urge for Maddy's sake.

"She's not answering her phone."

"Maybe she's at the library."

Agnes shoots me a look.

"We're getting close to finals," I remind her.

"Since when does Maddy care about school?"

"People change," I say with a shrug.

Panic flutters across Agnes's placid facade, and it sort of pleases me to see it. Still, I can't picture her as a rapist.

She steels herself, then says, "Are you hungry? I made a Cobb salad. And there's leftover paella in the freezer."

"Thanks," I say, confused by her niceness.

"I have a lab report to do, so . . ." She walks toward the basement and opens the door. "Don't you have to work today?"

I shake my head. She is unbelievable. "No," I say, "I got canned."

"Oh. Right." Agnes nods.

"How did you know? I never told you." *She is so busted!*

"Well, I didn't know for sure. Maddy had a suspicion. You know how she thinks she's clairvoyant and all. Who knows . . . maybe she really is. Anyway, I'm sorry about the job. If you need money, let me know." She starts down the basement stairs.

For a moment I seriously consider following her down to the basement and taking all of her cash. Or stealing her thirty-five-thousand-dollar doll and hocking it on eBay. It's ironic: after getting me fired, *she* owes *me* now. But why would she offer me money after getting me fired? Why not just let me keep my job?

Of course. Like Maddy said, Agnes wants control.

31

Maddy and I are at the mall. Not the "dead mall" but a slightly better one we found in Connecticut. Lately we've been spending a lot of time outside of the house. Sometimes we tell Agnes we're going to the library, and then go see a movie without her. Other times, like today, we ditch class and go shopping.

But I'm sure Agnes knows something's up. Still, she pretends not to notice. It's kind of sad—like she's given up. Maybe she's accepted the fact that *I'm* Maddy's best friend now.

When the mall gets boring, Maddy and I take a cab back to Wetherly. We decide to go home separately so Agnes won't get suspicious. Maddy asks me to go home first because she's afraid to be alone with Agnes. I'm still not sure about the rape, but something must have happened between Maddy and Agnes for Maddy to be so paranoid. I just don't know what that something is.

Back at home, I find Agnes in the kitchen with her head in the oven. A violin concerto by Mozart blares in the background. If

Agnes weren't wearing her green latex gloves, I'd think she was trying to pull a Sylvia Plath. But no, she's just cleaning.

"Agnes!" I shout over the music.

She pops her head out of the oven, her eyebrows arched. "What?" She brushes a lock of hair off her forehead with the back of her glove and gets up to turn down the music. "Where's Maddy?" she demands.

"I have no idea."

"You weren't with her?"

"No, I was in class."

"I thought you two were together. I tried calling her cell, but she's not picking up. Where do you think she is?"

Averting my eyes, I say, "I haven't seen her all day." I drop my backpack onto the floor. "Why are you so frantic?"

She claps her gloves together. A smile creeps onto her face. "I have some news. A surprise, actually. But we have to wait until Maddy gets home because I want to tell you both at the same time."

A surprise?

"Maybe I'll just go ahead and tell you first," she says.

"No, I can wait. I'll text Maddy right now."

"No, I'll just tell her later." She peels off her gloves and drapes them over the sink. "I might burst if I don't tell someone."

I hold my breath while Agnes digs inside her Pierre Hardy bag. She hands me a guidebook to Paris.

"What's this?" I ask. Is Agnes transferring to the Sorbonne?

"How does winter break in Paris sound to you?" she says, grinning. "I rented us an apartment in the seventh arrondissement. For an entire month. You, me, Maddy, and Paris."

Wow. Paris. The city of light, art, love. I've always wanted to see the Louvre, the Seine, and the cute French men. But I already have a ticket to California, and I know Maddy would never say yes to a trip with Agnes. Not now.

"That's amazing," I say. "I wish I could go, but I'm planning to go home for the holidays."

"Oh. That's too bad," she says in a detached tone. "For us, I mean. I'm sure you'll have a wonderful time in California." She doesn't look at all disappointed.

The truth is I'd give both of my ovaries to go to Paris (as long as it didn't involve blood or any type of surgery), but I know that to even consider the trip is a waste of time. It's pretty obvious that the only reason Agnes is doing this is because of her rift with Maddy. Paris is a peace offering.

Agnes clucks her tongue. "I had a feeling you wouldn't be able to go. That's why I only booked two tickets."

"Oh." My face burns. What a nasty trick!

"But Paris will always be there. You can go some other time. Maybe on your honeymoon."

Bitch.

"We'll send you a postcard from the Eiffel Tower."

Double bitch.

She clears her throat. "Well, I have to return to my cleaning."

Mozart comes back on and Agnes's head goes back into the oven. I'm tempted to shove her whole body in there. Then we could have a roasted Agnes for dinner. But who'd want to eat her?

I head up to my room and stretch out on my bed. I can't wait to see the look on Agnes's face when Maddy tells her she's not going to Paris.

Ten minutes later, the doorbell rings—once, twice, three times. I run downstairs. Agnes shoots me a withering look on her way to the door. "Coming!" she yells, beating me to it. She swings open the door and Maddy glides in.

"Did you forget your keys?" I ask her.

"No. I was just too cold to look for them."

Agnes beams. "Let's go into the kitchen. I have a surprise for you."

32

I'm going to kill Maddy. What the hell was she thinking saying yes to Paris? So she and Agnes are fine now? One minute she's my best friend, and the next minute she's Agnes's? One minute Agnes rapes her, and the next minute they're going to Paris together? And she was so excited about it, as if the mere mention of Paris ended the war between them. She fell right into Agnes's trap, and now they'll be in Paris for a month while I'm stuck in California with Nana. It's so unfair. I would *kill* to go to Paris. Had I known Maddy was going to say yes, I would've said yes too. I would've booked my own damn ticket, with or without Agnes's consent.

But I can't change my mind now. I'd feel stupid, and besides, Maddy doesn't even seem to care that I'm not going. She's still downstairs with Agnes, *ooh*ing and *aah*ing over that stupid guidebook. But I'm on to Agnes. She must have known I was planning to go home for winter break. The only question is: how?

I open the top drawer of my nightstand. The plane ticket is sitting on top of a box of L'Oréal Feria, just as I left it. But something's off. The placement of the ticket seems too deliberate, its bottom edge flush with the bottom edge of the box. I remember throwing it in there. Now it looks too neat, like it was touched by the hand of Agnes.

That bitch! I slam the drawer shut. Then a strange thought occurs to me: what if Agnes bought me my ticket to California? After all, she got me fired. Why not send me to California too? There was no note from Nana, just her address and mine on the envelope, typed—

No, no, no. I have to stop being paranoid. Of course the ticket was from Nana. It had to be.

But I still don't understand why Maddy would say yes to Paris. And why wasn't she disappointed when I said I wasn't going? She's impossible to keep up with, a different flavor every day. She said she hated Agnes. She said she couldn't stand to be alone with her. She said she felt closest to me.

So why is she doing this?

I need a Valium. I go into Maddy's room, open the top drawer of her bureau, and steal a pill. Then, changing my mind, I put it back. The last thing I need is an addiction to pills. I have enough problems. As I'm about to shut the drawer, I notice something unusual. In the back left corner is a pink Hello Kitty diary, secured by a shiny gold lock. I didn't know Maddy kept a diary. It wasn't here the last time I stole pills from her. She doesn't seem like the kind of person who would own a diary, much less write in one. She's lazy and not very introspective and she never wants to be alone, so when would she find the time to write? *What* would she write? If the diary weren't locked, I would definitely read it. Never mind that it would be an invasion of privacy and a terrible betrayal. After all, Maddy betrayed me by saying yes to Paris. All I want to do is understand. I hate how everything's such a mystery.

It occurs to me that I could pick the lock. It's a kid's lock; it'd be easy. I scan the drawer for a bobby pin. I find a blond one and position it in the lock, and then I freeze. I can't do this. I'm scared of what I might discover, and scared that Maddy will know I invaded her privacy and decide to end our friendship. She's certifiable, but she's all I've got at this point—my only raft in this raging sea—now that Agnes is tired of me and Reed is gone.

I close the drawer and tiptoe back into my room. I think I'll skip dinner tonight and just go to bed early.

It's the middle of the night and Maddy is standing next to my bed, wearing a thin white nightgown.

"Sarah," she whispers, caressing my hair for a moment before getting under the covers. "I have a plan."

I turn toward her. "Huh?"

She smiles and in a feather-soft voice says, "A plan for dealing with Agnes." She presses her palms together. "We're going to kill her."

I rub my eyes. "Very funny."

"I'm serious."

I sit up and search her doll face for clues, but there are none to be found. "Please tell me you're joking."

Maddy closes her eyes languorously, her eyelids two perfect rose petals. It's unfair, the monopoly she has on beauty. How could someone this beautiful be so diabolical?

"There's just no other way," she says, opening her eyes. "If we don't kill her, she'll kill me first."

"She would never—"

"She's sucking the life out of me, Sarah. You saw her earlier, how excited she was about Paris. Don't you know what she's trying to do? She's trying to win me back, because she can't stand the fact that you and I are best friends now. Obviously, she knows she really messed things up when she . . . violated me, and now she's going to do whatever it takes to get me back. I only said yes to Paris to throw her off. I've thought it over, and this is the only way. We just have to get rid of her. But we can't have her suspecting anything. She has to think everything's normal for our plan to work."

I snap my fingers in front of her face. "Get a grip, Maddy. We can't kill her. That's insane. And you're insane for suggesting it."

She turns away.

"Listen, I have to ask you something . . . Did you ever attempt suicide?"

She turns back and murmurs, "I swallowed a bottle of sleeping pills a week after my parents died." A pause. "Why? Do you think that makes me crazy?"

"No. I'm sure you were in a lot of pain."

Maddy nods. "I didn't think I wanted to live. But then I got a second chance—the doctors revived me—and after that, I felt more alive than ever. Now I just want to live forever."

"Committing murder is *not* living."

"No. But if I don't do it, I won't be able to live. Don't you see?"

"You can't just kill someone because they—"

"Raped you?" she says. "Yes, you can."

"Two wrongs don't make a right."

"What if murder was the only way out of a horrible situation?"

"But it's not the only way."

"She's going to kill me. The Gypsy said I was going to die before my birth—"

"She never said that. Be rational, Maddy."

She's quiet for a while and then I realize she's sobbing. "I hate her for what she did to me," she cries. "I'd rather kill myself than just sit here and be a victim."

"Don't say that."

"It's true. Help me, Sarah. You're my best friend." She pauses, touches my wrist. "Agnes is not a good person. She's not who you think she is."

"What do you mean?"

"I shouldn't even be telling you this, but you need to know. She told me she was getting tired of you and that she didn't want you to go to Paris with us. She's trying to get rid of you."

"How?"

Maddy shrugs. "Slowly. You don't even want to know the mean things she's said about you."

"Tell me."

"Well . . . she called you a freeloader. Loser. Liar. Whore. She said the only reason Reed liked you was because you were having sex with him—that sex is the only thing you have to entice a guy with. She called you weak, boring, selfish, useless, and she said you were ugly inside and out—"

"Jesus." I shudder.

"There's more. She wants you to move back into Haven House next semester. She told me she was going to talk to you about it."

My body turns cold. "When?"

"I don't know."

"But why? What did I ever do to her?"

"Nothing. That's just the way Agnes is. She throws people away when she's tired of them."

"So she doesn't want to be my friend anymore?"

Maddy shakes her head. "No."

Agnes wants to get rid of me. I never thought she would

stoop so low. But I can't move back to Haven House. I don't belong there. What am I going to do? I feel like I'm five years old again, desperate and helpless, clinging to my mother's ankles, begging her not to leave.

And then, strangely, the feeling goes away, and I become mesmerized by Maddy's eyes. Even though I've probably looked into them a thousand times before, they appear different tonight, brighter, more powerful. I can't seem to look away. I hear her say, "Will you help me?" And I hear myself say, "Yes." And it's not until much later, after Maddy has left the room and I'm alone in my cold, white space that I realize just what I've agreed to.

The next morning I wake up at seven, exhausted and jittery. Trying hard not to think about last night, I get dressed and tiptoe down to the deserted kitchen. I snatch my keys from the counter and slip them into my backpack.

"What are you doing up so early?"

I turn. Standing in the basement doorway is Agnes, a hateful look carved onto her face. It suddenly hits me why Maddy would want her dead.

But can I imagine killing Agnes?

No. I'm not a murderer. I don't know what I was thinking last night. Maybe I was possessed. Something took hold of me; it made me say yes to Maddy.

"Well?"

I don't answer her. She wants me out of her house and out of her life. There's no point in making small talk. I grab my backpack and bolt out the door.

* * *

Days pass. Maddy and I spend most of our time away from home. We don't speak of killing Agnes again. I guess Maddy came to her senses, and I'm relieved. She probably said those things out of anger. Like me, she's no murderer.

The weird thing is that I'm exhausted all the time and I don't know why. Is it my diet? Lately I've been eating all of my meals out. I've also been eating straight out of the vending machines on campus. Maddy usually has lunch with me, but then she goes home to eat dinner with Agnes. It's incomprehensible to me why she would spend any more time with Agnes than she has to. How can she stand being friends with someone she wanted to *kill* just a few days ago? Their bond is simply too complex for me to understand.

33

It's days before finals and Maddy and I are alone in the library basement, fortifying ourselves with coffee, Cheetos, and Snickers bars. I've learned that junk food doesn't taste very good when you're eating it as a meal. I'd take Agnes's cooking over this crap any day, but that's no longer an option. Agnes spends all of her time in the basement now, purposely avoiding me. Whenever she sees me—on the way to the kitchen or bathroom—she turns and goes the other way without saying a word. I'm like a ghost in her house. I feel like I shouldn't be living there anymore. Why does she hate me so much? Is it my fault that Maddy likes me better?

The stress of the situation is making studying impossible. Who can think about finals when your life is falling apart? I'm so tired all the time that I have to keep eating just to stay awake. The weird thing is, despite all the junk I've been consuming, I haven't gained a single pound. And now I have insomnia because I'm so afraid Agnes will strangle me in the middle of the night. *Freeloader, loser, liar, whore.* Her hatred for me is palpable. The only thing keeping me going is the thought of spending winter break in California, far away from Agnes.

I have three finals to take, a paper on van Gogh to write, and a whole semester's worth of information to cram into my head. The only class I can count on passing is drawing, and that's only because Professor Connelly happens to like the way I draw.

"Yoo-hoo, earth to Sarah." Maddy waves her hand in front of my face. "Where are you?" She sets her bag of chips on the table and methodically licks the salt off her fingers. "We need to start brainstorming."

"I know. I just can't seem to concentrate."

Maddy looks puzzled. "I don't mean finals." Her eyes grow large and round as she whispers, "I mean Agnes." The excitement in her voice is unsettling. "You know. Our *plan*."

"You're not serious," I tell her, shrinking away.

"I am," she says calmly. Too calmly.

"I thought things between you and Agnes were okay now. You guys have dinner together every night."

"That's so she won't get suspicious. It hasn't changed anything. I still hate her."

Flustered, I say, "I can't talk about this right now. We have finals."

"Fine. I don't want to talk about it here, anyway. We'll talk later. I just didn't want you to think that I forgot, or that I changed my mind. Because I *am* serious. We can't let her get away with what she did to me, Sarah."

I stare at her for a moment and we don't say another word.

Later, we head back up to our carrels, but I can't concentrate. Once someone brings up murder, it's virtually impossible to think about anything else. Memorizing a bunch of econ graphs suddenly feels obscene.

Maddy reaches into my carrel for a pen. I'm dizzy, feverish.

I feel her hot, caffeinated breath on my arm and I shudder. I have the impulse to run. I just want to be far, far away from her.

Calmly, I close my econ book. "I think I'm going to head home and take a nap," I say casually. "I'll come back afterward."

"I'll go with you."

"No. Stay. Study."

"I was starting to feel claustrophobic anyway. I could use a nap too."

Wonderful.

Maddy packs up her books and we exit the library. The sky is the color of rot, the moon a smirking crescent. The cold air gnaws on my face until my cheeks turn numb, and then my hands begin to shake. Maddy wraps her Burberry scarf around me. Is she a victim or a monster? Either way, she's terrifying. Her moods, her ideas, her hold over me. Why can't I say no to her? Even the way she likes me—so wholly, so devotedly—is frightening. And addictive. I walk faster.

"Slow down," Maddy says. "I want to talk. We have to be smart about this so we don't get caught."

I stop and turn toward her. "We'd definitely get caught, Maddy. And you wouldn't like prison."

"We just have to be careful. We have to make it look like an accident. Or a suicide."

"A suicide?" I say, meeting her eyes.

She nods. "I just haven't figured out how to do it yet. We have to be quick and we can't leave a mess. Maybe we could hang her?"

She's serious. She's actually serious. I feel sick to my stomach, but all I manage to say is, "That's morbid."

"Well, we're all gonna die someday," Maddy says, missing the point.

"I don't want to be a murderer. *We're* not murderers. Agnes isn't worth a life in prison. There has to be another way. We could move out, get an apartment together, stop being friends with her . . ."

"You maybe. But not me. She'll stalk me till the day I die. She told me she'd kill herself if I ever left her."

Agnes threatening suicide? I don't believe it. She's too proud. "Well, even better," I say. "Move out and you won't have to do a thing. Let her commit suicide."

Maddy turns to me and places her hands on my shoulders. "I shouldn't have dragged you into this, Sarah. It's my problem, not yours." Maddy removes her hands from my shoulders and lowers her eyes. "What she did to me was horrible, but who knows, maybe I deserved it."

"You didn't deserve it. How can you say that? What she did was completely wrong."

"No. Agnes was right. I'm a tease. I led her on."

I grab Maddy's arm. "It wasn't your fault."

She looks at me with vulnerable eyes.

"What are you going to do?" I ask her.

"I don't know. There's a part of me that still cares for her—that will always care for her—but I just can't be her friend anymore. She violated me. She's become a different person since we all moved in together. She even told me she was planning to give you a bill for all the money you owe her. The old Agnes never would've done that. I tried to talk her out of it, but she wouldn't listen to me."

"A bill?"

"Yeah. For your share of the rent, utilities, food, trips, gas . . ."

"*Gas?*"

"She says you owe her close to ten thousand dollars."

My heart contracts. "That's outrageous!"

"Plus interest."

"There's no way—why is she doing this?"

"Because she's jealous. She's going to do whatever it takes to get rid of you. She said that if you didn't pay her back, she'd call your grandmother and ask her for the money. She's heartless. That's why I have to do something."

I try to imagine Agnes calling Nana and demanding ten thousand dollars. What would Nana do? Refuse to pay? Disown me? Agnes is a beast. She's really trying to destroy me. All because I'm best friends with Maddy. It's psychotic.

"I'll find a way to pay Agnes back," I say. "I'll get a job over winter break and I'll pay her back in installments. I'll sell my eggs if I have to."

"You don't owe her ten thousand dollars, Sarah. And even if you paid her back, she'd find some other way to harass you." Maddy frowns. "Money just happens to be your weak spot. She knows that. And she knows that most of my money's tied up in a trust until my twenty-first birthday, so I can't really help you."

Hmm . . . is that why Maddy lets Agnes pay for everything? But what about all of Maddy's designer clothes? Did Agnes buy those too?

"I have to run every expense by my aunt and uncle," Maddy adds. "They can't stop me from buying clothes, but they would never give me ten thousand dollars in cash. I hate them, and I hate Agnes. She's out to get you, Sarah."

We don't speak for several moments. It must be nice to be rich, I think. Agnes not only has the means to destroy me, but she also has the daring that comes with privilege. She's pushed me into a corner. She raped Maddy and now she's terrorizing me.

I might not have any worldly power, but I do have the right to fight back. Rage warms my blood. I feel my pulse begin to race. And then, a strange sense of calm comes over me. I hear myself say to Maddy, "What if we gave her a Valium and drowned her in the bathtub?"

"*We*? But I thought you—"

"You're my best friend. And if you think getting rid of Agnes is what we have to do, then I'm with you. That's what best friends are for, right?"

Maddy's face brightens.

"So, what do you think?"

"You know Agnes. She won't take anything even when she has a headache. We'd be lucky to get her to take a baby aspirin."

"We could get her drunk first," I suggest.

"Except she doesn't really drink. No one can make Agnes do anything she doesn't want to do."

"*You* can. What if you pressured her? Say we have a little party at home to celebrate the end of finals."

"Or my birthday."

"Right."

"No, we'd have to do it before my birthday. We could do it the night before, right after finals." She rubs her chin. "But I want a sure thing. Maybe we should just hang her."

"Hanging someone . . . Maddy, that's hard-core. And we'd still have to drug her first. I mean, she's not just going to stand there and let us tie a noose around her neck." A flash of inspiration hits me. "Here's what we'll do. We'll get her drunk on champagne—it'd be easy with her low tolerance—then drown her in the bathtub."

"You think that would work?"

"Sure. People drown in their bathtubs all the time." *God, did I really just say that? Are these really my thoughts? How can I be so calm? It's as if I have no control over myself, but I feel fine.*

Maddy nods. "And we could leave a suicide note too."

I think of Agnes's meticulous cursive script. "You know how to forge Agnes's handwriting?"

"No, but I could type something up on her typewriter."

"I think it'd be better if we made it look like an accident instead of a suicide. Like she got drunk and drowned in the tub."

"Yeah, yeah," says Maddy. "I like that."

We stop talking when a gaggle of girls catches up to us. We wait for them to pass. The feeling of calm stays with me, and I feel connected to Maddy in a way I never have before.

When the girls turn the corner, Maddy says, "The night before my birthday is also the night before Paris. Perfect. Campus will be empty by then. And the next day, you and I will leave for Paris. Together."

"But won't that look suspicious? Leaving the country right after Agnes's 'accidental' death?"

"No, because we already had these plans. We could say we were so upset that we had to get out of town."

"I don't know," I say. "Maybe we should just forget about Paris. Besides, Agnes only booked two tickets—one for you and one for her."

"I'll book you a ticket tonight. With Agnes's credit card. We can't cancel Paris. I was so looking forward to it," Maddy says giddily. "I can't wait to go shopping!"

Suddenly I feel the craziness, the stupidity, the impossibility of our plan. I feel my nerve and confidence drain away. What was I thinking, entertaining the idea of murder? This isn't a game. Killing is serious business. And it's evil. I'm not evil. Am I?

We start walking again and I don't say another word until we arrive at our street. The house is dark and ominous in the distance—unusual, since it's typically an inferno of light when Agnes is home.

"Do you think she went out?" I ask.

"I have no idea." Maddy pulls me aside. "Sarah, listen." Her face darkens slightly. "I know this isn't going to be easy. There's a lot to think about—a lot of details—but we can do this. We've got each other, and that's all we need."

Here's my chance to stop her, to kill this crazy plan before it takes on a life of its own.

But instead, I stand silent.

She unlocks the front door, and I flip on the lights. On the dining table is a plate of sugar cookies and a note that reads:

M & S,
    Had a toothache, so went to bed early.
    Casserole in fridge if you're hungry.
    See you in the AM.
                    A

Maddy takes a cookie and devours it.

I'm in bed, twisting, turning. The sky shimmers like a cockroach through my window.

I want to believe that Agnes is malevolent. I want to believe this is why we're going to kill her. But I'm still not convinced. Yes, her plan to kick me out of the house and to force me to pay ten thousand dollars is truly low. And the way she smothers Maddy is downright revolting. But did she actually *rape* Maddy?

And even if she did, does this mean Agnes deserves to die? Are we really going to do this? Somehow it still feels like make-believe.

Maybe the world would be a better place without Agnes, but maybe it wouldn't. Maybe Agnes doesn't matter enough either way. Perhaps none of us matter—in which case, killing Agnes would be forgivable, like killing an ant or a cow. Besides, if there is no God, who's going to be there to punish us in the afterlife? Am I defective to be thinking this way? Like those serial killers who have damaged frontal lobes and can't feel empathy?

Or am I just vicious?

34

W hat if she struggles?" Maddy asks me the next morning while I'm still in bed.

I groan. "Jesus, Maddy. It's eight o'clock."

"Well, we have to talk about it. Time's running out." She stares up at the ceiling. "Remind me to buy the champagne. I wish I had a fake ID. Agnes does, but I can't pass for her and neither can you. I'll have to get some stranger to buy it for us." Maddy starts pacing. "But what if she doesn't drown so easily? Do you think she'll struggle while we're holding her down?"

I look at her in disbelief.

"I know she'll be drunk, but still."

A wave of nausea hits me. The image of the two of us getting Agnes into the tub and then holding her underwater while she kicks and quivers is just too horrific. What was I thinking, agreeing to this?

I block the image out of my mind, and my nausea goes away.

"So we get her drunk," Maddy persists, "but what if she doesn't want to take a bath? How will we get her in the tub?"

"You could offer to take a bath with her," I hear myself suggest. "Just the two of you. She wouldn't say no to that, and it would make our job so much easier."

Maddy frowns. "But it would be like reliving that night."

"I know, but you have to admit—it's pretty foolproof."

"I don't know if I could go through with it. I don't want to take a bath with her," she says, wrinkling her face in disgust.

"You wouldn't have to. You could make her get in first and then take your time, lighting candles and pouring her more champagne."

"And then you'll come in and hold her head under the water?"

I gasp. "No. You'd want to wait until she got really drunk. Then you could give her a little push."

"I don't think I could do it alone, Sarah. I'd be too scared. You have to be in there with me. I'll come get you when she falls asleep, and we'll push her together, okay?"

My nausea returns. "We shouldn't be discussing this in the house," I say.

"She's not here. She went to the dentist." Maddy studies her cuticles for a moment. "Get dressed. I'll make some coffee."

The mere mention of coffee makes me think of Agnes sitting in the kitchen with her cup of Italian Roast and *The New York Times*. There won't be many more of those mornings. Overwhelmed, I run to the bathroom, slam the door behind me, and throw up.

"Are you okay?" Maddy asks through the door.

"I'm fine." I wipe my mouth. "Just give me a minute."

"Are we still going to the library?"

"Later," I say. When I hear her move away from the door, I get up off the floor. I splash cold water on my face and then study my reflection in the mirror. I'm unrecognizable! My skin is shadowy and gray, my eyes dead. Agnes was right: I *am* ugly. Inside and out.

There's still time, I tell myself. I could put an end to this madness.

But then a voice inside me says, *You can't stop now. Maddy needs you.*

We talk about our plan in between cram sessions at the library, though it still doesn't feel real to me. Maybe it isn't real. Maybe Maddy is delusional, hanging by a thread, and I'm simply indulging her insanity.

I still feel exhausted all the time, like I'm on the verge of collapse. Yesterday I forced myself to go to the infirmary, where they poked and prodded but couldn't find anything wrong with me. Yet I know something's wrong. I'm just waiting for it to reveal itself.

Two finals down, one more to go. I don't think I did so well on the first two, but the last one is the one I'm really worried about. Microeconomics is a motherfucker. Right now I'm trying to memorize the whole textbook as well as Betsey's cryptic notes, despite the fact that I'm not grasping any of the concepts.

I look over at Maddy, who's asleep in her carrel, head resting on a ball of pink pashmina, oblivious to the stress that surrounds her. She still has to take her sociology final, but she quit studying once she learned about this rule we have at Wetherly: if your roommate dies during the academic year, you automatically get straight As. I told Maddy not to count on it, but she just looked at me and yawned.

Back at the house, Agnes is busy packing for Paris. Edith Piaf trills in the background.

"*Bonsoir,*" Agnes says when we enter the house. She smiles warmly. This is the first time I've seen her in over a week. The moment should be awkward, but it's not because she's in such a good mood. She even seems happy to see me. She probably aced her exams.

I notice the homemade éclairs and chocolate croissants cooling on the counter.

"Help yourself," Agnes says to me. "You look kind of sickly, Sarah. Have you been eating?"

"Yeah," I mumble.

"It's just stress," explains Maddy.

This is the first time Maddy has acknowledged my sickliness. I thought she couldn't tell because she sees me every day, but no. It must be evident to everyone. I look and feel like a zombie.

What is happening to me?

35

It's the night before my last, most dreaded final and I'm holed up in my carrel. Maddy is taking her sociology exam, so I'm here alone. I know I'm going to fail microeconomics, but I don't care anymore. It's trivial compared to what Maddy and I are planning to do. Besides, if all goes well, we'll both get straight As.

Feeling a tap on my shoulder, I look up to find Agnes standing behind me, ghostlike in her long ivory coat, cheeks rash-red from the cold. She looks strangely pretty, her hair tousled and free, her skin aglow. I feel a pang of nostalgia for the good ole days, when we were still friends. How different things are now. Tomorrow night Maddy and I are going to drown her.

"What are you doing here?" I ask, suddenly jittery.

"I have to talk to you." There's an edge in her voice.

"I can't right now. I'm studying."

"Here," she says, handing me a manila envelope. "Maybe this will help."

I accept the envelope but don't open it. "I don't have time for this, Agnes. I'm really stressed out and—"

"Open it. You won't be disappointed."

She has nerve doing this to me the night before my final. I bet it's an invoice for the ten thousand dollars I supposedly owe her. I open the envelope and extract what appears to be a copy of my microeconomics final with the answers filled in.

My eyes widen. "Where'd you get this?"

"Does it matter?" She taps her nails against my carrel. "Come on, let's go."

"Go where?"

She motions for me to follow her.

"My professor's going to know I cheated," I whisper. "I got a D on the midterm."

"So you got your act together in time for the final," she says through gritted teeth. "That's not unheard of. How much is the final worth anyway?"

"Fifty percent."

"So you'll get a B in the class. Believe me, your professor won't suspect a thing. And you're welcome, by the way."

While gathering my books, I start to panic. Why is Agnes helping me? Should I even be cheating on my exam? I'm desperate, but cheating is unethical. And what if I get caught? Then again, murder is unethical and I'm still planning to do that, so why not cheat too while I'm at it?

We exit the library and step out onto a blanket of blue-white snow. All of campus has been transformed into Narnia.

"First snow," Agnes says matter-of-factly, walking briskly toward her car. "Come on."

Why *is* it so intensely beautiful tonight—the night before Maddy and I commit our heinous act? And why does Agnes look so radiant? I don't like all this beauty. It feels depraved.

When we get close to her car, I ask Agnes, "Are you going to tell me what's going on?"

"Get in," she says, unlocking the doors.

Inside, Agnes cranks up the heat and then lights a cigarette, opening her window just a crack.

"Since when do you smoke?"

She shakes her head. "I don't, except when I'm in Europe."

"Why only in Europe?"

"I don't know. It feels right there."

"Well, currently we're in Massachusetts, so . . ."

"Stop talking, Sarah," she grumbles, gripping the cigarette with her first and middle fingers. Her hand, I notice, is shaking.

She steers the car out of the parking lot and onto the main road toward town.

"Where are we going?"

"In a minute," she says, agitatedly puffing away. She points to the bottle-shaped brown bag near my feet. "Hand me that, would you?"

I reach for it. "Wine?"

"Champagne." She takes the bottle from me and slides it onto the backseat.

"What for?"

"Maddy wanted it."

I feel a slight pain in the pit of my stomach. Maddy never told me she was going to get Agnes to buy the champagne. Probably because I never would have supported the idea. I would've told her how totally twisted it is to involve Agnes in her own murder. God, Maddy has nerve.

"Did she say why?" I ask.

"To celebrate the end of finals. Tomorrow night. I was hoping we could all celebrate together, but I know you'll be gone by then."

"My flight's not till ten."

"Yes, but you'll want to get to the airport early. Anyway, it's not going to be much of a party. I don't drink champagne, so Maddy will be drinking alone."

I stiffen. "You don't drink champagne?"

"No," she says, wrinkling her nose. "It gives me migraines. I never touch the stuff."

"Never?"

"Never." She looks at me.

My head spins. "Does Maddy know you don't drink champagne?"

"She should. She's only known me my whole life. Why?"

I shrug. "Just wondering." Suddenly I remember Agnes telling me about her aversion to champagne early in the semester. She was feeding Hope the champagne truffles her mother had sent her, because her mother apparently forgot that champagne gave her migraines. Maddy was in the room with us. And she *has* known Agnes forever. How could she have overlooked this one very important quirk of Agnes's?

"Look," Agnes says, startling me. "I'm sorry I haven't seen much of you lately. But schoolwork comes first." She blows out a wisp of smoke.

I blink at her. Why is she pretending that there isn't a giant rift between us? When is she planning to kick me out? When I'm in California?

She tosses her cigarette out the window.

"Sarah," Agnes continues, "I want you to know that I really did want you to come to Paris with us. But I thought it'd be best if you went home for winter break." She turns to me. "That's why I bought you that ticket to California."

"*What?*" I grab her arm. She instantly tenses. "I knew it! That's why the envelope was typed and there was no letter. I knew I wasn't being paranoid. God, Agnes, why would you do something like that?"

Shaking off my hand, she slips another cigarette into her mouth and lights it. "It was for your own good. I thought you and Maddy could use some . . . distance."

Her jealousy truly knows no bounds. "You still think I'm trying to take her away from you?"

"No, it's not that," she says. "I'm protecting you. Maybe you haven't noticed, but Maddy's been pretty manic lately. I think she's up to something and I'm concerned for your safety."

Does Agnes suspect that Maddy and I are plotting something against her? Maybe Maddy alluded to it in her diary and Agnes read it?

Suddenly Agnes makes a sharp turn and pulls into the parking lot of the Wetherly Inn.

"What are we doing here?" I ask her.

Ignoring me, Agnes puts the car in park, then gets out while the engine's still running. I follow her out and watch as she, with one hand, hauls my suitcase out of the trunk and drops it at my feet. She takes a long drag on her cigarette and exhales.

My face heats up. "You're kicking me out?"

"No." She closes the trunk.

"You can't treat people like this, Agnes. You think you can just get away with things because you're wealthy, but there are consequences."

Agnes narrows her eyes. "What are you talking about?"

"I'll pay you back. For the food and the gas and the rent and whatever else. You don't have to do this."

"I'm not asking you for money, Sarah. You don't owe me anything." She sounds oddly sincere.

"Why? Because you feel bad that you got me fired?"

She looks perplexed. "I really don't know what you're talking about. Look, I got you a room here, just for tonight. Take this," she says, handing me a key card and my plane ticket. "Room 404. Good luck with your final and have a safe flight. I packed all of your things so you needn't come back to the house. Have a good time with your grandmother. I'll call you."

"That's it? You're not even going to tell me what's going on?"

"Trust me, Sarah, it's better this way. Give Maddy some space. Everything will be fine by next semester. I promise."

Throwing up my hands, I say, "What did I do?"

"It's nothing like that." She tosses her cigarette onto the snow and then gets back in the car. "I have to go. Maddy will be home soon." With a quick wave of the hand, she says, "See you next year."

Before I can say "Wait," her car shoots out of the parking lot.

What do I do now? Agnes must have discovered something in Maddy's diary, because how else could she have figured things out? God, why does Maddy have to keep a fucking diary?

One thing's clear: I've got to read that damn thing before Maddy gets home. I glance at my watch: 9:32. I have twenty-eight minutes.

I drag my suitcase into the hotel lobby and leave it with the guy behind the counter. After all, Maddy and I may have to come back here tonight. Then I call a cab.

"Please hurry," I say into the phone. "It's an emergency."

36

Six minutes later, I arrive at the house. I pay the driver, wish him a good night, and sneak in through the back door.

The bottle of Dom Pérignon sits ominously on the counter. A faint glow emanates from the open basement door. I hear Agnes moving around down there, opening and closing drawers in a furious manner. What is she looking for?

Quietly, I start up the stairs, feeling my way to the top. When I get to Maddy's room, I flip on the lights, aghast to find the room in shambles. Clothes, books, and stuffed animals are strewn across the floor. Drawers are open and eviscerated, the bed stripped of its linens. Agnes must have been searching for Maddy's diary.

I peek into the top drawer of the bureau, where, strangely, the Hello Kitty diary sits untouched. So what was Agnes looking for? With a bobby pin I find lying on top of the chest, I pick the lock. My hands tremble as I turn to the first page:

September 1

Hate it here. Town is so boring and being around girls all the time totally sucks. It kinda makes me miss Sebastian, even though I don't miss giving him blow jobs.

My roommate is a weirdo. And she drools over Sebastian, just like every other girl. Too bad he only has eyes for me.

I don't know what I'd do without Hope. She's the only thing or person (?) I get along with. Why can't people be as nice as animals?

September 18

I HATE Sarah. Why won't the bitch move in with us? I wish she would just get into a car accident and die. I know she fucked Sebastian behind my back. That evil slut! She has no idea who she's messing with. Had a funny feeling the day Sebastian came to Wetherly to surprise me, but I didn't confront her. Didn't have to. My intuition is never wrong. And then the Gypsy went ahead and confirmed it. Plus she said I would die before my birthday. I knew my short lifeline meant something! I must do a human sacrifice. Of course the Gypsy urged me not to, saying that even if I succeeded in prolonging my life, I might be altered in some repulsive way. Said there were cases of people going blind, losing their limbs, and contracting yucky diseases that turned their lives into nightmares. But I don't care. It's worth the risk. And it's the only thing that's going to make me hate Sarah less. Plus, she has a long lifeline—exactly what I need.

Even though I know Agnes would do anything for me, murder is a lot to ask. She wouldn't murder someone unless it was out of jealousy, so I've got to make her jealous of Sarah. But first, I have to get Sarah to move in with us . . .

October 1

Brilliant moi *got Agnes to convince Sarah to move in, and now everything's falling into place. It's too bad because I kind of like Sarah. She doesn't worship me the way Agnes does, but I know she thinks I'm beautiful. I can tell by the way she looks at me. I bet she secretly wishes she could be me. Well, she can't.*

Finally told Agnes about my tea-leaf reading, but just about the circle, the number twenty-one, and the betrayal. She blew me off. Told me not to pay attention to "psychic nonsense." Fucking Agnes. If I didn't need her, I wouldn't even be her friend.

October 11

Broke up with Sebastian yesterday. He came to the house and I saw the way Sarah was looking at him, so longingly. Pathetic. He only wants me, doesn't she know that? She's sooo stupid. I was happy he ignored her, but I'm still disgusted with him for fucking her. Why her of all people? What does she have that I don't?

Finding Hope dead and rotting in the backyard was horrifying. At first I was so upset I couldn't stop crying. Hope was my one true friend. I used to tell her everything. Now I only have you, Diary. Anyway, once I realized I might die next, I stopped crying. I only have two more months to live unless I do something about it.

October 20

Trying to get tight with Sarah, but it's not working. I think she's still pissed about her eyebrows. Like who gives a shit about eyebrows? Guess the iPhone wasn't enough. She's been distracted lately. Makes me think she's fucking someone. Like she actually believes she can have a boyfriend after she ruined my relationship? Hasn't the bitch heard of karma?

November 28

Been so busy, no time to write. But VERY proud of myself. Successfully ruined Sarah's relationship with Reed and spent Thanksgiving in town alone with Sarah. Nearly drove Agnes insane.

December 2

Plan backfired. Got Agnes jealous but it's not working the way I wanted it to. She turned needy and angry. Tried to calm her down with a romantic night at the Wetherly Inn. Got all dressed up and looked sexy and cute just for her. Then I told her Part 2 of what the Gypsy said—that murder was the only way to reverse my fate and that if we made a human sacrifice, I would get the remaining years of the person we sacrificed. Tried to convince her to help me get rid of Sarah. Even told her about Sarah fucking Sebastian behind my back. But Agnes went ballistic. Accused me of being mentally unstable! Accused me of using her to carry out my own plans and making her do the dirty work and not really loving her. Not the reaction I was expecting. Then she came right out and asked me if I loved her. I lied to her face and she knew it too. She said it didn't matter, that she would

continue loving me anyway, that it would always be uncondi-
tional with her. But she would NOT help me get rid of Sarah. I
wasn't about to give up, so I ran her a bath to calm her down,
but she wouldn't get in the tub. She accused ME of being in love
with Sarah! Told her that was the stupidest thing I'd ever heard
and poured her a glass of champagne, but she wouldn't drink it,
so I took the bottle and chugged it down myself. Then I licked the
head of the bottle in a supersexy way and she just stared at me.
I pulled her down onto the bed with me and started kissing her.
She went along with it for a while, but when I put my hand on
her boob, she pushed me away. "Come on. It'll be fun," I said. "I
know you want to. I know you've been fantasizing about it." She
stood up and said, "I really haven't, M. I'm not interested in a
sexual relationship. With you or anyone else." Bitch. Who the
hell does Agnes think she is? She's turning ME down? Nobody
turns me down. I will make her pay for this. I hate her so much
I could kill her. I hate her so much I WILL kill her.

December 11
    Switching up the plan. Going to get Sarah to help me kill
Agnes instead. Doesn't matter who I murder, as long as they
have a long lifeline. And Agnes does. Plus, now I hate Agnes
more than Sarah, more than anyone in the world. That bitch is
going to be sorry she rejected me.
    Cast an Agree Spell on Sarah. The one I cast on Agnes
before Thanksgiving didn't work. But it's working on Sarah.
Probably because she's weaker-willed than Agnes. Decided not to
tell Sarah about the human sacrifice. Just going to tell her Agnes
did something horrible to me. Revenge sounds a lot less evil.
    Can't wait for my new life to begin!

I wipe my brow, slick with nervous sweat. There are no more entries. Still, I flip through every blank page of the diary. And then I find something hidden in the pocket of the back cover. A photograph of me with my Louis Vuitton purse. Maddy took this picture on our way to Harvard. But why is it in her diary? I flip over the photo. Taped to the back is a lock of long, black hair. *My hair.* She must have picked it up off the floor at Sally Jo's House of Beauty. Sick! Who does that?

Below my hair, in tiny handwriting, are the words: *My Sarah.* And below that, in even smaller writing, is a phone number: 413-555-9728. I take my cell out of my jacket pocket and dial the number. After two rings, a man picks up. Immediately I recognize the whiny, irritated voice of Dr. Shelby and hang up. I shudder. So Maddy's the one who got me fired. She actually told Dr. Shelby I had herpes and then blamed it on Agnes. And she lied to me about the rape. *Maniac!*

I close the diary and sit down on the bed. My blood is jumping. I can't believe Maddy wrote down all her plans, so casually, so stupidly. She truly believes she's above the law. She's truly psychotic! What should I do now? *Think, Sarah, think.* But crazy people are impossible to figure out. I'd have to be insane like Maddy in order to understand her. The Gypsy, the lies, the human sacrifice, the Agree Spell. What kind of monster is she? What kind of monster am I? For believing her, for agreeing to help her. Even Agnes knew where to draw the line. But not me.

Her hold over me was overpowering, and I know it wasn't just the spell. Somehow she was able to control me like a puppet and make me believe all her outrageous lies. God, if only I'd read her diary earlier.

Now what? I want to run out of the house and never come back. But if I do that, will I ever be able to escape the horror of what I've done? I traded in my moral code for Maddy's wretched friendship. I gave in to her charm, her beauty, her audacity, and then watched as the lines between right and wrong, normal and insane, love and hate, all blurred into nothingness. And Agnes still isn't safe. Maddy might try something even without my help. I glance at the Cinderella wall clock: 9:55. I snatch the diary, bolt out of the room, and call to Agnes while running down the stairs.

The basement is a wreck: the dolls yanked off the shelves and strewn across the floor. Agnes, crouching amid a sea of Barbies, rummages through a hatbox. She looks up at me, and her surprise quickly turns to irritation. "I told you not to come back here," she says.

Without bothering to explain, I grab her by the wrist and drag her toward the stairwell.

"What are you doing?" She yanks back her hand.

I wave the diary in front of her. "Have you read this?"

"Maddy's diary? You actually read it?"

"Oh, yeah. And you would too if you knew what she was up to."

"No, that's where we're different, Sarah. *I* would never betray Maddy's trust," she says, jabbing her index finger into my forearm.

"We need to get out of here."

Agnes smooths her ivory silk blouse. "I'm not going anywhere."

"You're in serious danger, Agnes." I point toward the door. "Let's go to the inn. I'll explain everything there."

"Maddy will be home any minute."

"That's why we have to hurry. Trust me, you don't want to be around her right now."

Agnes turns away and, in a condescending tone, says, "She's my best friend, Sarah."

"Well, your best friend wants to offer you up as a human sacrifice!"

Our eyes lock. The room goes still. Then Agnes lets out a short laugh. "You're delusional. Maddy needs me. I'm her family. You're the one who betrayed her with Sebastian."

I open the diary and begin reading aloud, *"Who the hell does Agnes think she is? She's turning ME down? Nobody turns me down. I will make her pay for this. I hate her so much I could kill her. I hate her so much I WILL kill her."*

Agnes pales slightly.

"You committed the ultimate sin—you rejected her." When Agnes doesn't respond, I say, "Let's go."

"I can't," she says, biting her lip. "Maddy took my gun."

Fuck. Shooting Agnes was never part of the plan.

"I don't know how long she's had it. I looked in my drawer today and it wasn't there. I searched my room, her room. God knows where she hid it—we have to find it before something terrible happens."

"Is it loaded?"

Agnes nods.

I ignore my accelerating pulse. "We'll worry about that later. Let's just go."

"She might hurt herself."

"She's not going to hurt herself; she's going to hurt *you*."

Suddenly the basement door slams shut, and Agnes and I freeze. A second later we hear the click of the lock.

37

I sprint to the door. While frantically jiggling the knob, I ask Agnes, "Where's your key?"

"On the kitchen counter." She comes up behind me. "I have duplicates, but the basement only locks from the outside."

"Fuck!" I bang on the door with the flat of my hand. "Maddy! Open up! This isn't funny."

Silence.

"That's it," I say. "I'm calling the police."

"Wait, Sarah, hold on." Agnes moves away from the door and begins to pace. "Let me think for a minute."

"What's there to think about? We're trapped in a house with a psycho bitch!"

"Don't worry. She's not going to leave us down here forever."

"Why are you still not getting this?" I say, throwing up my hands. "Maddy believes that killing one of us will give her longevity. She's *evil*. And sick. How can you still defend her?"

And then the answer hits me like a kick in the stomach: love. Agnes's unconditional, unrelenting love for Maddy. She'd never stop loving Maddy, no matter how many horrible acts Maddy committed, or how mentally defective she was. Though it's completely inappropriate, I feel a twinge of jealousy. No one has ever felt that strongly about me.

"She just needs to get past her birthday," Agnes explains. "Then she'll be fine. She's afraid of becoming an adult. Eighteen is a big step for a lot of people. It wasn't for me, but I've always felt . . . older," she adds. "And Maddy's life hasn't been easy. Her parents' death nearly killed her."

"And now she's going to kill us!"

I feel the room closing in on me. Maddy could gas us, burn down the house. For a second I see the entire house ravaged by flames. We're going to die in this doll-infested basement. "I'm calling the police," I say.

"Please don't," Agnes pleads. "Not yet. Let me try something first."

I exhale loudly.

She goes to the door and presses her palm against it. "M? Can you hear me? It's Agnes. Don't be upset. Sarah and I were just talking. I got the champagne you wanted. It's on the counter. See it?"

No response.

"Maddy?"

Still nothing.

Agnes shrinks away from the door.

"She's going to drown you, Agnes. She even tried to get me to help her."

"And what did you say?" she says, meeting my eyes.

"I said no," I lie. "Of course I said no." Blood rushes to my face.

Agnes opens her desk drawer and takes out her cell phone.

Thank God, she's going to call the police.

Instead, I hear the landline ring once, twice, three times. Then Agnes coos into her cell, "Hi, M. How did your final go?" A pause. "Well, Sarah and I are getting kind of claustrophobic down here, so would you mind opening the basement door? Please? Thank you, Maddy." Agnes hangs up, then says to me, "She's coming down. See? She's not as bad as you think."

"She has your gun. We still have to call the police."

"She's not going to do anything."

"I feel sorry for you, Agnes. I really do. You're in love with a defective human being."

Agnes ignores me.

Minutes pass and my intuition tells me that Maddy is going to leave us here to rot, so I take out my phone, dial 91—

Startled by the click of the lock, I drop my phone and bolt toward the door.

Agnes chases after me. I push the door open, and we step out of the basement just in time to see Maddy scrambling back up the stairs in a sheer white nightgown.

"Maddy!" Agnes calls out to her, but Maddy doesn't turn around.

I hear the tub upstairs running. Is Maddy planning to go ahead with our scheme a day early, even without my help?

Agnes charges up the stairs. Why is she going *toward* Maddy? But I can't leave Agnes, so I rush after her. Once we reach the top, Maddy's voice taunts us from inside the bathroom, "Come on in, girls."

Agnes and I exchange a nervous glance before entering the glowing bathroom. Lit candles adorn the shelves, the window-sill, and the sink. To my right, the claw-foot tub is filling up rapidly. To my left, Agnes's bottle of Dom sits on top of the linen chest, alongside a notebook, a pen, and a vial of pills. Maddy is facing the wall, with her back to us. Slowly she turns around, clutching the gun to her chest with gloved hands. She's a demon doll, her gaze fixed and unnatural, her cheeks flushed.

Suddenly she aims the gun at me. My breathing stops. "Close the door, Sarah," she says.

"Put the gun down, M," Agnes demands.

Maddy redirects the gun at Agnes. "Shut up. Sarah, do what I asked."

I kick the door shut, keeping my eyes on the gun.

With her free hand, Maddy points toward the tub—which I happen to be closest to—and says, "Turn that off."

My hands shake as I reach down to turn the knobs. What is she planning to do? Make me drown Agnes? Or just shoot me instead?

With the water turned off, the room goes quiet.

Maddy re-aims the gun at me. Then she points it back at Agnes. It's as if she can't decide who to shoot. "So, which one of you wants to die?" she asks.

"M, put the gun down," orders Agnes.

"Shut up!" She keeps the pistol pointed at Agnes. "The thing is, I'm conflicted. I can't decide which one of you deserves to die more. The Gypsy was wrong: she told me *one* of my friends would turn against me, not *both*." Maddy's face turns overcast for a moment and then brightens. "But I guess it doesn't matter. Only one of you needs to die tonight, and since I can't make up my mind, I'll take a volunteer." She pauses. "Who's it going to be?"

I avert my eyes. This is ludicrous. Maddy actually expects one of us to offer ourselves up as a sacrificial lamb? I don't want Agnes to die—of course I don't—but if I had to choose between the two of us, wouldn't I choose her? After all, I want to live. And Agnes is the one who got us into this mess and kept a loaded gun in the house. She wouldn't even leave with me when we had the chance.

"You'll never get away with this, Maddy," I say. "I read your diary. I know everything now."

"*I read your diary. I know everything now,*" Maddy mimics in a whiny tone. "So what?"

"I told Agnes what you were planning to do."

"Agnes knows you agreed to help me drown her?"

I don't dare look at Agnes, but I hear her slowly exhale.

"You lied to me," I say to Maddy. "You told me Agnes raped you, and then you said she was out to destroy me. Who does that? What kind of sicko are you?"

Maddy begins to squirm. "You're implicated no matter what, Sarah, so why don't you just keep your mouth shut. Unless you want to be our volunteer."

If only I could distract Maddy long enough to knock the gun out of her hand.

Still pointing it at Agnes, Maddy grins at me. "I'm leaning toward you, Sarah, because Agnes and I have history, and at least *she* never fucked Sebastian behind my back." Something slithers behind her eyes. "Sarah Weaver. Depressed student. Good at drawing. Drowned in a bathtub. Has a nice ring to it, don't you think?"

Fear shoots through my veins. I imagine Maddy sliding my drunk body into the warm, soothing water. I imagine her holding me down underwater, while I kick and squirm.

I look over at Agnes, who is twiddling her thumbs, avoiding my gaze. "I'll do it," she says suddenly.

Maddy's mouth falls open. "What?"

"No," I say. "No one should have to die. Be reasonable, Maddy. Let's all just take a breath, blow out these candles, and calmly talk this over downstairs."

Maddy gives me a dismissive glance. "If Agnes wants to volunteer, then that's her business, not yours."

"Maddy," says Agnes. "I'm only doing this to show you how much I love you."

"Well, don't write that in your suicide note." Maddy points to the items on top of the linen chest. "Grab that pen and notebook."

When Agnes has the two items in her hands, Maddy commands, "Write: 'May my next life be happier. Agnes Pierce.' And date it."

Agnes looks up from the page. "Now what?"

"Open the champagne and swallow those sleeping pills."

My eyes shift nervously between Agnes and Maddy. "Agnes doesn't drink champagne," I say.

Maddy glares at me. "Yes, she does."

"No, I don't, actually," Agnes quavers. "It gives me migraines. If you ever paid attention to me, you would know that, Maddy. But you never pay attention to me, even though you say I'm your best friend. Why is that?"

Maddy rolls her eyes. "I'm supposed to remember all of your food restrictions?"

"You're a complete narcissist. I don't know why I didn't see this earlier. Maybe I did see it, but I thought you could change, if someone loved you enough. But it doesn't matter how much I care, does it? You'll never love me. Because you're incapable of love."

"Drink up," Maddy says with a gleam in her eye. "You won't have to worry about migraines when you're dead."

Agnes picks up the bottle of champagne and twists off the wire hood. When she pops the cork, my heart jumps.

"You said you saw into my soul," Agnes says, taking a swig of champagne before putting the bottle down. "You lied. You used me. I was just a means to an end. But the thing is, I've loved you for so long that I don't know how to stop. Even now."

"If you really loved me, you would've helped me when I asked you to!" Maddy shrills.

Agnes shakes her head. "Some things are just . . . *wrong*. I wanted to protect you from destroying your life. I wanted to protect the part of you that was still pure and good."

"Are you finished?" Maddy scoffs.

"I would've done anything for you, just not—"

"Shut up, shut up, shut up!" Maddy covers her ears, pressing the pistol against her cheek.

I consider going for the gun, but somehow psycho-psychic Maddy senses this and the next thing I know, she's aiming it at me again.

Agnes picks up the bottle of pills. "Leave her alone. I'm already doing what you want."

The room becomes suffocating, the air pulsating with heat and fury. Maddy and Agnes exchange a glance that I don't quite understand. Is it repulsion? Longing? A mixture of both?

"Okay," Agnes says, breaking the silence. "I want out of this hell anyway. It's not worth it anymore." She opens the vial of pills.

"No-o!"

"Shut up, Sarah," Maddy commands.

While Agnes empties the vial into her mouth, my throat closes.

She chews the pills, chasing them down with the champagne without even a grimace. "Happy now?" she says to Maddy.

They stare at each other for a while, and I realize I'm witnessing something momentous, yet too tangled and intimate for me to comprehend. Outside, the wind moans. Maddy and Agnes just keep staring at each other. What is being communicated?

Finally Maddy turns to me and says, "I still think it should be Sarah," and then she raises the gun toward my chest.

My blood lurches. My knees turn to mush. She's really going to do it. She's really going to shoot me. I wait for the moment—the flood of memories, my life flashing before my eyes, the regret that's supposed to come—but nothing happens. My mind goes blank. I feel oddly numb. Even before my own death I'm numb.

Maddy pulls the trigger. I close my eyes and the gun goes off with a crude, earsplitting sound. I'm going to die, I think, I'm really going to die.

A force knocks me down to the floor. I open my eyes. Agnes is lying on top of me. *What the . . . ?* I try to get her to stand, but her body won't cooperate. "Agnes!" I shriek. "Say something, Agnes." When she doesn't answer, I slide out from under her and that's when I see it. Blood. Spilling out of her chest.

This isn't happening. *This can't be happening. Fuck!* What do I do? CPR? I don't know CPR. I look to Maddy, who's frozen in shock.

Agnes starts gasping for breath.

"Oh, God!" I howl.

She's twitching and she looks so scared and frail. Her ivory blouse is now crimson.

"You're going to be okay, Agnes," I whimper, reaching for a towel.

I place the towel over her heart, over the gushing hole in her chest, and press down. Miraculously, the blood seems to stop.

"Maddy!" I shout.

She just stands there.

"Maddy! Call 911! Hurry!"

Maddy doesn't respond. The gun falls out of her hand, hitting the tile with a loud crack.

I get up, bolt out of the bathroom and into Agnes's room, and reach for the receiver on the nightstand. As I dial the numbers, a million thoughts ricochet in my head, too loud, too fast to register. When the operator picks up, I sputter uncontrollably. Then I hear Maddy's bloodcurdling scream.

I drop the receiver and sprint toward the bathroom just in time to catch Maddy slapping Agnes's face. When Maddy sees me, she cries, "She's dead!"

"*What?*" I kneel down, place my fingers on Agnes's thin neck, and feel for her pulse. Nothing. *Nothing?*

"She's dead! She's dead!" Maddy shrieks.

No, this isn't real. It must be a nightmare.

"It should've been you, Sarah. She took the bullet for you. Why? Why? Why?" Maddy starts smacking Agnes's arms, torso, legs. "Don't leave me," she sobs. "Don't go. You can't leave me, Agnes. Wait for me. Please."

I yank Maddy's bloody hands away from Agnes. "Stop."

"I didn't think she would take those pills," Maddy cries. "I didn't think she really loved me that much."

So it was a test? *What the fuck?* Didn't Maddy get what she wanted—longevity in exchange for her best friend's life?

Maddy pushes me away and begins caressing Agnes's cheek with her fingertips, and the tenderness of the gesture shocks me. She leans forward and presses her lips into Agnes's.

A moment later Maddy stands up. She goes over to the gun, picks it up off the floor and, before I know it, jams it up against her temple.

"*Noooo!*" I cry.

She looks right through me as she pulls the trigger.

epiLogue

It's May and I'm back in California, living with Nana. I dropped out of Wetherly after getting automatic straight As—the idea of which still repulses me—and I've been working as a telemarketer for the past four months. It's mindless, consistent work, and it keeps me from thinking too much. Twice a week I see a shrink. In the fall I'll start school at UCLA.

Strangely, I don't remember much about the funerals. Not the eulogies, the flowers, the attendants, or even the clothes I wore that day. But I remember thinking that Agnes, at last, looked peaceful. Maddy had a closed casket.

The weeks that followed the funerals were excruciating. Almost every night, I dreamed that Maddy and Agnes were still alive, that they had faked their deaths and it was all a practical joke. When I woke, I felt like I was being clawed to death—survivor's guilt is hell—and I asked myself over and over: *Why couldn't I stop them?*

I spent days in a frenzy of puzzle-piecing and analysis, playing the events over and over in my head, each time with a different outcome. What would have happened had I not read Maddy's diary that night? Or had I made that call to the police while I was still in the basement? What if Agnes hadn't stopped by the library? Would Maddy and I have actually succeeded in killing her the following day? Is that even conceivable?

Perhaps Maddy and Agnes never should have met me. After all, I came between two best friends, and upset the balance in a relationship that was deeper and more complex than I ever could have imagined. Maddy and Agnes are dead, I'm still alive, and there's still no good reason for why things turned out this way.

And then there's the matter of the Gypsy and her prediction, or at least Maddy's interpretation of it. Maddy so wanted to believe she was going to die before her birthday that it ultimately became a self-fulfilling prophecy.

A few days after the funerals, I noticed that my weight had returned to normal. Almost immediately, my body grew stronger and, though I was still in the depths of mourning, I started to look healthy and feel more energetic. Perhaps Maddy's Agree Spell had caused my mysterious illness, and when Maddy died, the spell automatically broke. But I know I can't blame everything on the spell. After all, *I* made the decision to help Maddy carry out her plan. She might have tricked me into it, but she never used force. So, why did I say yes? The answer still eludes me. I suppose I'll spend the rest of my life trying to figure it out.

I like to believe that they are together now, wherever they are. Despite her insanity, Maddy was loved by Agnes with a fierceness I doubt I'll ever witness again in my lifetime. And, in her own sick way, I think Maddy loved Agnes back. Maybe love is all that matters in the end. Or maybe that's just my antidepressants talking.

A few weeks ago I had a dream. I dreamed that I was back at the house, in the red room, reading my microeconomics textbook. Maddy was outside playing with Hope, and Agnes was preparing dinner. It was just like old times. I was elated. I knew all along that they weren't really dead. It was all just a terrible mistake. Maddy joined me in the library. Strangely, she didn't smell like anything. Not like her usual crème brûlée or green apples or candy. That's when I realized she was dead, though I still didn't know I was dreaming. She apologized for everything and then proceeded to explain why things had turned out the way they had. Her story made complete sense. It was what I needed to hear. Finally I had an answer. Finally I could let go. And then she vanished.

When I woke up, in a pool of sweat, I couldn't remember a thing Maddy had said.

acknowledgments

My deepest gratitude goes to Rachel Orr, Margaret Miller, Kathleen Wallace King, Rachel Resnick, Rob Roberge, Eve La Salle Caram, Lyn Stimer, Chieh Chieng, Rhoda Huffey, Len Joy, Mark Childress, the Community of Writers at Squaw Valley, and the wonderful team at Bloomsbury. I am forever indebted to my parents, my extended family, and, most of all, my angels: Anna Boorstin, Michele Montgomery, and Constance Sommer.